SECRET SINS OF THE MOTHERS

First in the Mockingbird Hill Series
Revised Edition

BY
DOROTHY K. MORRIS

With the exception of certain place names, this book is a work of fiction and does not intend to represent any person living or dead.

"Secret Sins of the Mothers," by Dorothy K. Morris. ISBN 978-1-949756-32-6 (softcover).

Library of Congress Number on file with publisher.

Published 2019 by Virtualbookworm.com Publishing Inc., P.O. Box 9949, College Station, TX 77845, US.

IN MEMORIUM
Dorothy White
A beloved teacher.

NOTE TO READERS

The first version of *Sins,* published in 1999, was my very first attempt at writing a novel. It was published with many errors. I have learned so much in the process and art of writing that I have wanted for a long while to do a second writing and make corrections. This is the revised edition and I do hope you enjoy it as much without the mistakes as you enjoyed it with them, and that you will be tempted to read the next eleven books in the Mockingbird Hill series.

Happy Reading

1847

A lonely road near the
James River in Virginia

ONE

IN THE FOURTH DECADE OF THE NINETEENTH CENTURY a young man by name of Charlie O'Donnell travelled the roads in Virginia, looking for a wife; not an easy endeavor, because Charlie happened to be of mixed blood. An Irish wanderer had come into the life of Mary Bunch of Arrows, a member of the Catawba community, just long enough to leave her with child before he went away continuing his exploring lands farther west. Mary Bunch of Arrows descended from the revered ancient one, Charlie O'Donnell, and when her son came into the world, she gave him that name. Mary Bunch of Arrows reared her son in the culture of her people, where women owned land and inheritances; therefore, when she died, the land that had been under her care passed not to him but to his sister.

Much had changed in their Native culture during the past century. Young girls sought husbands among young white men who had moved into their land, thinking that they could make a much better match than with a man of mixed race. In their innocence, these young women seldom understood that the white man wanted their land much more than he wanted them. That they would lose all claim to it under the white man's law, did not occur to them.

Charlie O'Donnell earned his living as a seasonal turpentine man and chipped trees on various plantations in the Carolinas and Virginia. In off times, he was an itinerant handyman. He was old enough to want a son to whom he could pass down his trades. For this he needed a wife and if the Native girls sought white men, he decided that he might as well try to find a white woman. He had learned that passing down a trade to a son was important to white men.

Because of Charlie's wandering lifestyle, finding a white woman willing to many him had proved as difficult as finding an Indian maiden to wed. He had taken the better part of two years to search for a wife throughout the small towns and villages of Virginia and the Carolinas. He had looked at women on the plantations. He had spoken of his plight with travelers he met along his travels. He had almost given up hope, when one evening his luck seemed to change. Charlie sang as he drove his wagon along the hard-packed dirt of the high road leading up toward Jamestown, Virginia. It was twilight and Charlie wanted to reach a known camp site before dark.

"Just be a bit, Chinquapin," he called softly to his stoic, chestnut mule as he guided him off the high road and onto a narrow dirt trail leading into the woods, a path barely wide enough for the wagon to pass. A slight breeze brushed the tops of trees causing moonlight to send sparkles across water standing in mud holes left from the last rain. Charlie was glad that it was not far to the spot where he always tried to camp when on this route. There waited a wide glade on the bank and a river full of fish. After he put the mule to graze, he would take his fishing pole from

3

the wagon bed. Within a half hour, he would have a feast.

"There, now, see the light through them trees?" Charlie continued to talk to his sole companion, Chinquapin. "Right through there's all the grass you can gobble."

The mule knew the way and smelled water. He pulled eagerly until they were in the glade beside the slowly-running river. Charlie jumped down from the seat. The first job was to take care of his companion, so off came the harness. The mule needed no hobbles. He had never wandered off before because Charlie always kept a sack of dried corn kernels in the wagon. The sack was well protected from the nosey mule, but Chinquapin knew exactly in which box Charlie kept it. As soon as he had drunk his fill in the river, he settled down to grazing the rich, green grass by the bank. Charlie gathered kindling and a few bigger logs from the woods to start his supper fire. He filled his coffee pot with river water and poured in a stream of coffee grounds from his store box. Setting it down close to the flames, he took the pole to the river. Digging in the mud along the river bank, he found some crawdads. He put one on his hook and kept the rest in a cup, then sat—still and restful—while waiting for the inevitable bite.

"Chinquapin?" he called to the mule. "Tomorrow we go down to the ferry and cross over into Virginie. Soon we'll come up to Jamestown way. Long time since we been here."

Charlie liked to talk and realized that one of the reasons he wanted a wife was so he would have someone to talk to besides the mule—someone who would answer back — someone with a voice less harsh than his mule's braying.

He ate the fish with cold corn cakes left from the day before and washed it down with coffee. Darkness had fallen and nothing could be heard but frogs croaking, crickets rubbing their wings, the occasional, mournful call of a whip-poor-will met with the response of an annoyed mockingbird. Chinquapin had eaten his fill and stood by the wagon close to the corn box. His head was low and one rear leg rested at an angle. The mule's eyes were half-open and half-shut as he slept. Charlie looked up toward the wood's path that led from the high road, knowing that the noise he had heard could only be a horse snorting.

The man and horse came into view at the edge of the clearing and stopped. The stranger doffed a tall black hat and spoke, "Hello to the camp! Name's Hargrove, Reverend Hargrove. May I join you for my evening? I assure you, I am harmless. I saw your beacon through the woods and realized someone was camping in my usual spot."

"Come on in. Glad for the comp'ny. Tired of gabbin' with my mule."

"Does yon mule talk back?" The newcomer gestured toward Chinquapin, who was now wide awake, although he had not left the side of the corn box.

"Nary a word, preacher. Hope you will. This your spot? Mine, too. Close 'nough to the ferry to start early start in the mornin'."

The preacher came closer and Charlie saw that he rode a big bay gelding — both fat and shiny.

"Looks like tonight we will share our spot," Hargrove said as he dismounted and tended to his gelding. Untacked and hobbled, the gelding immediately lowered his head to graze, ignoring them all. The Reverend reached into his possible bag and pulled out a parcel wrapped in a dingy white cloth. He came over to the fire and asked, "Some of that coffee? I smelled it all the way to the highroad."

"Sit right down here. I'll get another cup," Charlie jumped up to fetch another cup from the cabinet on the side of the wagon.

The Reverend opened his parcel and took out two oat cakes and half of a stringy rabbit. The food had been blackened over an open fire but was now cold.

"I see you had success tonight as a fisherman," he said, eyeing the three remaining cooked fish still strung on the willow rod by the fire.

"Help yourself. Had my fill and there's more in the river." Charlie quickly reached for the fish, pulled two off the fire and put them on a tin plate. The preacher dug in hungrily.

They sat by the campfire, sipping scalding coffee. Having shared the meal, supplemented with the bit of sweet oat cake that the Reverend had brought, Hargrove began conversation by trying to see if Charlie had need of salvation. He was used to paying his way through life by offering salvation to all whom he met. It was an easy product to offer because it cost nothing to make.

As they held their tin cups of the strong, steaming liquid, Hargrove said: "I want to thank you heartily, my friend, for sharing your provisions with me. My journeys along God's route—doing his will and reaching out for his lost lambs — are possible only by the kindness and generosity of people like you. Now that you have provided me with sustenance of the body, how might I provide you with sustenance of the soul. I am a fisher of men."

The preacher's plump face took on a look of seriousness. Charlie's first thought was that people along God's route must be quite free with sustenance of the body. His guest was just about to break out of his tightly-buttoned vest — and if his clerical collar had been buttoned, it would surely have choked him. However, Charlie had learned Christian manners from his mother, who was a born-again Christian, and had been sprinkled by the Methodists. He knew what the preacher was after.

"Sustenance of the soul," Charlie responded. "Now that is a gentle way of puttin' it. It sure is necessary, I know. My Ma, she got Christianized and made sure I knew my prayers and who I am to thank for all my blessin's."

He hoped this would assure the Reverend that he was not in need of more soul food. He didn't like to argue the advantages of Christianity over his own preference for his Native beliefs, because the preachers always got him confused. So he thought of a sure way for the minister to help him.

"Tell you what I do need, though, and can't seem to find. Maybe you learned something in your travels and you can help me," Charlie suggested.

"Yes, Brother, I'll help if I can. What is it you need?"

"A wife," Charlie answered.

"A wife?" responded the surprised man. He had been asked many things on evenings like this, but never for a wife.

"Yes, sir," said Charlie. "I'm old enough to have me some young'uns, and bein' as how I'm on the road all the time, I ain't in no one place long enough to find a good woman — and even if I did, ain't none goin' to want to wander round the countryside with me. I done asked from the Carolina pocosins all the way out to the mountains. Ain't nobody been able to tell me 'bout a lone woman looking for to get married to a man like me."

Charlie's face showed his frustration and he looked up to the preacher with hope.

"Well, now, let me think." The preacher sipped his coffee, held the cup tight and sipped some more as he thought. Suddenly, he looked up at Charlie with a gleam in his eye. "Well, now, I think I might know of a likely prospect, if you don't mind one with a few years on her," the preacher announced, overjoyed to have this chance. "A few months ago while I was traveling up by Jamestown, Squire Kerry came to me with a problem." The preacher was surely enjoying himself now. "Seems his serving woman was about to serve out her indenture and he didn't need her any longer. Told me he wanted me to help him find a position for her." Charlie hunched closer to the preacher as the preacher continued, "Her being over thirty years old, none of his neighbors want her. Say she's too old to do much work."

The preacher thought to himself that he owed Squire Kerry a few favors, having eaten many a meal and slept in many a soft, clean bed while passing

8

through Jamestown—while bringing the word of God—all for free. It was Squire Kerry's way of doing his bit to help in the salvation of souls. This would be a good way to help the Squire.

Charlie answered. "I aim to have a son, so I need one young enough for that," Charlie said doggedly.

"Don't think she's more than thirty, thirty-one. That isn't too old."

"She live close to here?" inquired Charlie, his curiosity piqued. Finally, there was hope.

"Like I said. Outside of Jamestown."

"She a widder woman?"

"Nope. Never married that I know of. Believe she's what they call a spinster." He had the presence of mind to refer to the possible future Mrs. Charlie as a spinster—rather than an old maid—out of politeness to his host.

"What else do you know about her? How come you think she's wantin' to marry? How'd you know her?" Charlie shot questions at the poor preacher faster than he could answer.

"She works at an inn. She's an indentured servant and she's been there for many years. Spent two terms of indenture, seven years each, poor soul. I do know that she's soon to finish her time, though," said the preacher emphatically.

"What's her name? You know that?"

"Certainly, I do. She's one of my congregation on every Sunday that I'm able to be in the pulpit up there. Name is Miss Sharp, first name of Sylvie. That's what she goes by. A good and pious woman."

"'Bout thirty? That makes her almost ten years older 'n me. Kin women that old still make babies?"

9

Charlie asked. He felt a bit strange talking about making babies to a representative of the spirits, but he needed to know.

"In the Bible it says where God blessed women with child bearing at ages greater than that. God willing, you could get your son," the preacher assured him. "Reckon you better make another pot of that coffee?"

As the preacher warmed to the subject, Charlie put another pot of coffee on the fire. Hargrove was a natural talker. Being able to bring God into the conversation, he had found a subject on which he could expound. They sat up late around the campfire as he told Charlie all he had heard about this poor, unfortunate woman. This is the story he told:

"Sylvie Sharp was the daughter of a Liverpool dock worker who died of drink and a mother who died of consumption. Came to America, a young girl of fifteen, by way of indenture. That is, she got her passage money in exchange for agreeing to work after she arrived here in America for the man who paid the fare. She signed indenture papers on herself and her twelve-year-old sister, Margaret, the day after their mother's funeral. Maybe she didn't quite understand the agent. She just wanted to get herself and her sister away from the docks as soon as they could. Sylvie believed they were going to be apprenticed to learn a trade when they got here. Wanted for her and her sister to be dressmakers and had high hopes of growing up and owning their own shop. The fast-talking agent set up their passage money and gave the indenture papers to the ship's captain for safe keeping."

Here the Preacher paused long enough to reach over and refill his tin cup with more hot coffee. Charlie hunched forward expectantly, waiting for the story to continue. He could already picture the two helpless girls signing over their lives to strangers, going to a strange land. Already he felt sorry for this Sylvie Sharp. Aware that he had his audience hooked, the narrator continued unfolding the drama in his best sermonizing voice.

"They say the ship sailed from Liverpool, down to Barbados, before coming up to Charleston and then on to Jamestown, a long and bitter passage down in steerage. You know they only had canvas hammocks slung up between posts to sleep on down there. Then the fever broke out. Margaret, the little sister, caught the fever and died when the ship was three days out from Barbados. Sylvie begged the captain to keep her sister's body on board 'til they reached land, but due to the nature of the fever, he couldn't do that. Had to get the body off the ship soon, so's to keep as many passengers well as he could. Insisted the dead girl be buried at sea immediately, just like the others who died. So they wrapped her up in a shroud made from her hammock and over the side she went."

The preacher's face now showed the effects of this tragic story. Charlie ached with sympathy for the poor girls.

The story continued: "You know some people who signed on for passage to America slipped ship when they got to Barbados. By that time, they'd had enough of the sea and the fever and the moldy food. They could find work on the sugar plantations, and comely women could find husbands. Some people on the ship told Sylvie that young women were scarce on the island. Most of the women there were criminals sent out for crimes committed in England. They tried to convince her to leave with them—but not Sylvie. She had signed indenture papers for America and was determined to get there. Hadn't heard anything about Barbados except that it was full of savages, so she remained on the ship and continued to Virginia. Kept counting on that American agent to apprentice her to a dressmaker."

Charlie interrupted the story long enough to take a walk out to the edge of the camp. With his back to the fire, he relieved himself. Loudly, he asked, "How'd you find out about all this?"

"The innkeeper's wife, Mrs. Kerry," replied the Reverend, "but let me continue. Don't want to get ahead of myself. All in good time."

Charlie returned and threw a few more sticks of wood on the fire. The flames shot up and golden sparks flew into the night air. He settled again by the now brightly-burning fire to hear more about Sylvie Sharp. It amazed him to realize that he already thought of her as "his" Sylvie.

The preacher began to wonder just how much he should tell this young man. Young Charlie already seemed smitten and ready to go up to Jamestown. He knew he had to be careful not to tell this young man too much and dampen his enthusiasm, yet his conscience tugged at him—this way and that—as he tried to figure out just where to stop. There were bad things said of Sylvie. Not that she was a loose woman, not anything like that. It was her disposition, her moods and her sullenness that Squire Kerry and his wife had spoken of. They'd said that the wench seemed ungrateful that over the years they had given her a roof over her head, new top dress and under clothes every year and all the food she could eat. She had a mean streak, they'd said. Should he tell all this to Charlie or not? He wasn't a dishonest man, but he was a practical one. How could anyone know for certain? If the spinster found a husband, then that might be just what she needed to improve her disposition ... a family of her own and some young'uns might be just what the good Lord had sent him to this place to help arrange.

The preacher made up his mind and his conscience was clear. He would tell young Charlie just enough to get him to Jamestown. This way, he could make young Charlie happy by finding him a wife. He could repay his debt to the Squire by helping him dispose of the serving woman and he could make the Lord happy by leading a woman and man into holy matrimony.

TWO

THE FOLLOWING MORNING Hargrove and Charlie broke camp early and rode north together. Charlie was anxious to meet his prospective bride, yet he doubted that she would have him. As they rode on Charlie's wagon, with the preacher's horse tied to the rear, Charlie asked, "How you know they gonna let me take her away? What if they don't want no mixed-breed to have her? What if she don't want me? What'll I do then?"

Knowing there was no chance that Squire Kerry or his wife would refuse the marriage, he reassured Charlie. "They'll see right off what a fine, upstanding Christian man you are. You have a trade — you work hard — and you'll be willing to accept a woman who's older than you. I don't think they'll have any objections."

A man of good disposition, kind and gentle, Charlie came from a family where his mother had seemed always happy and she'd handed that trait down to her offspring. His mother's brother was good- natured, except when Charlie had played his youthful pranks. Charlie was also honest. It never occurred to him not to answer every question with the truth. Not knowing how to dissemble, the truth simply tumbled out of his mouth each time he spoke. All this made for quite a bit of naivete. That a preacher would be less than forthcoming and tell him a partial truth did not occur to him.

Reverend Hargrove lowered his broad-brimmed hat over his brow to shield his eyes from the sun as he tried to doze. He still fought a deep feeling of guilt as the rest of the untold story played over and over in his mind. Some of it he had heard from the Kerrys. Other bits and pieces he had heard from various members of the congregation who found occasion to comment to him about the sour faced spinster. They had told him that upon arriving in the port of Jamestown, the ship's Captain had delivered Sylvie along with her papers of indenture to the American agent. Within a few hours, she found herself indentured to work at the inn of Squire Kerry. When her new master discovered that the sister he had also paid for had died, he'd informed the now thoroughly frightened, disappointed and unhappy Sylvie that she would be required to work off both terms of indenture — fourteen years. For those long years — in exchange for her food, clothing and a small attic room that was hot in summer and freezing in winter — she had toiled at the inn. Now thirty years old, she was completing her servitude. She'd learned no skills except cleaning rooms, scrubbing, cooking, waiting and cleaning tables, washing linen and other drudgery. Her difficult life, with all its misfortunes, had not helped her to grow older with a good disposition. Cheated of her dreams, her family and her youth, she had grown sullen and mean. It was said that when she believed no one was looking, she would take out her relentless feelings of anger and hopelessness on the dogs that hung around the back door of the kitchen. People also said she seemed to enjoy the most repulsive of chores like killing fowl.

She would hold down the bird—chopping off its head with a small hand ax—and toss the flopping, bleeding chicken into a barrel where she slammed down the wooden lid. Then she would stand by and listen to the noises coming from the barrel until they finally stopped. People said that they had seen her smile when she lifted the lid of the barrel took the dead, headless, filthy and bloody bird from it. She would then throw it into a pot of boiling water. Those who had seen her do that said it brought them to shivers.

Now her situation had come to this: after the fourteen long years of indenture had been done, Squire Kerry had purchased two slaves to do the work she had been doing. The inn was successful. The squire had prospered and he felt compelled to display the wealth that it had earned for him and his wife. The fashionable way to do this was to have slaves. He had no more need for an aging, white servant. Sylvie had nowhere to go but to the poor house, unless someone could help to find her a place to live out the remainder of her years.

As the preacher had heard these sad tales, he could almost understand how she could have become so unhappy, but how could he tell the prospective bridegroom any of this? Anyway it was only hearsay. He had never seen any of this with his own eyes. Convinced that the Good Lord was guiding him, he preferred to believe that He had given him the task of leading this tragic woman to happiness.

The parson and Charlie arrived in Jamestown early one evening in mid-October, Charlie driving the mule while the Reverend gave directions. They bedded down just out of town at a sheltered spot beside a creek. It was a site familiar to Hargrove as he had camped there many a night while still a young man, before receiving the blessing of Squire Kerry's hospitality. Up at daybreak, Charlie bathed in the river, wet his long, dark hair and tied it with his one, clean black ribbon. Wearing a clean but thoroughly wrinkled shirt and some almost-clean trousers — both of which were almost too small — he cut a striking figure. He stood about six feet tall, with a well formed, muscled body. His eyes were of the darkest brown and his skin color a healthy tan. Most women would privately find him appealing, no matter what they might have said aloud.

It was early morning when they pulled up behind the inn. Charlie waited out back, sitting on the wagon seat while the preacher went to call at the back door. He saw a woman open the door and the preacher went inside. Charlie waited. He tried to get a glimpse of Miss Sylvie Sharp. A couple of times thought he saw a shadow move in front of the window, but the curtain was drawn. Finally, Preacher Hargrove appeared, his florid face flushed and smiling. He motioned Charlie to come inside, so Charlie, nervous as a courting man should be, jumped down from the wagon seat. In his haste, he caught his heel in the axle and almost stumbled. Steadying himself and forcing his face into an appearance of sternness, he walked toward the open kitchen door. Inside, Hargrove stood beside a stout man whose hand rested familiarly on his shoulder. He presided over the introductions with as much flourish as he could muster.

"Squire Kerry, I would like to present Charlie O'Donnell, the young man of whom I have been speaking." He pushed Charlie forward as Squire Kerry held out his hand. "Charlie, meet Squire Kerry, a very good friend ... a God-fearing man."

"How do you do, young man?" asked the squire in a hearty voice, obviously pleased with the preacher's description. Quickly sizing Charlie up and liking what he saw, he smiled as Charlie made his manners.

"I ... I'm just fine, Squire Kerry. I'm happy to meet you, sir," Charlie answered. He took the squire's hand in his own — shaking it mightily — then quickly glanced around the large kitchen. It was empty, save for the three of them.

The squire continued: "Reverend Hargrove here ... he tells me that you are on a sacred mission."

Charlie quickly looked into the squire's face at the term "sacred mission," not quite aware what was meant.

The Squire explained quickly. "I mean, you're looking for a wife, that is. The Reverend here, he thinks that's a sacred mission and he also thinks he is the hand of God," the squire stated pompously. "He says you are perfect for our Sylvie. But before I'm sure ..." he continued as though he genuinely cared for this Sylvie ... "I must know if you'll make her a good husband. I won't just allow her to go with anyone. If you didn't come with the Reverend's recommendation," he said with self-righteousness smugness, "I wouldn't even consider this."

The Reverend Hargrove, afraid that Charlie would spoil things if he said too much, jumped into the conversation to sing Charlie's praises. "Yessir," he began, "this young man has a profession and a second skill— if that one isn't needed. In addition to being a jolly good turpentine man, he is mighty good with a saw and hammer."

"That right, Mr. O'Donnell?" asked the squire.

"Yessir. I do ... I mean, I ... that is, I can chip turpentine with the best of 'em and when they ain't no trees around I can do carpentry and fixin' and all that. Right handy' round the farm when they's buildin' needed," Charlie stammered.

"Take you traveling quite a bit, does it?" inquired the squire.

"Well, now," the preacher interjected, "Charlie says he's on the go now and again, but he's been free as a bird. No need to settle down. Besides he was hunting for the wife. Now that he's found her, he can settle, can't you boy," he asked, looking sharply at Charlie.

Charlie was no dummy and got the message right quick. "Yessir. I kin settle. Lots of plantations down south of here got lots of pine trees and some planters they want they own chipper right there on the property. Likely I can find a place like that," Charlie assured the two gentlemen. "It can be a good life." He was getting anxious. He wanted to meet his Sylvie.

Squire Kerry, having taken pains to show that he was a *protector* rather than an *exploiter,* now was ready to allow Charlie to meet his serving woman. He walked around the great wooden table, marred with marks from chopping tools and sharp knives, past the tremendous fireplace where pleasant smells drifted from steaming black kettles hung over glowing coals, to the doorway where a thick curtain separated the cooking room from the dining room. He made as though to call but was startled to see that Mrs. Kerry was huddled just beyond the curtain.

"It's time to fetch Sylvie, my dear," he addressed his wife sweetly. "You've talked with her as I asked?" His smile stayed just a bit too long, as though it were pasted there on his face.

"Yes, Mr. Kerry. I've spoken with her." The wife addressed her husband as though he were her employer.

"Was she receptive?" he inquired softly, his eyes denying the smile that was just about to make his face tired. "You know Sylvie," she whispered, pleadingly. "She never says anything. Just sits there. How do I know if she is receptive?"

Under his breath, with the smile vanished, he said harshly, "Like it or not, she will be receptive. It's this marriage or the poor house." Taking his wife by the skin of her upper arm between his meaty fingers and pinching her, he pushed her toward the stairs. "Go and fetch her and warn her that those are her two choices. She'll leave with this man tonight or go to the other place. It's up to her. The man is waiting. Go!"

Mrs. Kerry, rubbing her arm, ran toward the stairs to do her husband's bidding. The Squire turned a smiling countenance to his guests.

Sylvie sat on the edge of her narrow cot in her room high on the third floor of the inn, listening to the voices below. She had seen the preacher and the man parked in the wagon out back and suspected that the man had come for him. Squire Kerry would be anxious to send her on her way. Her faded blue eyes, which had been soft and brilliant so long ago in Wales, had now turned to a flinty gray, without life, joy or brilliance. Her feelings were well bundled up, deep inside. She looked around her tiny room, seeing the dingy wallpaper and the room's meager furnishings. There was a small table that held the wash basin, its porcelain broken both around the rim and at the bottom. A long, rusty nail held her washrag and the bit of cotton cloth that she used as a towel. She could cover her floor from end to end in three strides.

Now her garments were rolled up and packed in the bundle, which sat beside her on the cot as she waited. Sylvia heard Mrs. Kerry knock and call softly. She stood up and tucked in a wisp of graying hair that had loosed itself from the pins, then slowly opened the door.

Mrs. Kerry was about to speak—to tell Sylvie about the handsome young man who wanted to marry her, to try to convince her to accept him—when her eyes caught sight of the small bundle on the cot. Startled, she spoke. "You'll go then? You'll marry him?" She stopped for a moment as the woman in her connected with the woman in Sylvie and she thought to herself, how can she agree to go with a man she hasn't even met? Should I even allow it? Then she remembered the difficulties they all had in dealing with their sullen servant and found relief in being obedient to the stern command of her husband. She could even squirm from under any responsibility or guilt because it was her husband's command. That, as always, was her refuge but for an instant, the older woman's face betrayed her empathy and allowed Sylvie to read her thoughts.

"It don't matter none, Mrs. Kerry. It don't matter none." Turning to gather the bundle, she said, "Let's do it and be done."

Mrs. Kerry sat down on the cot beside Sylvie. With a pinched, pained look on her face, she began, awkwardly, to speak.

"Sylvie, the young man has come to marry you. I know that Squire Kerry will give you to him and we need to speak of things that you will need to know," she said with intense embarrassment, remembering how her own mother had spoken to her the night before her wedding day. She tried to take Sylvie's hand in hers, but Sylvie would not allow it, sitting rigid and unyielding in the face of Mrs. Kerry's discomfort.

"My dear," she began, her face contorting into something of a smile, "you are to be married. I feel it my Christian duty to help you with your questions. I'm sure you will have many. Feel free to ask me anything you wish." She waited, but Sylvie said nothing. She only sat with her head lowered. Mrs. Kerry persisted.

"I know you are no child, but I'm not sure you know what to expect as a wife ... that is, on your wedding night and many nights thereafter." She blushed as she continued. "There's things a husband demands his right to, you know, and if you don't permit him to have his way, he can throw you back. He doesn't have to keep you as a wife."

"So that's what you're a'feared of," sad Sylvie in a matter-of- fact tone. "A'feared I'll come back to your doorstop. I know enough, I reckon. I seen things. And this is an inn. I hear things." Then seeming to enjoy the brutality of her tone and her words, she added, "I seen the dogs. I'll get by." She was silent for an instant as she looked up at Mrs. Kerry's stunned face. Then she asked, "I got one question. How often does he do it?"

A horrified Mrs. Kerry could only stammer, "As ... as ... as often as he wishes."

Sylvie rose from the cot and led the way out of the room, striding down to the kitchen ahead of Mrs. Kerry, who struggled to keep up. Sylvie looked at the young man standing by Reverend Hargrove. The preacher turned to her with a smile. Seeing Hargrove smile, Squire Kerry realized they had company and turned to Sylvie to commence a hearty introduction — none of which either Sylvie or Charlie heard. They were too busy looking at each other.

Charlie was surprised by two things. How boldly Sylvie looked at him and how old she looked. Thin, graying, pinched of face, there was nothing left of the bloom of her youth. Sylvie was surprised at how young the man looked up close. Black eyes, dark brown hair, rugged and muscled — she half expected him to reach for her and drag her from the house.

The squire finished speaking and there was an awkward silence as they all began to size up the situation, each with his own thoughts. Charlie knew that he was tired of looking for a wife. Here was one willing and available, one who came with good recommendations from a preacher and a man of means. Sylvie had never had anything she could call happiness and did not expect to have it now. She knew that she had only two choices and could not—would not—spend the remainder of her days in the poor house.

The squire broke the silence by suggesting, "'S'pose you two would like some time alone to become acquainted?" He was about to suggest that he and Mrs. Kerry leave them, when Sylvie answered.

"No need for that. The man here wants to get married, guess I do too." Then she made her one request. "Only thing I want is a proper weddin'. Right now. Don't want to go off with him now and step over a broom somewhere. And he got to be a Godfearing Christian man!" She turned to the preacher and demanded, "Is he?"

Charlie answered for himself, "Yes, Ma'am. My mother was a Christian woman and she brought me up right. You've no need to fear that I'm a heathen," Charlie explained rather defensively.

"I can perform the ceremony right now." Reverend Hargrove came to the rescue. "No need for you to go away unwed. As a matter of fact, I would not allow it. I'll go fetch the Good Book from my valise. It's in the wagon." He hurried from the kitchen and across the sandy yard to the wagon, untied his gelding from the wagon and tied him to the hitching post in front of the inn. He found his Book and returned to his ceremony.

Mrs. Kerry simpered, then began to hustle about, calling to the two slave women. "Charity, come in here and see about fixin' a weddin' breakfast." Not

24

hearing a response, she waddled out into the dining room to look for them, but not before hearing Sylvie.

"No, ma'am. Don't want no fancy breakfast. Already et." All heads turned to her as she continued. "Just want to marry and go." Then turning to Charlie, she addressed him directly for the first time. "Less'n you take to somethin' fancy." With her eyes looking straight into his, she continued. "I ain't fancy. You ain't fancy. This weddin' ain't fancy. Why we gonna pretend it's somethin' special by coverin' it up with a fancy breakfast?" She turned to the door as the preacher returned carrying the Good Book in the bend of his arm.

Squire Kerry, seeing that Sylvie was going to be true to form and not even allow him to pretend that the relationship between them was civilized, lost patience with her the final time. "Then get on with the words," he said to the preacher. "And make them short." He stomped out of the kitchen to find his wife and to stop any further preparation. "By God, we'll be rid of her," he muttered under his breath. "Finally, rid of her."

Charlie, Sylvie and the preacher stood together in the large kitchen. Charlie was bewildered, not quite knowing the ways of white people and unsure of what was expected of him, so he kept silent. The preacher was anxious to have this harridan wed and hopeful that God would help this man in his endeavor to rule her and bring her to gentle womanhood. Sylvie wanted nothing more than to get away from the hated inn and the man and woman who she blamed for all her sorrows. They all stood together as the man of God said the words that made these two man and wife as quickly as he could without being sacrilegious. They stood in front of him—not touching—and he spoke as loudly as though he were in front of a magnificent congregation: "I now do declare you man and wife." His words were barely out of his mouth when Sylvie reached for her bundle—which she had laid on a chair by the table—and started toward the door. Charlie shook the preacher's hand as the man of God, his face ashen, whispered to Charlie, "May God be with you, my son."

When Charlie reached the wagon, Sylvie had already climbed up and sat stiffly on the wooden seat. As he stood quietly and looked up at his new bride, she ordered, "Git up here and drive!" Not being able to think of anything else to do, Charlie climbed up into the wagon, sat down beside her, picked up the reins and spoke gently to wake the dozing mule, "Back up, now, Chinquapin, back up, back up." He gently tugged on the reins and the mule slowly backed the wagon a few steps until they could miss the tree under which he had rested. "Giddy up, now, Chinquapin. Giddy on up." They rolled away from the inn and onto the sandy high road leading out of Jamestown as the sun climbed toward its zenith.

THREE

CHARLIE FELT EXTREMELY UNCOMFORTABLE sitting beside this stiff, silent woman who was now his wife. It took five hours for them to wend their way southward from Jamestown toward a familiar turpentine farm where Charlie had chipped trees some months back. He knew the farmer would remember him and would allow him to stay overnight in the spacious barn where he had slept during the weeks of his previous work. Charlie didn't mind sleeping out in the open himself, or under the wagon, if necessary, but he wanted to furnish his bride with a soft marriage bed of sweet hay under his blankets and a roof over her head.

Several times along the way Charlie had attempted to begin a conversation. "The preacher told me you came from Wales. Said it's a country close to England, 'cross the sea." He waited for a response, but none came. After a few more miles he tried again, "Said you been at the inn for fourteen years or more." Again, she said nothing. Charlie couldn't think of anything else to say, except to maybe tell her about his mother. He'd remembered that the only thing she had seemed anxious to know about was if he was a Christian man, so he thought he might tell her about his mother.

"I want you to know that I'm a Christian man, like I told you. My Ma ... she was a real good woman and she raised me right. She learned how to read, real writin' out of books. Used to talk to the preacher when one came out our way." Charlie waited for Sylvie to ask a question or say something, but she just looked down at the mule as it slowly pulled them along. Charlie's discomfort grew with her silence and he tried harder to get her to talk, but with no success. He might as well have been talking to himself. "Ma, she still lives out in the hills with the Catawbas. That's what my Ma is. Full blood almost. She got some white man's blood from way back and that's who I'm named for. After the big war, long, long time ago, some of 'em stayed out in the hills and some went over to the Cherokees. Lots of us come closer to the whites and live close in. Ain't seen my Ma for a few years, though. Hope she ain't ailin'."

There was still no response as Sylvie, who, with a face like stone, just looked ahead at the ruts in the road. Charlie let more time go by. Turning to look at Sylvie, he spoke softly: "Preacher told me 'bout your Ma 'n Pa and sister. I'm sorry 'bout that. You havin' to come here alone and all that." He was sure her silence was from fear, embarrassment and a sense of strangeness. If he did all he could to make her feel comfortable, he thought she would begin to talk, but he was wrong. When the journey of that first day was over and they pulled up in front of the farmhouse, the new Mrs. Charlie O'Donnell had not spoken a word. Charlie went up to the back door and knocked, the sound joined by the joyous baying of three coon hounds who recognized him from those months before. He spoke with Farmer Tate, but not wanting any special treatment and being afraid that Sylvie might not be sociable, he didn't tell the farmer that he had brought a bride. Receiving permission to stay overnight, he drove the wagon inside the barn, unhitched and watered the mule, then led it into a stall with a pile of hay. He took his bedroll from the wagon bed and laid it out in a clean stall, then went outside to wash up in the water trough and stayed a polite length of time before going back inside the barn. Drying his hands on his shirt, he returned to the barn, the stall and Sylvie.

Charlie knew what was expected of him on his wedding night. He did not know quite what to expect from his bride, but in all his imagination nothing had prepared him for her to behave as she did. Opening the stall door, he found Sylvie lying down on the bedroll, her night shift pulled up above her knees, her legs apart — no sign of modesty or tenderness toward him or even to herself. With clinched fists, she lay still and silent, waiting for Charlie to accomplish what she knew he must. Not knowing what else to do, Charlie quickly removed his trousers and got on top of her but was inexperienced and rough as he fumbled with unfamiliar places. At the instant of consummation, Sylvie emitted such a howl as to frighten all the sleeping pigeons and send them shrieking throughout the rafters and set the hounds to baying. The sound so terrified Charlie that he tumbled off her and rolled away, stopping up against the rough oak boards of the stall, trying to gather his wits. When he turned back toward Sylvie, she was lying with her back to him, silent, her night shift pulled down over her tightly closed knees. Charlie did not know if he had succeeded in his manly duty or not.

FOUR

DURING THE REST OF THE FALL AND EARLY WINTER, Charlie wandered southward with his new wife in the buggy, still drawn by Chinquapin, the patient mule. He did make one concession to married life. He rigged a thick canvas cover for the wagon and hung it over curved wooden frames and fastened it along the sides of the wagon with loops of small rope. For the front and back openings, he made flaps that rolled up and out of the way during daylight hours and rolled down during nighttime. He also cleaned up the clutter off the wagon floor and stacked the various articles in little cabinets he built on the outside of the wagon. In this way they traveled southward through Virginia, and North Carolina, stopping for a few weeks at a time to gather turpentine while the season lasted and doing odd chores for food and a place to camp when there were no trees to tap.

Sylvie proved to be an inventive cook, making hearty stews of the wild game and edible roots and plants that Charlie brought in. He showed her how to cook his favorite dish, sofkee, made from coarsely ground corn, water and a pinch of salt. When he worked a stand of trees on a plantation, they were furnished with potatoes, vegetables and farm-raised meat or poultry as part of Charlie's pay. Occasionally, Sylvie would be asked to do a special chore for the wife of the overseer and would be compensated with used but clean bedding or other necessities to augment her meager housekeeping articles.

Unfortunately, their personal relationship did not change. Sylvie answered when her husband spoke to her, but never ventured to begin a conversation. Charlie tried, but was always met with her resistance. Coming back to camp one evening, he brought a brace of pheasant, fresh shot, which he had already plucked, gutted, and cleaned in the river. He put the two birds on skewers cut from a young sapling and set them to roasting over the open fire. All the while, he tried to entice Sylvie into talking with him the way he believed married folk should talk. He called it "bread and butter" talk.

"I come across them birds down by the edge of the woods. They was jist a-sittin' there a-peckin' in the dirt. Didn't see me coming up on 'em." He paused, hoping she would comment. Getting nowhere, he changed his tactic and asked a question. "You like turkey? I can shoot you a nice hen turkey soon. They got lots of 'em down in the woods on that turpentine farm." He went over to the log where Sylvie sat by the fire, occasionally getting up to stir the pot of greens steaming on the coals. He sat down beside her, but she moved away from him and replied, "Don't matter none. Turkey, pheasant, duck, all taste alike to me. Bring what you want."

"You do a good job with them greens." Charlie tried a compliment. "Them little wild onions you mixed in and them chinquapins does 'em right good." He didn't know if she liked the compliment or not, or even if she'd heard him, but he kept on talking.

"We 'bout finished here. Next week we'll go down Carolina way. They's a lot of pine trees in them woods, lots of big plantations, and the people is nice. You'll like it. Think you'll like Carolina. 'Ceptin' for the skeeters, it's nice."

"Don't make no never mind, north or south." Turning her back on him she muttered, "I gotta go where you go."

Charlie might as well have been talking to himself. Sometimes he did, just to hear an adult voice. Much to his displeasure, she also continued to be withdrawn, sullen and lifelessly submissive in the dark of night, so when his wife began showing signs of carrying a child, Charlie began to sleep most nights on his bedroll under the wagon, leaving his wife to enjoy her solitude. Their marriage bed had not turned out as Charlie had expected. He remembered from his childhood the laughter, giggles, and other noises of pleasure he had heard coming from cabins in his mother's village. This was another strangeness of the white people that he did not understand.

Summer found the ill matched, unhappy couple traveling southward, with Charlie gathering turpentine from the piney woods and pocosins in the Carolina low country and sullen Sylvie cooking and cleaning. Months passed as Charlie wondered why he had married, until in November of 1849, his baby daughter came into the world. He was as delighted as any father could be for now he had someone with whom he could converse, in a few years, of course.

He named her Margaret for Sylvie's sister, and Mary for Charlie's Christian Catawba mother.

FIVE

During Maggie's early years, when not at work or doing chores, Charlie tried to nurture his little girl, relieving Sylvie from what she considered a burden. If Sylvie's attitude and biting words had not eventually driven Charlie away from the home fire to seek companionship with other workers and their families, Maggie may have had a different childhood, but that was not to be. There was only so much of Sylvie that anyone could take. Charlie escaped what Maggie endured.

What Margaret remembered most from her young life was excruciating, bone breaking loneliness. Until her fourth year she knew nothing but the wandering life of turpentine gatherers, staying any one place only a few weeks or months at a time. She and her mother slept on folded quilts laid on the floor of the wagon. Only in very bad weather did her father stay inside with them, preferring to sleep outside even in winter. On many warm summer evenings, the child would creep out from under her blankets, climb down from the wagon and curl up beside her father to sleep. Her only playmate was a doll he made from corn shucks, Indian fashion, like those he had made for his sister when they were children. Her only feeling of closeness came when he could spend time with her, letting her sit at his feet while he whittled or sometimes keeping her close to fetch his tools when he was doing a repair job. Some evenings he combed and braided her hair, which had grown thick and long. He toted her on his shoulders and swung her around and around, holding her by her wrists while she squealed with delight in high-pitched childish laughter. She would plead with him to toss her high in the air and catch her. At the end of his day, when she saw him coming back to camp from a day of work, she would run to meet him. He would reach down, pick her up and throw her up to his shoulders for a ride. Sometimes he would tease her, walk by and pretend not to notice her waiting for him. Then she would sit down in the dirt, stamp her little bare heels and cry until he came back to pick her up again. She worshipped him.

The same could not be said of her feelings toward her mother. A bright and quick child, early in life Margaret learned to be quiet and obedient lest she anger her mother, who expected instant and total obedience — always. Any explanations made in self-defense or to justify her feelings or actions brought an instant rebuke followed by a slap if Charlie was not around.

Sylvie's sullen quietness had begun to give way to a constant tendency to scold. She was approaching middle age and had never had a real home since she left England. Her early years spent in servitude, the itinerant lifestyle, her difficult and lonely pregnancy and Maggie's birth, these had all done their part to make her almost crazed with unpurged anger at what life had done to her. She could hold it in no longer. Charlie was someone she could blame for her pain, so she did blame, upbraid and scold him. Charlie could not abuse his wife, yet he did not know how to defend himself.

The woman seemed to hate her husband's and daughter's happiness. Not being able to find any for herself, she would find a way to ruin that of her husband and daughter instead. The very glimpse of a smile on either Charlie's or Margaret's face seemed to touch her painfully, so that she was compelled to do or say something to take away their joy. It was as though she wallowed in her pain from the hardships that life had dealt her and was determined to make everyone around suffer with her. The playfulness between her husband and daughter was more than she could tolerate.

One of her expressions of sarcasm when she observed them playing and laughing together was, "Laugh today, cry tomorrow!" It was enough to take the joy out of any occasion. It seemed that everything Charlie and the child did made her angry. If they accomplished a task that she had asked, then it was not done well enough. They could do nothing to please her.

One of Margaret's memories concerned a Christmas when her mother had complained, "There ain't no place to put nothin' anymore. Wagon's too little. No cupboards to put the cookin' things in."

Then every evening for several weeks right after supper Margaret saw her father go away with his axe and saw and tool box. On the evening before Christmas, as they sat around the cook fire after finishing off bowls of hot sofkee laced with molasses, Charlie brought out the chest he had made from cedar wood. He placed it on the ground in front of Sylvie.

"I heard you talking 'bout not havin' 'nuf room to put things in. This here box, it's smooth inside. You can put anything in it. It'll fasten on the side of the wagon for easy gettin' to." Ever the optimist, he waited for Sylvie to show her pleasure over his gift. He had secretly made the box for her to keep her personal belongings in, but if she wished to put pots and pans in it, he wouldn't mind.

Instead of a smile and a word of thanks, Sylvie burst into tears, "I don't want no old home-made box. I wanted that trunk! You knowed I wanted it!" She ran from the fire and climbed into the wagon, buried her face and sobbed.

Charlie turned to Margaret in bewilderment. "What trunk she talkin' 'bout? I thought she wanted me to build her a box to put on the wagon."

Little Margaret put her coffee cup down on her stool, came close to him and placed her hand on his shoulder. "She saw a red trunk in that store winder, Pa."

"What store?"

"The one we wuz in jist a while back. You know that last town we come through. It was in the winder of that place where we went in to buy flour and coffee. She stood there at that winder and looked at it a long time.

"Why didn't she say she wanted that trunk? I'd 've tried to buy it. Or I could have painted that one I made red. Could have got red paint somewhere."

"That one in the winder it had shiny hinges on it. Maybe gold?" the child wondered.

37

"Not gold, Maggie. More'n likely brass," suggested her father with a long sigh. "Why don't she jist say somethin' when she wants it. I ain't no mind reader."

"Sorry, Pa," Margaret had few words of comfort for her father and knew that their meager Christmas had been spoiled for all of them. "The sofkee and 'lasses was good!"

Charlie reached inside his coat and pulled out a small slingshot he had carved for her. "I'll show you how to use it come sun up. You might bag some mighty tasty birds with that if you practice," he suggested.

"Thank you, Pa." Margaret held the sling in one hand and hugged her father with the other.

"You have to learn how to use that 'un before I teach you how to use the squirrel gun. Got to grow up a bit, too."

After that Christmas, to avoid his wife's ire, Charlie began to stay away from them as much as he could. He never did realize his dream of having a son to whom he could pass on his profession, the way white men did. There were no more children because Charlie was never allowed to touch her that way again. Gradually, he became distant and withdrawn. He began to take long lonely walks away from the wagon to get away from his shrewish wife and, although unintentionally, away from Margaret. When they were in the vicinity of a church or a place where a traveling preacher would give a sermon, Sylvie insisted that they all attend the service, which often lasted all day. Sitting for hours on a hard bench and listening to a traveling preacher tell tall tales did not appeal to Charlie, but he went. His mother had accepted the white man's beliefs, so he tried to learn and to understand what had appealed to her, but the words of the preacher and the sort of world that the preacher wanted them to live in, just did not suit Charlie. Not much about life with the whites suited him. He missed the easy flowing natural ways he had known in his mother's house. He missed the humor, the rowdiness, the good times his family had shared while sitting around his mother's cooking fires. He missed being Indian. Sometimes he thought he should return to the mountains and his old life, but he knew that his wife would not accept Indian ways and he had his little one to think of. As months passed, he became aware that Sylvie had driven a wedge between him and his daughter.

SIX

THE VILLAGE OF MACLIN sat in heavily wooded, swampy land in the mid-coastal pocosins of South Carolina, a bit north of Charleston. Most of the citizenry of the area surrounding Maclin were descendants of very early settlers from England, Scotland, Ireland and France. Adventurous younger sons of England's aristocracy, political refugees from Scotland and Ireland, and religious refugees of France, had become planters with very large land holdings. By the early nineteenth century, most of them had acquired dozens of slaves. Some even had hundreds, so that there were many more blacks than whites. Those members of the gentry, *quality folk*, who did not live and work on plantations were doctors, wealthy merchants, and lawyers — almost all of them relatives of the wealthy cotton planters.

Into that bi-cultural citizenry of owners and slaves, in 1850 migrant workers began to drift down from the north; landless, itinerant wanderers who were welcome here only because they had brought with them the skill of gathering turpentine from the pine trees that grew profusely in the swampy woods. After the completion of the first railway connecting the north with the south, workers hopped cars from settlement to settlement. Still others came in wagons, bringing travel weary wives and shy, frightened children. At first, they went from plantation to plantation asking permission to harvest the sap of the pine tree. This given, they would tap the trees, gather resin, hand it over to the plantation owners who would sell the turpentine resin to brokers at cities on the coast — like Georgetown or Charleston — and give the gatherer a small percentage of the profits. Some of these gatherers were multi-skilled and hardworking. They might be offered other work so that they could stay on the plantation to work the pine trees in a permanent arrangement. These men might earn less of the profit, but they would have a settled place for their families. There would also be a chance for their children to attend school. An experienced turpentine man was a good thing to have on a plantation. Some people were convinced that war was coming and turpentine would bring a lot of money. Landowners began exploiting their resources of pine trees, harvesting all the resin they could. A few of these turpentine men were industrious and wise enough that they were eventually able to save enough money to buy their own small farms. A very few became rich men and eventually were accepted into society — if not in the closed societies of Maclin or Charleston, then into the more entrepreneurial atmosphere of the growing merchant class.

Sylvie's constant complaining caused Charlie to believe it might be time for settling down. He remembered her comment from long ago, "I gotta go where you go," and thought that maybe a house to live in and one place to stay might help her temper. He recalled Tally's Nook, a large plantation located near the small town of Maclin where he had worked the pine trees many times before. The overseer had asked him more than once to stay and take charge of the turpentine operation. However, at that time he was still young and had the itch to roam. Now he needed to settle, so he led his small family in the direction of this promising place.

Working his way southward, Charlie brought his small family to Tally's Nook, at the beginning of spring, just after Margaret's fourth birthday. By the time they came near the place, buds were beginning to bloom in the heavy woods that lined the narrow, sandy road. Ditches, half filled with stagnant rainwater, bordered both sides of the road. It would be here — in these ditches, in the heat of summer — where multitudes of malaria bearing mosquitoes would breed. They were the bane of existence to the people who lived here, but there were compensations. The woods were a pageant of early dogwood blossoms, wild magnolia and the pungent scent of wisteria that climbed high up into the tops of the trees and mingled with the heavy hanging Spanish moss. Wild cherry and plum battled for space with the hearty oak and pine — sending their lovely, petite blossoms out to fetch a ray of sunshine. Old fence rows were covered with thick vines and tiny pink blossoms of the wild rose and honeysuckle. In the morning, one could hear bobwhites cheerfully calling to their mates and, in the evening, the yearning sound of whippoorwills hiding in the shadows could send chills down a man's spine.

Charlie drove the wagon slowly, letting the mule set its own pace. Sylvie sat up front on the wagon seat beside Charlie, while Margaret sat on the back of the wagon, her slim barefooted legs swinging with the slow lurch of the wagon and her toes wiggling in the sunshine. Bird sounds mixed with the creak of the wagon filled her ears. Her bright mind was filled with pleasure at the beauty all around her. Noon approached and she felt hunger pangs. She left her seat at the end of the wagon and made her way to where her father sat driving the mule. Quietly coming up behind him, she reached as if to put her hands on his shoulders, then caught herself and dropped her hands at her side, stealing a quick glance at her mother to see if she had seen. Sylvie did not like for them to touch playfully.

Like children everywhere, she asked, "We almos' there? I'm hongry."

"You jist et," came a retort from her mother. "We'll eat when we get there. I ain't gonna unpack and do fixin's now."

"It ain't far now," came her father's soothing voice. "I 'member right, it'll be up ahead, round that there stand of pine. I done worked them pines a couple year back. Wait a bit. After I talks to Mister Anthony, we'll eat."

"All right, Pa." Margaret went back to the end of the wagon and sat down to dangle her legs again.

As her father had said, just around the heavy stand of pine, the road took a bend to the left. As they cleared the last few stands of trees, fields of corn came into view. Margaret thought they would see the house like her father had said, but she didn't see one — just field after field of corn and then more fields of cotton. She called from the back of the wagon, "Whar's the house, Pa? You said 'round the trees."

"Don't yell at your Pa," Sylvie scolded. "It ain't good for young'uns to yell."

"Yes, Ma." Margaret climbed up from the back of the wagon and went again to the front to quietly ask her Pa, "These fields all belong to one farm?"

"Yes, girl. All to one farm. Tally's Nook. One of the best plantations and one of the richest in this part of the state."

"What all they grows? Only corn and cotton?"

"No. That ain't all. They has a big hog farm. Out back is pens and pens of hogs and pigs, and they smokes hams and bacon and side meat."

"I reckon all them hogs makes the place smell good, huh?" Sylvie puckered her nose as though she could already smell the pig pens.

"I likes pigs," Margaret laughed as she remembered. "I helt onta one befo'. Up at that farm we wuz at when it snowed. He wuz almost big as me and…"

Before she could finish, her mother's sharp voice cut her off.

"Pigs is dirty. I ketch you holdin' one agin, I'll lay a switch to you."

Margaret wanted her father to say it was all right for her to hold a pig. It had been a tiny pig and not too dirty. It had squealed and wiggled and made her laugh, but her father said nothing, so her mother had her way. Margaret would be afraid to hold a pig again, for fear her mother would find out and punish her.

Just then, Margaret glanced up over her father's head and saw the plantation buildings come into view. A jumble of buildings and cabins on one side of the big house hid most of it. Only when they had driven another half mile did the big house come fully into view, but after hearing Charlie talk about the "big plantation," Sylvie was disappointed that it was not more magnificent.

"Ain't no big house, a'tall," grumbled the woman. "You said it was a big plantation!"

"It is a big plantation," Charlie defended himself. "Big like in lots of acres. Hundreds of acres, maybe mor'n a thousand. See all them buildings on this side and out back? Them's the smoke houses where Mister Anthony makes them hams what sells all over here 'bouts."

"They got young'uns here?" piped Margaret. "I want a young'un to play with."

"Well, you ain't going to have time to play. You'll have chores to do," warned Sylvie.

"Now, Sylvie," defended her father. "Girl's got to play sometime."

"You heard me, girl." Sylvie had spoken her final word, and that was that! Margaret knew better than to say another word on the subject, lest she get her mother's hand on her cheek. She went back to her seat on the end of the wagon and watched the pattern of the wagon tracks that framed the prints left by the mule's hoofs.

"My, my," she whispered to herself. "He shore got tiny little feets. How do he pull all this, I wonder?"

The wagon rolled past the west outbuildings and on past the Big House, where a small road led from the high road onto the plantation property. The big two-story house was mostly hidden by huge magnolia trees. In front was a large yard with a circle

45

drive where a fancy buggy stood empty, hitched to a beautiful bay horse. The reins were loosely tied to the brake handle. They could see people sitting on the wide veranda.

"That buggy, it belongs up at the other plantation, just down the road, name of Mockingbird Hill. Neighbors," explained Charlie.

"How you know that?" Sylvie demanded to know.

"I been here before and I seen it before."

Margaret thought her father marvelous. He knew so many things. She came up to the front again, curiosity getting the better of her fear. She stood quietly behind him as they drove on past the big house. Just behind it was a smaller, still elegant, house.

"This is the overseer's house," her father said as he pulled the mule to a stop by the kitchen yard. Charlie jumped down from the seat and walked to the kitchen door, knocked and waited.

The door opened and a small, dark face of a girl child peered up at him. "Yassuh?"

"Mister Anthony to home?"

"Naw suh. He ain't to home." The small, round dark face broke into a sly grin.

"Anybody home but you?"

"Yassuh. Aunt Leah, she to home, but she up to de big house. Took tea to Miz Tally. She be back t'reckley." The child stuck her head outside, just to peek around the door-sill to see who else was in the wagon.

Charlie didn't remember either this child or anyone named Aunt Leah from before but knew that she would have to come down the covered walkway that led from the main part of the house to the kitchen. "Thank you," he said, then he settled down on the kitchen stoop to wait. It wasn't more than five minutes before the back door of the house opened and a tall, very plump and very black woman emerged. Her dress was the color of indigo, covered by a starched and sparkling white apron. Charlie stood up so that she would see him before she came upon him and would not be startled.

"Aunt Leah?" he inquired.

She looked up quickly, looked him up and down, took in the covered wagon close to the yard and sternly said, "I ain't yo' Aunt nothin'! An' we don't feed no Gypsies heah! Go on 'bout yo way."

"Ain't no gypsy. Looking for Mister Anthony. I knows him. Worked here befo'," Charlie quickly explained. He knew well how the locals hated Gypsies.

"Mistah Anthony, he up to the smoke houses. He know you comin'?"

"He knowed I might. He asked me to last time."

"When that?" She was a spirited, haughty black woman, protective and snobbish, like only a treasured, black house slave could be.

"Three, four year ago." Charlie was tired of sparring with her. "I'll wait here in the wagon 'til he comes." He turned on his heel and left her. He could hear her frump and strut on into the kitchen and heard her say, "Shet dat door, chile!"

But the child had spied Margaret peeking out from behind the canvas of the wagon and before she closed the door, Margaret saw her stick out her little pink tongue as far as she could and wiggle it; the ultimate insult that one child could give to another! Margaret felt her face go hot with anger. And she had wanted to play!

When Anthony Parish, the overseer, returned, it was obvious that he remembered Charlie and his greeting was warm.

"Charlie, glad you came back." Anthony slapped Charlie on the back as the two gripped hands. "And just in time for spring tapping. I wondered who I'd get this year." He had been looking toward the wagon and saw Sylvie sitting in her bonnet on the buckboard, ignoring him. "Wife? You bring a missus?"

"And a young'un. Hidin' in the back," Charlie grinned.

"Good for you! Decided to settle down? Come here for good?"

"If you still want me ... and mine ... and have room." Charlie fidgeted, shuffled his feet on the ground and twisted his old hat.

"I told you before that when you were ready to settle, to come back. I don't aim to go back on my word. Besides, I'm happy you came ... and we need you something awful. The pork business is going strong, and what with the cotton growing and peanut stuff, I haven't any time left for the resin. I need you."

Charlie could see that this was a good move. He was proud that he had done well. "Well, my wife— her name's Sylvie—she's tired of traveling. We been up and down for 'bout four-five year now. Time to settle down. My gal soon be ready for schooling and I hears you got schools here 'bouts."

Margaret and her mother watched from the wagon as the two men greeted each other, shook hands and conversed in the way of men. They could see that this was a reunion of friends. Sylvie was envious.

"That we do. Just on the other side of the village store, next to the church. Easy walking distance. Let me meet the missus and see your child." Walking over to the wagon, he intended to cover Charlie's social awkwardness by introducing himself to Sylvie, but Charlie beat him to it and quickly walked in front.

"Mister Anthony Parish, this here's my wife. She's Sylvie ... and this young'un here, she's my daughter, Margaret. Come on Margaret. Don't go hidin' on me. Mister Parish ain't gonna bite," coaxed her father. "Say hello, Sylvie."

Sylvie turned to look at Anthony Parish, her face almost hidden by the wide brim of the poke bonnet. "Mornin', Mister Parish. Glad to meet you." She turned away and looked straight ahead, her back a bit stiffer.

"Morning, Ma'am. Want to welcome you and Charlie here. Glad he's back. Charlie's just about the most dependable turpentine man I ever hired ... and he knows about the smoke house operation, too. Matter of fact, a long time ago his people taught us a few things about how to smoke meat. We do it their way with charcoal from the hickory tree."

Then he turned to little Margaret. Her green eyes met his directly on and he instantly recognized

49

intelligence and strength in the child. He could see that she would someday grow into a striking woman.

"Come on, Charlie," he said, "lead the mule and we'll see about a cabin for your family." He walked beside Charlie as Charlie led the mule and wagon a few hundred feet past the kitchen to an empty cabin. "It isn't very big, seeing you have a child, but right now, it's the only one empty with a full room and a kitchen out back. You'll like that when summer comes. No good having to cook and eat and sleep in the same room. Gets too almighty hot," the overseer explained.

"I'm sure it'll do fine. It's more'n we expected. Glad we kin stay. Like I said, the missus, she done getting' tired of bein' on the road all the time. We're grateful, Mister Anthony."

"I am the grateful one. Remember all the quail we used to shoot? They're still here, so you get settled and we'll go shooting again."

"Yes, sir," Charlie grinned. Charlie knew that Anthony was a younger son of Mrs. Tally's brother and was considered "quality," like the folk in the big house. They could not socialize, but the opportunity to go quail shooting with the overseer would furnish him with the companionship and conversation he did not find at home. Only a year older than Charlie and still unmarried, Anthony had never treated Charlie like trash or considered him a "breed." He seemed genuinely happy to have his old companion and worker back on the farm. Away from the big house, they could believe they were friends.

SEVEN

WILLIAM TALLY HAD NURTURED his family's reputation for breeding prize hogs. At a time when most planters were running wild hogs in the swamps to fatten on roots and acorns, Squire Tally continued to import prize Berkshire hogs from England, as his ancestors had done. He continued to breed these to their homegrown free-range sows, while also keeping separate the Berkshires for showing at the local fairs. Ancient smoke houses, constantly being repaired, lined the back of his property behind the slave cabins. Some of the best smoked hams and bacon in Carolina were produced there.

With young Anthony as overseer, Charlie in charge of the turpentine crew, and the breeding expertise of Squire Tally, the plantation continued to flourish as it had for generations. Pork production remained the top moneymaker. They had tried indigo in the early days, and then rice, but both were too labor intensive and required slaves. The original owner of Tally's Nook had banned slavery and had turned to stock and pork production for profit. Only with the advent of cotton and newer members of the family in charge, did slaves come to Tally's Nook; however, income from pork was almost as good as the cotton grown in the west fields, the east acres being used for corn and peanuts to fatten the hogs.

The O'Donnells had been at the plantation less than a month when Margaret saw Mister Anthony walking down the narrow dirt path toward their cabin one evening, a small object cradled in his arms. She knew her father liked this man and she did not fear to run out to greet him.

"Evenin', Mister Anthony. What you got?" She asked as she stood on tiptoe to get a closer look. He knelt to show her a small black and white piglet.

"Oh, a piggy!" she squealed, looking up at him quizzically. "It ain't pink. I only seen pink pigs."

"This is a hybrid. One of Master William's. She's half Berkshire."

"What's a Berkshire? And what's a hybrid? You mean she's half pig and half Berkshire?"

"Yes .... no ... yes—she is half Berkshire and no--she is not only half pig. She is all pig," he laughed as he explained. "A Berkshire is a kind of pig from England. That kind was her papa. Her mama is one of the swamp sows That makes this one a hybrid."

"Why?"

"Because a pig that has one parent that is of a particular sort and another parent of another sort... well, that makes it a hybrid."

"Oh, then I'm a hybrid," she blurted with a giggle. "Ma's from one kind, and Pa's from another. That makes me a hybrid, don't it?"

"You bet it does." Anthony stood up and began to walk towards the cabin with Margaret doing her best to step in his footprints. "It also makes you stronger than most. That's one of the best things about hybrids. They're better than either the one or the other of their parents. Come on, now. Let's give this to your father."

"It's for Pa?" she asked gleefully. Quiet for a moment as they came up to the back porch, she finally whispered, "Better not let Ma see it. She don't like pigs. She says they stink."

Anthony gave the female shoat to Charlie as the start of their very own brood. When she had grown into a big healthy sow and had been bred to one of the Berkshire boars, she presented the O'Donnells with a litter of thirteen pigs, their beginning as hog breeders. Charlie took example from the plantation methods and instead of notching the ears of his pigs and allowing them to run wild in the pocosin, he built a sturdy sty in which to keep them. Margaret loved the tiny, squealing creatures, some of which were her preferred pink color. Others were black and white like the sire. When her mother was not looking, she would run down to the pigpen and watch them suckle. From those thirteen, Charlie kept three sows to breed again, sold two other sows and three gilts, then returned one sow to Master Tally as payment for the original loan—leaving three to fatten for their use. Hog killing time—at the beginning of each winter—was one of the most difficult times for little Margaret. She had to listen to the pigs' frightened squeals and the blows that killed them, then had to work all day with her mother preparing the meat for curing and smoking. Margaret's job was cleaning the intestines to use for stuffing sausages.

His new life at Tally's Nook enabled Charlie to provide a reasonably comfortable existence for his little family. Master Tally was generous with payment from the turpentine operation and there was also money to be made selling a few pigs each year. The soil around Maclin was extremely fertile and Sylvie's garden produced enough vegetables for them year-round. Peach and plum trees grew in the orchards. Blackberry bushes and Catawba grapevines grew wild everywhere in the swamp. The swamps were also full of coon, rabbit, squirrel, possum and turkey, and the rivers full of fish. There was enough food in this land of milk and honey for little Margaret to grow strong and healthy physically but nourishment for her mind was not so easy to find.

The small log cabin with the kitchen in back was adequate, if not luxurious. Warm and snug in winter, there were windows on all sides to catch breezes in summer. It was well and comfortably furnished with a table and chairs, two rockers and one double bed with a mattress of clean straw and quilts for winter. Charlie had constructed a pantry in one corner of the kitchen with shelves for storing food and a place for brooms, mops and buckets. In the kitchen, also, was the small cot where Margaret slept alone.

However, it was a house where there was no togetherness ...no pleasant family conversation ... no kind words or loving dialogue between mother and father. It was a place where Sylvie ordered and Margaret and Charlie obeyed. Most of the talk came from Sylvie as she criticized and berated both for their inadequacies. For days on end, except for Sylvie's scathing words, they remained silent.

Margaret found it better not to speak, for speaking brought notice and notice brought her mother's ire and criticism.

As "white trash," young Margaret was not invited to socialize, associate or learn with the grandchildren of Master Tally. She had no playmates or friends, no brothers or sisters, no pet of her own to play with. Under the abuse of an unloving mother and a father who spent most of his time working, Margaret's sense of isolation was complete. From her front stoop she could see the play yard of the plantation where children played tag and tossed a ball. From the back of her cabin she could see the stable yard where the fortunate grandchildren learned to ride their ponies.

It was then—when she felt utterly lonely, misunderstood, unloved, and terribly sad—that she went to her father's pig pen, sat on the log fence and talked to the pigs. They were alive. At least, they grunted and looked at her occasionally while they rooted in the mud for the last, lost bit of watermelon rind or peanut hull. Careful not to let her small, dirty bare feet go too far below the top rails for fear of being bitten, she would sit there and listen to the pigs commune with each other until evening shadows brought the mournful cries of whippoorwills. Then, afraid of the dark, she would climb down, say goodbye to the pigs, and run on the narrow pathway back to her lonely home and her cot in the kitchen.

Margaret's feelings for her mother were clear and ordered. First, she feared Sylvie; then she thoroughly disliked her. Margaret never sought her out for comfort or companionship, knowing already that those motherly qualities would never be received. If

Sylvie were in an exceptionally bad mood, Margaret knew she might be punished for any infraction of one of her mother's rules, no matter how small or insignificant. A thing dropped accidentally brought a slap to Margaret's face with the full force of her mother's palm. Sylvie would find a reason to punish her, even if only to relieve some of her anger at her own life.

One spring morning, Sylvie hitched the mule to the wagon and prepared to drive into Maclin to purchase coffee, tea, some cloth and other necessities that could not be produced at home. She left after admonishing Margaret not to forget her chores while she was away.

Margaret's first chore was to run down to the section where Charlie was tapping resin and give her father his lunch, but when she got to the place where he should have been, he was nowhere to be found. She looked everywhere she knew but could not find him. Disappointed, she walked back toward the little cabin on the road that passed the play yard and saw Master Tally's young grandson having his riding lesson. He was learning to jump his little bay pony over low poles under the watchful eye of his grandfather. Margaret thought it the most exciting thing she had seen. She stood out of sight behind a tree throughout the entire riding session, then followed the boy and the pony to the stable—at a distance, so that she would not be reprimanded. She watched as the young boy turned the pony over to an equally young slave boy who untacked the sweaty pony and began to rub him down and brush him dry. Margaret watched from around the corner of the stable door. The hay smelled good and sweet. The odor of sweat from the pony hung in the springtime air. Margaret lost track of time. When she remembered that she had been given a second chore to do while her mother was away, and when she realized that she had forgotten what it was, she panicked. Leaving the stable and rushing home as fast as her little legs could pump, she hoped that once inside the cabin she could recall her task. She could not. She checked all the usual things she was expected to do. They were done. Try as she might, she could not remember. She heard the wagon in the yard.

Her mother called, "Margaret! Come out here and tote one of these bags."

Margaret ran out and accepted the cloth bag containing containers of coffee and tea. It was almost too heavy for her to carry.

"Your chores done?" demanded Sylvie.

"I couldn't find Pa," she answered fearfully.

"I said whar he wuz. You go there?"

"Yessum. I looked. He warn't in them woods," she lamely replied, frightened, because she knew her mother would be very angry. "I brung his lunch back and put it in the kitchen."

"Your pa will be hongry!" yelled Sylvie, as though she cared. Then she asked, "What about the other chore. You do it?"

"No, ma'am. I forgot what you told me to do." Margaret expected her mother to become enraged and to hit her. She ducked instinctively.

Instead Sylvie simply said, "You got one hour to remember what it was and to do it. Ain't done in one hour, you go get a switch!"

It was an hour of emotional torture to be followed by physical torture. Margaret could not remember the chore. Her mother would not tell her what it was. What made the torture worse was that Margaret could see that her mother was enjoying the cruel game. When the hour of agony ended Sylvie declared, "You ain't remembered what it was and you ain't done it." Then she demanded, "You know what to do now. Go pull me a switch off that peach tree. And mind you, don't you go bringin' in a little spindly one. I'll send you back and beat you harder!" Margaret knew her mother was telling the truth. She had done it before, increasing the number of strokes of the switch on her bare legs if the first switch had not been big enough. Sobbing and terrified of the coming punishment, the child walked to the edge of the yard where the peach tree was just putting forth the plump green buds that would result in delicious fruit in a few months. The small switches that held the buds were still green and limber. She reached up and tore one from the limb that held it tight. She dragged it behind her in the dirt, took it inside to her mother and gave it to her.

"Pull up your dress, pull down your drawers and bend over. I'll teach you to fergit when I tell you to do something."

The child did as she was ordered. As the first blow hit her bare legs, she cried out, "Don't, Ma! I won't fergit. I promise. I'll do it. I won't fergit" But as the blows continued, she could not remain still.

The thin, limber switch stung and made large red welts where they struck. She began to dance around to avoid the blows and tripped over her dropped drawers, lying helpless on the floor as her mother hit her blow after blow with the peach switch until the switch itself went limp and useless. It was only then that Sylvie was able to control herself enough to stop. Margaret was lying in a heap on the floor, sobbing, her legs flaming from the blows of the cruel switch. In some places the welts were bleeding.

"You gonna fergit when I give you a chore to do?"

"No ma'am. No ma'am. Ain't never gonna fergit no more," she answered between hiccups, her face covered with tears mixed with mucous.

"Then wash yo' face and go scrub out that pantry floor like I tolt you! Got to store this coffee and tea in them barrels in there and I tolt you them rats has been in there. Want them rat turds cleaned up and that floor scrubbed 'fore I put this stuff in there. That's what I tolt you to do!"

EIGHT

LIFE ON A PLANTATION in the years before the big war required endless work. Water had to be drawn from the well. Firewood had to be cut and stacked by the outside wall or brought into the kitchen. Yards had to be swept clear of chicken waste and leaves. Gardens had to be tended, vegetables gathered and put up for winter. Rugs had to be beaten, clothes and bedding had to be washed and ironed.

They all worked hard—Sylvie, Charlie and the child. Margaret had been put to work as soon as she was old enough to bring wood into the house. She helped to scrub floors, wash the dishes and make beds. She toted the night jars out to empty into the privy. She helped her father feed the pigs. She worked with her parents in the garden, helped to preserve vegetables and fruit as they were gathered. They all had few clothes, only one set for daytime and another for Sunday, but these must be washed each week, summer or winter, in the iron washtub in the back yard. The wet clothes were stirred around in the lye soap and boiling water with a long thick stick, because the water was too hot to touch. When the water had cooled just enough, the clothes were pulled from the water and rubbed against the wash board until knuckles were often raw and bleeding. In summer and winter, freshly washed clothes were hung to dry on lines strung between two poles and held up off the ground in the middle with a third.

When the clothes dried, they were brought in and pressed with irons on a metal plate set over the coals in the fireplace.

Late summer brought suffocating heat. On a swelteringly hot August day, one of the kinds called "dog days," Margaret had been in the kitchen with Sylvie since early morning. Pots of tomatoes lay in scalding water be peeled and preserved with beans and corn. It had been a particularly difficult day with her mother, cross and scolding her for everything she had done. Sylvie was in a pouting mood and Margaret knew her mother was looking for an excuse to send her for a switch from the peach tree. As soon as she could, she quietly escaped. "Ma, I got to go to the outhouse."

"Go on. We finished here. It'll be time to start supper in a bit. You pick up some collard greens from the garden on your way back. And don't you fergit!"

Once out of the outhouse, Margaret stole a moment to climb to her favorite perch on the pigpen fence and sat on the top rail watching the pigs at their usual pastime, rooting in the mud. Just then, she saw a large hound skulking along the road at the edge of the woods. The hound — a big black and tan — looked hot and tired. He was searching for water in the ditch by the roadside, but now amid the dog days of August, the ditch was dry. The hound looked too weak to walk all the way to the river. Margaret thought to fetch a pail of water from the well and offer it to him. She climbed down from the fence, ran to get the water and began to walk towards him with the bucket, but as she drew close the creature stared at her for a moment then snarled, his upper lip curling to show two sharp fangs. He turned and staggered towards the woods, slowly picking his way through the briars bordering the ditch and disappeared. She did not remember having seen him before—however, she knew better than to follow him. On her way back to the cabin, she went by the garden and gathered the collard greens as she had been told. Margaret forgot the encounter with the hound and several days would pass before she would recall it.

Three days later, the stray hound came into Margaret's life again, bringing with it the most powerful trauma that she had yet experienced. The August heat still lingered, the humid, sweltering air making the late morning too hot even for house flies to move. The back-yard clotheslines were heavy with clean clothes drying from the morning's wash, the black iron wash pot full of yet another batch. Margaret stirred and prodded the clothes with a piece of broken broom handle, being careful to continually push each piece to the bottom and pull another up to the top. When she glanced up from her task, she saw two black men walking toward them on the path from the big house. Behind them came a white man. They walked slowly, looking from side to side into the weeds and briar bushes on each side of the road. As they came closer, she could see that one was an older slave called Uncle Ned and the other one was his son, young Ned. Not allowed to carry guns, they carried sharp garden hoes and held them in front of their bodies like defensive weapons, their faces showing fear. The white man carried a shotgun. Uncle Ned called out to Sylvie, who was just beginning to take down the dried sheets from the clothes line.

"Miz O'Donnell, Ma'am, y'all go in de house rat now. A houn' dog is out here 'n he's mad. Frothin' at de mout, he is. He gonna go under a cabin fo' sho'. Massah he got de big gun ... we fines him, he gonna shoot dat mad dog. Now you go in de house, Ma'am, and take de young 'un, so's you stay safe. Y'all stay inside 'til we find dat dog. We's gonna come back to let ya know when dat po' ole dog's dead."

Margaret could sense their fear, could see her mother's reaction to the words "mad dog." She, too, became frightened. Without saying a word, Sylvie piled the linens in the basket. Lifting it and placing it under her left arm with her right hand, she took a firm grip with her fingers on the loose skin of Margaret's upper arm, hastily pulling her into the cabin. She closed and bolted the door, then closed the shutters tight.

Margaret rubbed her arm where her mother's fingers had pinched her and fearfully asked her mother, "What's a mad dog?"

Sylvie replied gruffly, "It's a dog what's mad ... and when they go mad they're shot!"

Margaret ran to the window to try and peek out through the crack in the shutters.

"Come on now, ain't no time to stop chorin' to watch. We got to do the ironin' 'cause no tellin' how long it'll take the boys to find that dog. But they will ... and Mistah Tally, he'll kill it. Mad dogs is dangerous."

One by one, Margaret fetched three irons from the corner behind the wood box and placed them on a hot stone resting among the live coals in the fireplace. She thought about her mother's words. In her small vocabulary, "mad" meant people who lost their tempers. She became worried. Her mother was mad all the time. Margaret began to think that the dog had gotten sick and was going to be killed because it had become angry. She vowed that never, ever would anyone know that she sometimes felt mad. Mad at her mother — mad at her father — mad at the children of the big house who made fun of her, would not play with her, and who could be so mean. And most of all, mad at the little slave, Flossie, who still stuck out her tongue at Margaret each time they met. Yes, she often felt mad, but she vowed to always keep it to herself, lest she, herself, get sick and old Master Tally might come for her with his shotgun, too.

Margaret ironed clothes until the iron cooled — then, wrapping a thick cloth around the handle, picked up another iron from the stone in the fireplace and replaced the cool one to heat again. This was repeated over and over throughout the afternoon. She needed air, but her mother had closed the shutters tight. Margaret grew faint from heat and from the fear that gnawed at her. The interminable afternoon dragged on as the two women worked in the tightly closed room. Finally, Margaret finished the ironing and was helping to shell peas for supper when they heard a shot in the distance. The shot was followed by yelling and sound of men's voices shouting that the mad dog was dead. Sylvie opened the shutters and air rushed into the hot, stifling cabin. Margaret had thought that she might faint from the heat and fear.

"We finish washin' tomorrey. Fire's dead and water's cold," Sylvie grumbled, opening the back door just in time for Margaret to see one of the black men lift a limp, lifeless dog with a big shovel and toss it into a wheelbarrow. She had seen it before; the black and tan coon hound that had been out by the pig pen; the one she had thought to give water and pet. Now the poor creature had been shot dead because it got mad. She wondered if someday her mother would get too mad and sick and someone would have to shoot her.

The poor school in Maclin's district stood at the edge of the village and a little less than two miles from Tally's Nook. Shortly after they had arrived at their new home near Maclin, Sylvie had learned about the school. Free schools had been authorized and established in South Carolina as early as 1805 and cost nothing to the families of the working poor. The first one in Maclin was built in 1811. Planters and professional families could afford private governesses and school masters for their children to be taught at home until their young gentlemen were ready for a university and the young ladies were ready for marriage. The wealthy considered it beneath their class to send their children to free schools, so they accommodated only the poorest of children, thus the nickname *poor school*. In Carolina's Low Country it was generally agreed that reading, writing and ciphering was enough learning to be taught in the free schools for the children of landless laborers so they would be of some use and benefit to the upper class.

When Margaret was soon to be six years old, time had come for her to begin her formal education. One evening in early September while they were cleaning up from supper, Sylvie said to Margaret, "Tomorrey morning you got to go to school. I'll wake you up daybreak so's you can eat and be there on time. You late," Sylvie threatened, "I'll give you a lickin'."

"Yes, ma'am. What's school?"

"It's whar you learns to read and write and cipher," replied her mother.

"You gonna come too?"

"No, I ain't gonna come, too. You go by yo'self. Ain't far. Just a couple miles. It's this side o' town."

"What do they do at school?"

"I don' tol' you! They learns how to read and write and cipher. Now don't ask no more fool questions. Jist go and you do what that teacher tells you to do. I hear you give trouble, you'll earn a lickin'. I ain't gonna let you grow up like me. You gonna learn schoolin' so's you won't never need to be nobody's slave. You're gonna be a teacher!"

Now quite knowing what a teacher was or did, Margaret sensed for the first time that her mother had some sort of concern for her, however out of character it might seem. Her mother had never expressed any thought about her daughter's needs or future before. She did not realize that Sylvie had lost her own dream and was clothing her daughter with a new one. She stared at her mother as Sylvie continued.

"If I'd knowed how to read and write, I would 'a knowed what I wuz puttin' my mark on 'fore I got on that ship," Sylvie said almost to herself. "If I'd knowed how to read and write," she repeated, "I could 'a had my shop."

"I think I heard about school once," the child said timidly, not quite sure if it was something she should have heard about. She added hastily, "I think I heard Mister Anthony talking to Pa about Squire Tally's grand-young'uns gettin schoolin. They go to this school I'm going to?"

"Them young'uns got they own teacher what goes to the big house. Then when they's growed up, they'll go to some fancy school far away."

This was more than Margaret had ever heard her Mother say about anything, except when she was fussing. She was intrigued and wondered if she dared ask another question.

"Will I be the only one at school?" she asked bravely.

"No. They's other young'uns hereabouts."

"Like me? Or will they be too old to play with me?"

"You ain't a-goin' to play!" Annoyed, Sylvie threw the dishcloth down on the table. "You'll go jist to learn what I said. You'll behave, act proper and keep your dress down! I hear you causing trouble or bein' bad, you know what I'll do."

"Yes, ma'am." Now she had gone too far and upset her mother.

"Now go to bed."

Mister Dellinger was school master at Maclin's little one-room school. To the boys and girls who attended, he taught the three R's, basic reading, writing and arithmetic. He tried to give a smattering of history and the bit of rudimentary science that he knew. He had to be careful, because the parents of these children did not have a clear understanding of the concept of education. They believed that learning the three R's was all that was necessary. Most of those parents did not know that much. The young students were often tired and sleepy, having to do as much time in work as they did in school. If Mister Dillinger taught them too much, or if they took home strange ideas, they might be withdrawn from school or he might lose his position and be replaced with another — not quite so adventuresome. The children seldom remained in school past the fourth level because they boys were needed to work in the fields or at their father's trade, and the girls had to help tend their younger siblings. One needed to read so that one could read the Bible and letters and contracts. It was necessary to count so that one would not be cheated. One must write so that one can add new names to the family Bible. Beyond that, more learning was a waste and not good for a working man or woman.

Mister Dellinger was a Charleston man. Tall, thin, with a shock of black hair, pale blue eyes and spectacles that slid down his long thin nose, he ruled the classroom with an iron hand. Young boys might chafe at being in a classroom with small children and girls, but in his school they behaved. Too much mischief from any one of them would result in a visit behind the woodshed. Then he would send them home with a note for their fathers, who would give them another thrashing.

Two of the boy students, William and Edward Baxter, were twin sons of Maclin's blacksmith. Janet Wills, who at fourteen was the oldest student in class and was considered almost grown and ready for marriage. She was a daughter of the Abner Wills, the sturdy couple who operated the post office and the village's only general store. This would be her last year in school. Mrs. Wills liked to pretend that they could have sent Janet away to Miss Julian's school for young ladies in Charleston if they had wanted to part with her, but everyone in town knew better. Allison Anderson and her towheaded little brother, Tommy, were children of the widow Anderson, the village dressmaker.

The seventh student was Thad Ball, the unfortunate son of Jethro Ball, the ne're-do-well, scrappy drunkard who owned and operated the lumber yard and sawmill on ten acres of land that he owned himself. Thad's mother had died giving him birth. While still a small boy, he had been crushed under a falling tree limb and his left leg was so damaged that it had not grown straight like the other. It was inches shorter, causing a marked limp. He also seemed to be simple-minded, but it was possible that this condition had been caused by the brutal beatings that were regularly delivered from his drunken father's fists. Thad should have finished his schooling, but because the other students often teased him, he stayed away for months at a time. Not long after Margaret began her studies, Thad ceased coming to school, preferring to remain at home and accept the physical blows of his father, rather than the verbal blows of his schoolmates.

Jethro Ball was Irish and the grandson son of a trading man who years ago had made a shrewd deal with a local native woman. Old Mister Ball had accepted ten acres of land deep in the piney forest from a Catawba woman in exchange for a wagon load of pots and pans and sharp steel tools needed by her village. He had quit his trading ways, bought an indentured servant from Ireland and married her. On these ten acres, he had established the area's only sawmill within a twenty-five-mile radius. Now new homes — or additions to existing ones — could be built of boards cut in Maclin and residents did not have to pay freight costs to have lumber delivered from farther away. When his father died, Jethro kept the mill going and intended to leave it to his crippled son. He believed that with the promise of ten acres of land, he would be able to procure a wife for the unfortunate boy.

Within a few months Margaret settled into the routine of arising early, breakfasting on a bowl of sofkee with home-made butter and a cup of milk. She dressed herself in her only everyday dress, made of homespun. Her drawers were made from flour sacking. She had almost received some fine dresses when Mrs. Tally had come to their cabin one afternoon to speak with her mother, while Margaret was at the butter chum on the porch.

"Mrs. O'Donnell at home, child?" she had asked.

"Yessum. She's out back. Want me to fetch her?"

"Yes. That would be fine. You going to school now?"

"Yessum," Margaret repeated.

"Good." Mrs. Tally smiled at her. "I believe in schooling for girl children, even though some don't. I want to ask her if you can have some of the dresses that my granddaughter has outgrown. Would you like that?"

"I guess so. I'll go get her." She quit the churn and went to call her mother. "Ma, Mrs. Tally's here. She wants to talk to you," she said hoping that her mother would allow her to have at least one dress.

"What she want?" was the abrupt response, grumbled as she walked around to the front stoop where Mrs. Tally waited.

Before she could say howdy, Mrs. Tally spoke up. "I came to offer little Margaret here a few dresses that my granddaughter has outgrown. I'm sure they would fit."

"She don't accept no charity." was her mother's firm reply. "I sew her dresses myself."

"Well, I don't think of it as charity. Just hate to see lovely dresses go to waste. They'll just linger in the trunk. No more granddaughters to wear them," suggested Mrs. Tally.

"Thank you kindly for the offer, but we can't accept." Sylvie was firm and Margaret was crushed. She had seen some of the pretty dresses the granddaughter had worn while playing with Flossie. The little black slave child had been elevated to the position of companion and personal maid when Mrs. Tally's granddaughter came to visit at Tally's Nook.

The dresses were denied her. The following week Margaret saw Flossie, pigtails tied in white ribbons, wearing one of the hand-me-down dresses — the most beautiful dress Margaret had ever seen. It was of the sheerest white muslin, with sky blue ribbon bows on short puffed sleeves and a wide blue sash tied around the waist, finished with a huge bow in back. When the slave child saw Margaret staring at her, she twirled around and around, showing off her new finery, then stopped, stuck out her tongue at Margaret and ran into the kitchen behind the big house where her Aunt Leah would protect her if there were trouble. Margaret felt her face go scalding hot with shame and anger.

The walk to school took the better part of an hour, so there never seemed to be enough time for Margaret to play with Tommy Anderson before class was called to order. A pot-bellied stove in one corner heated the little room. Those who sat close to it were apt to get too warm and those too far away would shiver. The well behind the schoolhouse furnished drinking water and an outhouse served their other needs. The alphabet and numbers were practiced on slate boards, which were rubbed clean with shirt sleeves. Sometimes, Mister Dellinger allowed Janet to help teach the younger two while he worked with the twins and Allison.

Before leaving for school each morning, Margaret did her chores. She fed the chickens and gathered eggs before fetching her lunch bucket, which usually held a portion of leftovers from the previous evening's supper, the same as the other students. Occasionally, there would be a portion of fried fatback and sometimes a fried spot fish from her father's catch to eat with cold cornbread and collard greens. Weather permitting, at noontime they gathered for lunch around a wooden table in the school's backyard by the well. One of the Baxter twins would draw fresh water from the well to wash down their food. After eating, there was time for a game of tag, marbles or some hopscotch before they returned to the classroom. When winter came, they remained indoors huddled around the pot-bellied stove in the corner. After they ate, they listened to Mister. Dillinger read from a novel. One of their favorites was *The Life and Adventures of Robinson Crusoe.*

After returning from school each evening, Margaret fed the chickens once more, looked again for eggs and filled the wood box from the pile of wood that her father had chopped, and worked the butter churn if needed. After a supper of more cornbread and greens, or biscuits and fatback—washed down with buttermilk—she helped clean up and then practiced letters and numbers on her slate by candlelight.

As years passed in this atmosphere, as simple as it might be, Margaret learned. She began to know that there was another world much different from the one she had known. As she learned, she began to sense that there was even more to herself than she had ever suspected. As her sense of self began to grow, she found that she had a natural love for reading—that Pandora's box which becomes the curse of all tyrants.

Months turned into years and Margaret grew into a strong, quiet, careful young girl, no longer a child— not a great beauty, but with a pleasant, deep, attractiveness that expressed itself through the intensity of her gaze. Her dark brown hair contrasted with her fair skin and deep grayish-green eyes. Seldom happy, often painfully lonely and exhausted by the constant unreasonableness of her now half-crazed mother, she was coming into her early youth acutely aware of the separation of social caste between her family and folk who lived in the big houses. It also pained her to realize that, to the white neighbors who knew that Charlie O'Donnell, even though he carried a white man's name and boasted a bit of white man's heritage, he was mostly Indian. He was a breed and as such would they consider her.

They might hire him and pay him fair wages for work—extend him respect for doing a job well done—but never, ever would they consider socializing with him. To the black slaves—with their own strong sense of pecking order—he was white trash, brass ankle, or red neck. Anthony might go shooting with Charlie, but Sylvie would not be asked to tea. The O'Donnells were beneath the respect of even the snobbish house servants. Flossie, the house brat, now grown through the years along with Margaret, continued to stick out and waggle her tongue at Margaret whenever her Aunt Leah was not looking, because she knew that their white masters would never socially accept trash.

NINE

IN 1861 MARGARET HAD HER TWELFTH BIRTHDAY and officers from *The Citadel,* Charleston's military college, fired on the Yankee ship, The Star of the West, from their encampment on Morris Island. The War Between the States had begun and life in the deep South would never be the same. In the beginning war did not bring much difference to Margaret's life as it did to the families who had sons. All the wealthy young men left their plantations and universities and young boys left their farm tools and plows to go marching off to enlist while singing patriotic songs. They felt thrilled to be given a chance to give the Yanks a beating, a task which they assumed their own braves souls would accomplish in a matter of weeks. They would be welcomed home as heroes with glorious adventures to tell and feared the fighting might be over before they would have a chance to earn their laurels.

War hardly touched those left at home until notices began to come of sons, husbands and fathers killed, missing in action, or taken prisoner. More and more men were needed to fill the depleting ranks. Those not so young and not so wealthy left their chores and went off to do battle against the enemy.

Mister Dellinger was among this second wave of men to join the fighting. With no suitable men available to be schoolmaster, the school shut down. Quite soon after he left, the school master was also a casualty— the first person close to Margaret to die in the war. His widow, Mrs. Dellinger, a skilled milliner, supported herself by making hats for the Maclin ladies, but the time came when there was no fabric to be had for fripperies such as new hats. Everything was going into the cavernous maw of the war. With no income, she needed work and encouraged by Maclin's women, Amy Dellinger reopened the little schoolhouse with herself installed as the schoolmistress. The children once again began to attend class with a school mistress, unheard of before this war, which would see many women take the place of their men who had gone to war and do well the tasks that only men had done before.

The departure of Mister Dellinger and the closing of the school had given the reluctant students much joy and some were not happy about its opening again, but Margaret looked forward to time away from the miserable little cabin and she missed learning. She was glad to begin her studies again under the kind eye of the new teacher.

Margaret's ability to read was excellent. Mrs. Dellinger complemented her by saying that she was reading far beyond her years. Her skill at arithmetic was not so good, as she struggled mightily to learn the multiplication tables. A shy and quiet student, not outgoing, she could not bring herself to ask for help. Her only recourse in any time of difficulty was to suffer in silence, to bear the frustration and emotional pain within herself. Mrs. Dellinger saw this and had a special way of reaching into the mind of her young student.

On the battlefields the fighting dragged on interminably. What had begun with enthusiasm and glee, fueled by a belief that the conflict would be brought to a swift close with glory for the South, turned into a seemingly endless struggle. When all the young men had been used up, older men were called to arms until there was no one left at home but children, women, invalids and grandfathers. Whole and healthy men of fighting age were away and only the most loyal of slaves remained on the plantations, the remainder having fled the yoke of slavery. There were few left to till the soil and bring in the meager crops. This chore fell to the children, the womenfolk and those few loyal slaves. As women always do when their men are off doing battle, spoiled though they might have been and unused to manual labor just as their gentlemen had been—these women of the South rolled up their sleeves. They had to survive. They planted crops and gardens in spring and harvested in autumn. They cared for the pitiful supply of cattle and livestock remaining. They suffered hardship. They did without soft cotton cloth, which went to make bandages for wounded men. No longer did they have the luxuries which had previously come into Charleston. Life was more difficult than most of them had ever imagined it could be.

There were other womenfolk besides the women of the plantations. They were the women of the turpentine men, wives of laborers who had earned a living for their families through their brawn or by trade or skill. These women had no land and were at the mercy of those who had. In the settled turpentine families, there was the cabin they lived in, which belonged to the plantation, the clothes on their backs and the ones in the wash tub. Their families could just about feed themselves by working small garden plots, but they had no warm clothes for winter. No shoes or blankets could be bought from the stores in the village. There was enough food for their families—maybe enough seed saved to plant the next year. They were not yet starving. Where there were no male children, young girls learned to shoot game, snare rabbits, and catch fish and crabs from the river. They became crack shots and filled the soup pots with possum, coon, and squirrel. When the garden seed was no more, their mothers gathered swamp cabbage, wild greens and whatever else they could find to eat.

Time came when Charlie could no longer resist the call to join the fighting. Turpentine was a wartime necessity and Charlie and Anthony had stayed as long as they could at Tally's Nook to help provide this commodity. For months they had considered that the hog farm—which provided provisions to the fighting men—was as important as fighting. They believed it to be what they needed to be doing; however, there were no more young men to go to battle. With the war not nearly won, their feelings about joining the army grew stronger. They felt that they should be fighting and leaving the pig raising to the few loyal blacks who remained. Now, even the turpentine gathering had to be given over to women.

One quiet moonlit evening, Anthony walked down to the cabin. Margaret was asleep in her cot by the kitchen fire. Sylvie and Charlie were sitting idle, staring into the flames. They heard Anthony call softly.

"Charlie. It's me, Anthony. Come out. We have to talk."

"Right," Charlie called in return, then turning silently to Sylvie, who continued to stare into the fire, he arose from his chair and went out the door, closing it quietly behind him. Anthony stood out in the yard away from the cabin, hands in his pockets, his head lowered, his right foot gently kicking up dirt in the yard. He didn't look up until Charlie stood no more than three feet in front of him. Still, he said nothing. He didn't have to. Charlie knew what he had come for. It had been an unspoken torment on both their minds for days. Neither one wanted to be the one to say that they should desert the plantation and abandon their families, though both knew that they must. They both knew that Old Squire Tally was too old to do a day's work and Mrs. Tally was beginning to lose her sight. They would be leaving their families unprovided for just like the others. A full minute passed before Anthony raised his head to look at Charlie.

"Time, ain't it?" Charlie said.

"Yes, it's time."

"When?"

"Hour before daybreak. I'll stop by."

"I'll be a-waitin'. Ridin' or walkin'?"

"We'd better walk. Best to leave the stock here with the women. They'll need the mules to plow. You got good walking shoes? Good soles, I mean?"

Charlie looked down at the heavy moccasin boots he still wore, then lifted first one foot, then the other to check the rawhide soles. "I reckon these'll do."

"Fine. We'll most likely have to walk to wherever we get sent. You got the boots, I'll bring extra socks."

"Thank you kindly. I accept. What about Mister Grenville down at The Hill? He comin' too?" asked Charlie. He was referring to the only other able-bodied white man in the county who had not gone off to fight, except for Jethro Ball, who was too drunk to stand, and his crippled, simple-minded son, Thad; although it was questionable whether Thad was able bodied.

"No. Not yet. General Lee still needs the river barges to haul supplies and ammunition and John Grenville is the only one left to run them. I suppose that when there are supplies to send in from Charleston, he'll be needed there. He feels bad about staying. Spoke with him two days ago. Wants to go with us, but he'll do what the Army needs. For now, anyway." Anthony turned and walked away.

Charlie watched him go until he was out of sight. He looked up at the sky. The moon was out and he could see only the brightest of the stars. The night was still. There were no owls or whippoorwills.

"Too late, now," Charlie said solemnly to the night air, "I decided to be white. Now I gotta go fight." He smiled and shook his head. "Damn, if now ain't a funny time for me to make a rhyme. My God!" he laughed.

When he went back inside, Sylvie was lying on their bed, the covers pulled up and her face to the wall. She didn't move when he climbed in beside her. He didn't touch her.

He had not slept a wink when the first birds began to chirp outside the window and the roosters began to crow. Charlie got up, dressed, got his coat and hat, pulled his shotgun off the wall and walked to the kitchen cot where Margaret lay sleeping. She was a young girl now, almost a woman. She would be able to take care of herself and Sylvie. He had taught her to shoot. She could hunt and fish with the best of the boys.

"Bye, Maggie," he whispered, closing the door quietly behind himself. He only had to wait for a few minutes before he saw Anthony coming toward the cabin. He walked out to the road to meet him, Silently, they fell in step side by side and walked away from Maclin.

Margaret did not know for two days where her father had gone. When he was not at home for supper the second night, she asked, "Where's Pa? He's not home again tonight."

"Gone," her mother answered. "He's gone."

"Where...," she started to ask, then stopped suddenly, as she really knew where. There could be no other explanation. Margaret knew that her Pa had gone to fight. Almost gently, she told her mother, "Don't worry none. We'll get by. And Pa, he'll be all right. He'll come back."

"Don't make no never mind," was Sylvie's only response. She allowed Margaret to clear the supper bowls from the table and went to sit in her rocker to stare into the fire while the girl rinsed them and put them back on the table for the morning meal.

TEN

THE WAR DRAGGED ON INTO ITS THIRD YEAR. Throughout Maclin and the surrounding miles, women, children and old folk were becoming destitute. Those women who still had land and a means of providing for themselves organized into aid societies. Through these groups, they gathered clothing, meager crops and other necessities of life for those who had been left behind, unprotected and unprovided. Rich and poor alike, they now had a kinship in suffering. There were charity cases in Maclin, a place previously known for its very wealthy or well-fed citizens. Margaret and her mother might have been among these charity cases had it not been for the skills that Margaret had learned from Charlie. He had taught her well. They would survive.

Margaret attained the upper class in school. Mrs. Dellinger, continually impressed by Margaret's interest in reading, began to loan her selections from her own meager collection. At first, there was a book by Emily Bronte, which Margaret happily took home to read, but as soon as Sylvie saw Margaret curled up in her cot reading the book, she became angry. "Wha' chu' readin?" she demanded to know. Margaret showed her the cover and replied, "It's a book Mrs. Dellinger gave me to read."

"That your lesson? You got to read it?"

"No, ma'am. The teacher just thought I'd like it. She knows I like to read."

"You can read your Bible," came the sharp retort. "Readin' other stuff is just a sign of laziness! Now put da book down and do your chores."

Reading the wonderful stories her teacher gave her had become her only path of escape from a sad and depressing life and Margaret refused to give up that one small pleasure. She devised a way to satisfy her blossoming appetite for literature. She continued to accept the loaned books. She read on her walk from the schoolhouse, but before reaching her cabin, she wrapped the book in an old torn towel and hid it under a wooden box under a tree trunk. Each morning, she retrieved the book from under the box and replaced it before she got back to the cabin in the afternoon. On the long walk to and from school over the quiet dirt coach road, she kept her head bent over a book while reading. After a while, she learned to do this quite efficiently. She could keep her eyes on the words in the book and—at the same time—could keep her eyes just enough on the path in front of her to avoid tripping or stumbling into the ditch. The thrilling stories of romance, descriptions of beautiful people and happy times, artful words of poetry that she found between the covers of the books—these things became Margaret's escape. It was her only way to relate to life and people in other than the ways that she had learned at home with her mother and father. With these stories in her heart, her dreams began. She dreamed of finding some better way for herself—a way to live like the people in her world of stories.

The road to school led Margaret past the Ball lumberyard and sawmill. Always looking down at her book, Margaret never noticed that she was being watched, daily, by Thad Ball, now a young man of seventeen. Thad had begun to think about marriage, but he feared that no girl would marry him because of his physical appearance. Long ago, when he had first set his eyes on Margaret, he planned to have her. Someday, when she was of age, he would have his father ask the O'Donnells for Margaret to be his bride.

His father, Jethro, had also watched her grow up and had encouraged Thad in his dream. Even though she always ignored him, never glancing his way, he allowed himself to believe that she was simply playing coy with him. He continued to weave his fantasies around her and a future life with her until he became obsessed. That he might repulse her did not occur to him, since they were both from the lower class of society. Thad considered himself her equal— even her better because he stood to inherit property all his own.

One day several ladies sat before a fire in the parlor of the Episcopal parsonage in Maclin, rolling bandages and exchanging the latest war news. The minister's wife had made root tea and corn muffins for the ladies while they worked. There was talk of crops, of runaway slaves, of the difficulty of keeping their young boys at home and in school when all they wanted to do was follow their fathers and older brothers to war.

"There is only one boy over thirteen left in class now," said Amy Dellinger. "Robert Clark and Johnny Eldridge left last month. They were both fourteen."

"I heard," replied Polly, the minister's wife. "Going off to war so young. Both their mothers came and talked with us. Tried everything they could to keep them home," she sighed.

"It's not easy. They know they must be men. They don't know whether to be men and keep the home together or go and fight. Always worrying about what the other boys will think of them," observed Elizabeth Perry.

"Robert was a good student," continued Amy. Her fingers deftly rolled a long swath of cotton cloth into a bandage. "He was good at his numbers ... better than I ... and soon he'd know more than I could teach him." She shook her head. "I so wanted him to go on to learn
more."

"Yes, The Reverend would have been glad to help him if he were here," said Polly, as she served more tea. "He was right good with figures. Trouble is, most of the men who are good with figures, they're already gone."

"I hear you have a good reading student ... a little girl?" asked Elizabeth.

"Well, not such a little girl. She's on her way to growing up," replied Amy. "And yes, she is excellent. Margaret can read anything I give her. And reads it well. I don't have any more books to loan her. She's read them all. She's a quiet and pleasant girl."

"Do you think she would come to Mockingbird Hill to read to me?" suggested Elizabeth. "I would enjoy the company."

"Why, what a splendid idea, Elizabeth. You have such a great collection in your library at The Hill." Amy suddenly frowned. "But I don't know about her mother. She might not allow the child to visit with you."

"Difficult, is she? Seems I've heard something of that sort. Name is O'Donnell?"

"That's it, Sylvie O'Donnell. The young lady's father left not long ago with Mister Anthony Parish to go up to General Lee's army.

"I'll think on it and see what I can arrange," Elizabeth assured her.

Elizabeth Grenville Perry was the daughter of John Grenville, the master of Mockingbird Hill Plantation and the young wife of Major Andrew Perry of the Charleston Perrys. A true-blue blood and member of the landed gentry of South Carolina, Elizabeth Perry considered it one of her responsibilities to discover and nurture talent and ability wherever she discovered it in her community. She thought on the problem of how to arrange for young Margaret to visit and not anger her mother at the same time, then came up with what she believed to be the perfect solution.

One afternoon as Margaret walked down the steps of the school house, she saw a pretty lady sitting in a buggy under the shade of the big chinaberry tree. In the driver's seat, holding the reins of a fine bay gelding, sat a black coachman. Margaret recognized the lady — having seen her at church — and knew who she was. She motioned for Margaret to come closer. Margaret walked slowly over to the buggy. Shading her eyes against the sun, she spoke, "Yes, ma'am?"

"You're Margaret?" the pretty lady asked.

"Yes, ma'am. I'm Margaret."

"Do they call you Maggie?"

"No, ma'am, they call me Margaret. Maybe my daddy called me Maggie sometimes. When he was here. I was named for my mother's sister. She's dead."

"Well then, Margaret it will be," the lady declared emphatically, then smiling with the most beautiful smile young Margaret had ever seen, she introduced herself.

"I am Mrs. Elizabeth Perry. I live at Mockingbird Hill. I've heard from your teacher about your interest in books. She told me that you have gone through her small collection and she hopes that I might find a few volumes in my library that might interest you. I've brought three and would like for you to choose one," Elizabeth said as she held out the three small books.

Margaret did not know quite what to think or how to feel. She wanted to see the books and wanted to read them. She felt a sudden rush of heat to her face as she realized that this wonderful person was praising her. She felt almost overwhelmed.

Seeing that Margaret stood off and mistaking her expression for fear, Elizabeth encouraged her. "Come on over, Maggie. I won't bite and neither will the horse," she said with a delightful laugh.

Margaret was not afraid of the horse, nor was she afraid of the black driver of the buggy, but she was awed by the lady. In her experience, the only person who had ever befriended her had been her teacher. To have someone like Elizabeth Perry come to her to offer books had to be a daydream come true.

Just then Mrs. Dellinger came down the school house steps. Seeing Margaret still standing away from the buggy, she walked over and gave her a gentle push forward. "Go on, Margaret. It's all right. I asked Mrs. Perry to come with the books, but I didn't know she would come today or I would have told you. It's all right for you to accept her offer."

Margaret walked closer to the buggy and stood still, arms to her sides. She watched as the lady looked at the titles, chose one, and lay the others on the cushion beside her. She handed the book she had chosen down to Margaret. Margaret reached up and took it carefully in both hands. It was beautiful— bound in real leather, dyed dark green with the title in gold letters. It was more beautiful than any book she had ever held, except her Bible. She read the title: *Jane Eyre.*

"This is rather a new book, Maggie, but already it is one of my favorites. Please read from the first page for me—aloud. Do you mind?" asked the lady. "I want to hear you read."

"No, ma'am. I don't mind." Margaret answered. She began to read the first paragraph of the book in a bright, clear voice. Although her pronunciation of some of the words that she did not recognize was awkward and slow, she read with a sense of knowing what she was reading, giving meaning to the words.

Mrs. Perry glanced at Mrs. Dellinger and smiled her approval. "You were right. She reads beautifully. I'll be happy to work with her." Turning to Margaret, she spoke again. "Mrs. Dellinger tells me that you read while walking to and from school. Why is that?"

Margaret hung her head and did not answer, but Mrs. Perry had heard of the peculiarities of Sylvie O'Donnell and thought she knew the reason.

She asked, "Is it because you may not read at home?"

Margaret, keeping her head down, remained quiet. She could not admit this to anyone for fear her mother would be told and punish her again.

"Well then," spoke Mrs. Perry. "I have an idea. Since my husband is away, I need someone to visit with me for a few hours each week. I know your father is away in the war, too. If I asked your mother to allow you to come to Mockingbird Hill on some afternoons after school would you be willing? Then you could read to me and I would pay you forty cents a week. I'll either give all the money to your mother or some of it to her, and you could keep some for yourself. I would leave that decision to you. Will you come?" she pleaded.

For the first time Margaret lifted her eyes and really looked at the lady. She had not expected that she would ever meet someone like Mrs. Perry, much less be asked to come to her house to read for her. For the first time, a bit of excitement born of hope came into the pit of her stomach. Before she really thought about what her mother would say, she replied, "Yes, Ma'am. I want to come."

"Good, then it is settled. You climb right up here with me. Toby and I will drive you home and I will speak with your mother."

Margaret climbed aboard and rode home in the buggy, seated beside her new mentor. She was too excited to say a word. Leaving the girl to her thoughts and feelings, Elizabeth said nothing. They rode in silence. When the buggy pulled up in front of the O'Donnell cabin, Margaret jumped down and ran up to the front steps to call her mother, but Sylvie was already at the front door, peering out from under her poke bonnet, trying to see who had arrived. With her snuff stick wedged in the corner of her mouth, she demanded through clenched teeth.

"What you done girl? You in trouble?"

"No, Ma'am, no trouble," Margaret hastily replied.

Simultaneously, Elizabeth Perry spoke from the buggy and came to her rescue.

"Mrs. O'Donnell, I have come to ask a great favor of you. I have need of someone to read to me some afternoons and I have just been to the school and have spoken with Margaret's teacher. She says that Margaret is doing quite well and that she could be a suitable reader for me."

Sylvie slowly walked down the steps and out into the yard. Looking up into the buggy, she had to further shade her eyes from the glare of the sun. Without even a pleasant hello or greeting for Elizabeth, she spoke: "Margaret's got chores. She's needed at home."

"I hadn't planned to keep her from her chores," explained Elizabeth, "and I fully intend to pay you for her services. I thought thirty cents a week. Would that be enough?" She didn't look at Margaret and Margaret kept her silence. This meant that she would give Margaret ten cents a week all her own. It was as though they were already co-conspirators against her mother. She dared not look at her mother when she heard Mrs. Perry continue, "I promise I'll not keep her late, or ask for her every day. Since my husband is away at war also, I need company and will be very grateful."

"How far you live?" Sylvie gruffly asked, knowing full well that Mrs. Perry lived at Mockingbird Hill, the neighboring plantation. "How long it'll take her to walk there and back?" she demanded to know.

"No need for her to walk. I'll send the buggy to fetch her." Elizabeth was a lady, a person of quality, and this old woman's meanness did not cause her to flinch. She could imagine what it must be for a young girl like Margaret to live under this tyranny.

The old woman stood her ground for a bit, then as she realized that this was a great opportunity to further her aims, she boldly asked, "Will you promise to help Margaret teach at school on her own when she's of age?"

Elizabeth studied her briefly, then assured her, "Of course, I will if that is what she wants to do."

"Don't matter none what she wants. She's too young to know what she wants. She can go for a couple hours three days a week. When do you want her to come?"

"Tomorrow acceptable with you?"

"I reckon it is." Turning to Margaret she said, "Now go start your chores. Enough foolin' for one day." She said loudly as Mrs. Perry turned to say goodbye to Margaret, "That'll be in advance, I reckon? The thirty cents?" As she held out her hand, Elizabeth reached into her velvet bag, extracted the thirty cents and placed them in the palm of Sylvie O'Donnell.

During the first few weeks that Margaret went to Mockingbird Hill, the old woman was resentful of the intrusion into her domain and made a fuss each time the buggy came for the child. Soon though, with the extra thirty cents a week tucked away in a covered jar in the back of the cupboard, she grumbled less and less, since Margaret also continued to do her chores. In addition, she was proud that she had been such a shrewd bargainer with Mrs. Perry by extracting a promise that Elizabeth would see to it that Margaret would secure a teaching position when she was of age.

ELEVEN

THE GRENVILLE AND PERRY ANCESTORS had come to the wild shores of what is now South Carolina, this low, swampy, mosquito-pestered land from England and Wales, from Massachusetts and from Barbados. They carved out of this new, raw place a little bit of England transported—complete with nobility, landed gentry and all its trappings. They made grand plans, laid out marvelous baronies, built houses and towns, fought Indians, and died from fevers when they brought African slaves to till the soil. Those who survived lived to create one of the most beautiful towns on the Southern coast—Charles Town.

The first Grenville, an aristocrat, had come from England in an early migration, sailing from Bristol, via Barbados. He had settled in the primitive village that was to become a lovely city. The following generations of Grenvilles left the protection of Charles Town and helped to push the original native Coosa and Yamasee tribes further inland. Reaching the domain of the Catawbas, the settlers took that for themselves and built more and more settlements in the surrounding low country and toward the foothills of the big mountains.

Certain among the slaves brought from the west coast of Africa knew secrets of growing and processing rice and indigo, and plantations grew wealthy. The settlers drained the swamps, cleared the woods and used this raw new land for crops and stock raising. They were among the first cattlemen in the new land. They left their cattle loose to fatten and roam the swamp lands, rounding them up with some of the first cowboys on these shores. They shipped the cattle down river on special barges to the city. Then came King Cotton. Life in this southern Eden seemed complete when the Grenvilles built their ancestral home, Mockingbird Hill, in the early Eighteenth century.

John Charles Grenville came into the world in 1810 into one of the best families in plantation society, one of the wealthiest in all the anti-bellum south. A true aristocrat, he inherited Mockingbird Hill as the first son of Charles Beardon Grenville. His was the typical upbringing of the scion of a wealthy southern planter family. Schooled at home by private tutors until ready for prep school and university, John married Anne Elizabeth Perry, a daughter of another old, aristocratic family.

As a young man, John Grenville did no manual labor. He rode blooded horses and entered them in races. He went shooting, danced and gamed, then studied the classics at university. He rode over the plantation occasionally, but often, he left the entire care of the place and the managing of his numerous slaves to his trusted overseer, as his father had done before him.

In that time of early settlement in the low country, rivers were the main highways from the plantations. Part of the operation of Mockingbird Hill was a fleet of river barges used to take cattle and harvested crops to the ports at Georgetown and Charleston. As a lad, John had taken a young boy's pleasure in riding the barges in the summertime. Young John did not work while riding the barges. Slaves worked and he accompanied the barge captain for the simple joy a lad derived from a summer's outing on the river. He fished, swam alongside the barge and listened to the slaves singing while they worked.

John was not a lazy exception to aristocratic life. He was not to be looked down on as simply an idle man. He was the son, grandson and great-grandson of gentleman planters. He was brought up to be the same kind of gentleman planter — to live the lifestyle of other wealthy gentlemen planters. He had been born to this life just as his ancestors had been born to it in England. His ancestors had been able to duplicate the lifestyle of landed gentry as it had been lived in England — with the added advantage of having slaves to do the work.

John Grenville was capable to a point, but with an overseer completely controlling what happened with the crops, the barge captain dealing with the river shipments, a clerk to keep finances, and his wife, Anne, in charge of the house, there was very little of substance for him to do. The first of life's grim realities hit John when Anne died of fever, leaving him with their young daughter, Elizabeth, to rear. However, after the first shock had worn off, with the everyday task of caring for her given over to the house slaves, he continued life as he had always known it.

When Elizabeth attained young adulthood and had completed her years at finishing school, she came out at the annual debutante ball. Then her father depended on her to be the woman of the house, planning that when she married she would bring her husband to live at with them Mockingbird Hill. In time she was betrothed to Lieutenant Andrew Perry, her mother's second cousin and the third son of his family. He would not inherit his family home, which would go to his eldest brother, leaving him free to make his home at the Grenville estate.

Life continued idyllic, peaceful and profitable until the shock of the war that came in 1861. Within days after the shots had been fired at Fort Sumpter, Elizabeth and Andrew married. His regiment immediately went away to war. Elizabeth remained as chatelaine of Mockingbird Hill.

John Grenville was already middle aged, his medium build still trim and fit, the gray at his temples tendering softness to his dark hair and blue eyes. His overseer and barge captain left to enlist, so responsibility of working both the plantation and barges fell on his unaccustomed shoulders. During the first part of the conflict, John managed to maintain the fleet of barges for transporting harvests to Charleston and taking supplies to the army but as months wore on and the fighting became uglier, their huge cash crops dwindled. Harvests were barely enough to sustain the populace. Grenville's barges became the primary conveyance for supplies and whatever food was available to maintain the army.

Elizabeth busied herself with many charitable works in the community. She was always ready to help others less fortunate than herself, so John was not surprised to return home one afternoon and find his daughter in the company of a comely young girl, helping her with reading.

Elizabeth arose from the parlor settee where the two women had been sitting when she heard her father come in. She pulled Margaret up by her hand and led her out to the entrance hallway that ran down the center of the house.

"Father," she said. "Please say hello to my young friend. She is coming to keep me company while Andrew is away. Margaret, say hello to my father, John Grenville."

John was tired and ready to retire to his study, but his manners required that he be polite. Barely stopping, he tipped his head.

"Hello, child. Welcome to Mockingbird Hill. We have little gaiety here now. Make sure my daughter entertains you well."

"I'm happy to meet you, sir," Margaret answered, so softly he could barely hear her. Then, as an afterthought, she attempted a curtsey and almost lost her balance. She felt very inferior to these people and was almost overcome with shame at her awkwardness. Their clothes, their speech and their manners seemed to be like something out of the books she had read and not from real life. She could think of nothing else to say.

"All right, Father." Elizabeth rescued them both. "Go on into your study and leave us. We will sit in the parlor for a while longer. Someday, you'll have to listen to this child read. She is really marvelous," she said, as her father took his leave.

John had barely taken any notice of the child throughout the ritual, but later, while sitting in his study, three things came back to him. He remembered her intelligent expression, her awkwardness when she had tried to curtsey. He remembered the luster of her hair but he could not recall her name.

Throughout the next year Margaret continued her weekly schedule. Three days a week were devoted to reading with Elizabeth. Margaret received instruction in how to understand the message of the writers, instruction in diction and in grammar. She became more at ease with the two Grenvilles. Many evenings, John would come in from the river — his boots muddy and his body expressing exhaustion — and see her with Elizabeth. He would quietly make his way to his room or to the library, leaving them alone. He was happy that Elizabeth had a pleasant companion. Some afternoons he would hear the child reading and would quietly take a chair out of their sight, simply to listen to her gentle voice; a calming and soothing effect that he relished and needed.

Throughout that year, as the fighting raged about them and they feared the war was being so painfully lost, Margaret spent as much time as she could with her new friend. She often stayed through supper time, being driven home in the buggy by Toby — except that now there was no shiny bay gelding to pull the buggy, just a big, rawboned mule, already tired from his day behind a plow.

During the spring of 1863, Andrew Perry made a brief furlough to visit Elizabeth. One week later news came to them that he had been killed in battle. Very soon after receiving this horrible news, Elizabeth realized that she was with child. Margaret was needed more and more at Mockingbird Hill to soothe grief-stricken Elizabeth.. Sylvie allowed the extended visits only because of the generous payment of money and food that Elizabeth gave her for Margaret's companionship.

As fighting between the North and the South dragged on and on, the Southerners' attitudes changed. Adventure turned into chaos. The adrenaline of excitement became the gall of fear. Confidence in their invincibility gave way to the dread of possible defeat and humiliation.

War came home to Maclin in the form of wounded soldiers leaving the front lines, some on bleeding feet, some on the backs of scrawny mules, and some drifting down river on log rafts or rowing in rickety canoes. When they reached their destinations or simply could not travel any further, women sheltered them in makeshift hospitals or churches. They were lucky if there was a doctor to care for them.

All healthy women and young girls were called upon to become nurses in addition to all the other responsibilities that were heaped upon them. Only married women could care directly for the soldiers. The unmarried girls were kept busy washing bloody sheets and bandages and preparing them for further use. Many women encountered each other who normally would not because of class distinction. Margaret found herself working in the hospital with several young ladies of class. She felt very confident and proud knowing that she had been able to care for her mother and herself and that she had not needed charity from anyone. She might be poor, but she was self-sufficient; however, she did accept a gift of two of Elizabeth's dresses, as her friend's middle expanded and she could no longer fit into them. The dresses fit her blossoming figure becomingly. Elizabeth had also given her a diary. It was a brown leather-bound book with blank pages. Elizabeth explained how she could write all her secrets in it, yet still use it to practice her penmanship and writing skills. Margaret's manners had become more like the those of Elizabeth Perry's class than of her own class. Her way of speaking had greatly improved. She was not yet a real lady but had begun to see the way.

Sylvie's tiny garden kept Margaret and her aging mother going along with the small game that Margaret brought home. Several days a week, when she was not at Mockingbird Hill or rolling bandages, she attended to her snares and fishing; going out into the woods alone and unguarded except for Charlie's old bird gun that she always took with her. Often, as she left her cabin at Tally's Nook and walked toward the river and woods, she did not notice Thad Ball watching her as she passed the sawmill.

There had been no word from her father since he and Anthony had left Tally's Nook. Charlie did not know how to write, so there was never a letter. After many months had gone by, a returning soldier told of seeing Charlie alive, but could not remember where or when. Sylvie and Margaret never knew which battles he fought, or if he fought at all, and for a long while they did not know if he was dead or alive. His wife hardly cared, seeming to be quite content with him away. Margaret missed him but did not talk about it with her mother.

In 1864 the war was lost. No one had surrendered, but a generation of good men had almost been annihilated. Many rotted in Yankee prisons. Others died from eating rotten food and drinking contaminated water, from gangrene, fever, or pneumonia. If not dead, they were crippled or missing. What had begun so gloriously in lovely Carolina was ending not so gloriously. The little bit of England was no more. It had become a little bit of hell.

During the closing months of the war, violence did not confine itself to the battle field. The territory was open to drifters, deserters, thieves, and ne'er-do-wells. Young women had to protect themselves, their older parents and younger siblings from accident, from roaming thieves who would kill for a piece of bread, from unprincipled men of all ages and all origins who were always ready to violate a woman found alone. In the deepest parts of the swampland, this type of man could hide and exist very well for weeks living off the land. Lawlessness reigned throughout the south.

Elizabeth was aware that Margaret went out alone to hunt and fish for her mother and herself. She had warned Margaret to be careful and Margaret assured her that she always took along her gun and kept it ready. Maybe two times a week, she would find a plump rabbit in her snare—then there would be rabbit stew or roasted rabbit for dinner. Coming on flocks of quail, she would bag eight or ten of the plump birds and that would be dinner for several days. On other days, she fished in the river. Sometimes, there was even enough fish or game that she and her mother could share with Old Lady Tally who was living up in the big house all alone, Squire William having passed away two winters past. Margaret remained unaware of the hungry eyes silently watching her as she walked past Ball's sawmill on her way to the river.

One morning, as Margaret walked by the Ball place on her way from fishing, Thad Ball stepped out from behind a tree and blocked her way. Tall, skinny, with sandy hair and watery blue eyes — a homely face adorned with crooked, yellow teeth — she found him repulsive and tried to move around him. He moved quite quickly despite his twisted, shortened leg and continued to keep her there, holding out both his arms to prevent her from going around him. She could see the strength in his arms, muscled by endless hours of sawing logs with his father. He laughed at her and her disgust became fear.

"Better not go in dem woods by yo'se'f, girlie. Dey's full of deserters hidin' in der jest waitin' to jump on you," he teased. "Better you let me go wid ya."

"Let me pass, Thad Ball," she demanded.

"Now, girlie, don't be in sich a hurry," he sneered, wiping his nose with the back of his hand. His clothes were dirty, patched with a man's awkward stitching, his pants held up with an old piece of wire twisted together at the ends. "I ain't lettin' you go by 'til you be neighborly and say hello, nice like," he replied. "I got plans for us. For you 'n me. Soon, I'm gonna talk to your ma. I done seen her a couple times and done hinted. It don't seem like she don't like me. You gettin' growed up, girlie, and when Paw's gone I'll have this place for me own. I'll be landed, with ten whole acres. Yo' ma said you gonna be a teacher. Don't matter none to me. You can teach all you want. It's time I'm gettin hitched and soon I'm gonna ask yo ma."

At this declaration, Margaret curled her lip in disgust. How dare he presume that she would even consider him. She might be poor, but no longer was she trash. Holding up Charlie's old bird gun in front of her chest, she threatened him, "You get out of my way Thad Ball or I'll fill you full of bird shot!" With this she ran around him, leaving him grinning at her until she was out of sight.

"Let her go for now," he said aloud. "I knows how to make her marry me." He shook his head and laughed, "Uppity li'l thang!"

Margaret was now old enough to be considered a young woman of marrying age. Girls married young because many died young. It was not unusual for a man to have two or even three wives during his lifetime and rear two or three families. Except for war, the odd accident or a rampaging fever epidemic, a man could expect a rather long reproductive life. Women, however, suffered the added danger of dying during childbirth and might live only until their late teens or early twenties. A wife was lucky to live until her thirtieth birthday, have several children — the last of which might still be her cause of death — leaving her husband to take another young wife of fourteen or fifteen years and begin again. Even though all the eligible and acceptable unmarried men were either away fighting or crippled, Margaret believed that there had to be better for her than Thad Ball. Never in a million years would she stoop so low as to marry him, no matter what her mother expected her to do. And Sylvie might! Just from meanness and the promise of ten acres of land, Sylvie might consent to hand Margaret off to Thad.

Margaret intended to become a lady ... almost ... and she wanted a suitable man. She would let Miss Elizabeth take care of that for her. Maybe she would find a merchant for her—or a skilled craftsman. Either would be better than the likes of Thad Ball. The very thought of him touching her made her shiver in disgust. That night, as she lay in her cot in the kitchen, she wrote in her diary about her encounter with him.

TWELVE

ALTHOUGH VISIBLY BEATEN, the South would not lie down because its spirit had not yet been crushed. There had been so many casualties that not one single Confederate regiment had enough able-bodied men to make a full company to send into battle. Then most of the remaining old men who could walk and tote a gun, and boys old enough to leave their mothers, who had not yet gone to fight, joined the fray.

For John Grenville the time came when his barges sat idle at the river's edge. There was nothing left to transport. No supplies, no troops, no more machines of war remained to ship. On the plantation, only four slaves remained out of the one hundred thirty he had owned at the beginning of the war. There remained Toby, his woman, Nellie, and two women field workers. There was nothing to plant or to harvest except for greens and sweet potatoes from the kitchen garden. There was nothing to keep him at Mockingbird Hill any longer. John knew that he must go to the front in Virginia. There, he might be able to do some good. As he readied himself to join General Lee, he arranged for Elizabeth to go to her husband's family home in Charleston. There, with the two Perry sisters, she could await the birth of her child and remain until the war ended and he returned, if he was lucky enough to come home. Toby and Nellie would be left in charge of the plantation.

Margaret went to Mockingbird Hill to help Elizabeth pack and to set everything right at the plantation before Elizabeth left. As they were in Elizabeth's dressing room filling the trunks, Elizabeth pleaded once more.

"Margaret won't you reconsider and come with me? You won't be safe here."

"I can't leave Ma. She needs me."

"Won't they take care of her at Tally's Nook? Surely Mrs. Tally will care for her?"

"She's too old — Mrs. Tally is--and we take care of her now. You know she's almost blind. Can barely see her hand in front of her face. For some reason, Ma and Mrs. Tally get along. Most all the blacks are gone. Aunt Leah's the only one left in the house, and she can't do anything. Keeps saying she's a cook and don't know how to do anything else."

"Doesn't know," corrected Elizabeth.

"Doesn't know," Margaret repeated. "Uncle Ned and Young Ned do all the outside work. They got lots to look after." She looked up at Elizabeth with a smile. "Besides, you know how Ma is. She's old and getting crankier, but she depends on me. I'd best stay here."

"I'll give you the address in Charleston where I will be staying. If you need me, just post the letter with Mrs. Mills at the post office in Maclin. She'll make sure I get it."

"Yes, ma'am."

"Don't say 'ma'am' to me. You've become like my own sister," she said gently. Then, in a stronger tone, she admonished, "You continue reading, and write in the diary every day. Write everything that happens." Then she cautioned, "Don't forget to practice proper grammar and sentence structure, and don't let yourself slip in diction either."

"Don't worry, I'll keep up with it all, even though now I'm reading the same books over and over."

"I know ... it's this war. Won't it ever end!" Elizabeth sighed. "Until it's over, there won't be any new."

Everything was packed and loaded on the rear of the buggy. Time had come to say farewell. Margaret stood in the yard and shivered in the early autumn air. She watched with tears in her eyes, as Toby helped Elizabeth up into the buggy and then climbed onto the driver's seat. Elizabeth waved her handkerchief and Margaret waved in return as the buggy, pulled by the lone mule remaining on the plantation, drove out of sight.

THIRTEEN

TOWNSPEOPLE STILL REFERRED TO ELLEN PERRY RADLEY and Alice Perry Beton as The Perry Sisters. They lived in the spacious Perry family townhouse just off Tradd Street and had never lived anywhere else, although they had both been married. The morning after the declaration of war they stood together with their young men in the chapel at St. Philips and were married in a joint ceremony. Cadet Beton and Cadet Radley, both upperclassmen at The Citadel, were more interested in the war and fighting the Yankees than in romance and the begetting of sons. They enlisted directly after the wedding ceremony and went straightaway to their regiment. The young wives returned to their ouse off Tradd Street.

On what was to have been their wedding night with their young husbands, Ellen and Alice slept in the same bed while they held and comforted each other as they cried themselves to sleep. Within weeks they received news of the death of Lieutenant Beton, killed at Haws Shop. On the following Wednesday, Lieutenant Radley was killed at the battle of Cold Harbor. First their brother and then both their husbands had given their lives. The Perry sisters — Alice, aged sixteen, and Ellen, aged seventeen — donned widows' black. They were still virgins.

When the sisters heard that their sister-in-law, Elizabeth, was expecting a child, they had been filled with joy, wanting nothing more than for Elizabeth to come and live with them so that the child would be born in the Perry home. After several letters of invitation, Elizabeth had written to accept, believing that her father would go to war as well.

It was a special reunion of the three young women when Elizabeth arrived in Charleston. Ellen and Alice were excited to see her and took turns sitting beside the big bay window in the front room watching for the buggy all afternoon. Finally it came into view.

Ellen called out to Alice, "It's here! I see the buggy. It has to be her. My God, that poor mule! Doesn't she have anything better to hitch to her buggy? I hope the neighbors do not see."

"You certain?" Alice ran breathlessly to the window and pulled the other side of the curtain away to look. "I do believe it is. Let's go out."

She ran to the door and threw it open, just as the buggy stopped in front of the half-circle stair steps. With Ellen directly behind her, she ran to the buggy door and opened it.

"Sister," greeted Elizabeth as Alice reached in to help her sister-in-law climb down.

"You're so big," Alice commented with youthful vigor, to the consternation of her elder sister.

"Alice! Your manners! You shouldn't say such things to Elizabeth!" she reprimanded.

"Oh, it doesn't matter, Ellen," said Elizabeth. "I'm just so happy to be here and out of that cramped buggy seat that Alice could call me anything." Turning to Toby, she instructed, "Toby, tie the mule to the hitching post and come inside for supper before you go back. I wanted you to stay to rest overnight, but Father said you must return immediately. I don't know why, but there you have it."

"Yessum, Miz Elizabeth. Just 'low me to tek 'im to de trough to drink. You go on in. I'll come up to de kitchen terekly."

"Come on up into the parlor, Elizabeth. Alice, call for Malcom to come down and help Toby get the trunks," Ellen ordered.

Later that afternoon, after Toby had been fed and sent on his way and the three ladies had dined, they sat together and talked.

"Ellen," asked Elizabeth, "why are you both still wearing black? It's been a long time. No one would expect you dress as a widow for more than a year."

"Alice and I decided to wear black until the war is over," Ellen explained. "It seemed the right thing to do. With all the men gone, there's nothing to dress up for—no one to try to be pretty for. There's just sadness everywhere we turn."

"Yes," chimed in Alice, "we almost changed our minds once, but then Andy got killed and we just kept on wearing it ... but you know," she added excitedly, "I might just go back to colors when your babe comes. That would be all right, wouldn't it, Ellen?"

"Yes, I think be all right... and so will I!" Hugging her sister-in-law carefully, she said, "You don't know what this means to us; your having the baby here. He'll be a Perry! It will be so good to have a new Perry in the house. It will make it seem like life can go on after all. He will give us something to look forward to."

"I can't wait to hold him," gushed Alice.

"You know it will be a 'him'?" laughed Elizabeth.

"Oh, yes. I just know it," Alice laughed as she danced around the room. Then, city girl that she was, she asked, "Now tell us, Elizabeth, what do you do out there on the river to keep busy."

FOURTEEN

MARGARET CONTINUED THROUGH HER LONG and exhausting days of going to the woods for game, the river for fish, doing the work of a man, and trying to care for both herself and her mother. She was lonely. No conversation, no reading and talking about the message in books, no evidence of civilization, made for a bleak existence. The only things that gave a bit of joy to her day was her diary and the few books Elizabeth had left with her. She had written in the diary many times, but not every day as Elizabeth had suggested. Now she turned to it as a dear companion. Sylvie still would not allow idle reading in the cabin, so Margaret would take the books with her when she went into the woods. There, in a clearing by the river, was a huge oak tree. She would prop up her shotgun and lay down her sack of rabbits or squirrels. There, at the foot of the oak, she could take time for herself and simply read; until that dreadful day in October.

She did not hear or see Thad Ball follow her into the woods. She did not see him drop to his knees behind a cypress stump to watch her take her book out of her coat pocket and lie down on her belly to read. She was so engrossed in the pages that she did not know he was there until he was standing over her, looking down with a drawn, ugly face.

Before she could get up, he was on her. Straddling her back, he pinned her to the ground and grabbed her wrists in his big rough hands. She struggled, trying to dig her toes into the soft ground, but her shoes kept slipping on the wet grass. She tried to turn over so she could get her knee into his groin, but she could not. Screaming at him, she kicked her heels into his back, uselessly. He knew nothing but the rush of wild passion as he felt her helplessness. He was silent. Shifting position, he slammed his knee in the middle of her back, shutting off her breath in mid scream. He let go her wrists, took her shoulders and flipped her over on her back. Then, before she could scream, with all the force he could muster, he hit her across her face with the back of his hand. His palm came down again. The second blow left her dazed — her eyes blurred and her body limp. He grabbed both her wrists with one hand and placed them above her head, then — with his free hand — he reached under her skirt and ripped at her underclothes. He ripped the waist loose and pulled it down to her knees, then all the way off. She tried to move, to fight him, but her body would not obey her. She tried to scream, but no sound came. She felt the cold air on her bottom as her dress was flipped up over her face. She fought to sit up, to get her arms free, but he hit her again with his fist... and then there was darkness.

When he finished with her, he got up and stumbled off into the woods, leaving her lying on the soft damp ground — bruised, battered, bleeding and practically senseless. She tried to move, but pain shot through her body, so she lay still with the foul odor of his filthy body still all around her.

Minutes that seemed like hours passed as she lay there fighting nausea. She struggled to her hands and knees, vomited and then fell over. She lay still again until her senses slowly came back and her breathing become normal. She shut her eyes in shame, recalling in anger the horror of what he had done to her ... recalling it again and again. Remembering her shotgun, she pushed her hair away from her face. With relief, she saw that it was where she had left it — propped up against the tree. There was only one thing she wanted to do with that shotgun. Hunt him down and kill him, but she knew that she could not. She must hide what had happened to her. No one must ever know. Not her mother — because she would surely marry her off to the monster. Not Miss Elizabeth, nor Mrs. Dellinger, because if they knew that the vile creature had touched her, she would never be given a teaching position. She would never be a wife to a decent man.

Margaret limped to the water's edge and splashed river water over her face. She stared at her reflection and wretched again. All she could think about was her mother's reaction, if she ever found out. Sylvie would never cease to blame her, just as she blamed herself. She would say it had been Margaret's fault. And her mother would be right. She should never have been so relaxed under the circumstances. If not Thad, it might have been a deserter, or even a Yankee. *It was her fault. It was her fault.*

Looking down at her skirt she saw smears of blood and dirt. She waded out into the river to wash the stains from her clothes and from her body. She must go home and into the house as though nothing serious had happened to her. Never again would she put her gun down.

She could hardly walk. Her body ached, her head seemed ready to burst and her belly flamed with pain, but when she got close to the cabin she did her best to walk straight, showing nothing amiss. Sylvie was sweeping the yard and hardly looked up as her daughter approached.

"You late comin' in," her mother observed, continuing with the chore.

"Yes, ma'am." Her voice was shaky enough that Sylvie looked sharply at her.

Seeing the wet dress and boots and the general disarray of her daughter she asked, "What happened to you? Fall in the river?"

"Almost," replied Margaret, thinking quickly. "Got my foot caught on a root, dropped the game bag in the river and tried to grab it. Current took it and I got all wet and muddy trying to reach it. I had two fat quail and a rabbit."

"Did ya bring 'em?"

"No, ma'am. They fell too far out. Didn't bring nothing home. I'm sorry. I'll go out again tomorrow and for sure I'll bring something back."

"Well, they'll only be biscuits and 'lasses for supper tonight and breakfast tomorrey. I wuz looking to have to a mess of quail tonight with gravy for the biscuits."

"I'm sorry, Ma."

She was sorry indeed, but not for her failure to bring home supper. She was sorry that she could not even tell her mother what happened to her. It was bad enough for it to have happened. To have no one in whom she could confide and find solace was more than anyone should have to bear. That night she took out her diary—feeling that just telling something, if not someone, would help. And so she wrote about what had happened to her. Her face flamed as she wrote the descriptive words, her eyes burned as she wrote the name Thad Ball. She wrote that no one must know—not ever, but she still did not cry.

FIFTEEN

SOMETIMES PROMISES MUST BE BROKEN — even those made to one's self. Three and a half weeks from the day of the rape, Margaret became aware that she had passed her monthly time and nothing had happened. She had hoped that she could forget the incident and put it behind her, but now she could not. Sylvie also noticed that her daughter was late.

"You late," she stated one evening as she sat in front of the fireplace, mending her stocking. Margaret was putting away the supper plates. When she heard her mother's statement, she knew exactly to what she was referring.

"Yes, ma'am," she quickly admitted. Then added, "But my back is feeling poorly and I think it's coming."

"Why you late?" her mother asked harshly.

"I don't know why. Maybe 'cause Miss Elizabeth left. I'm missing her something awful," was her lame explanation.

"Ain't never heard of no reason like that one. You been doin' somethin' you shouldn't oughta, girl?"

"No, ma'am! I ain't!" Then under her breath she corrected herself. "I haven't."

"Ain't come by tomorrey, it's a dose of castor oil. That'll bring it on."

The next morning before daybreak, Margaret made a show of getting out of bed, stripping the sheet and placing it with her nightgown in a tub of water.

She vigorously washed and rinsed the sheet and garment and hung them on the line. When Sylvie awoke Margaret informed her, "It came this morning. I had to get up and take care of things."

Margaret kept pretending that her period had come, used the cloths, washed them, and hung them on the line as she did every month. During the next few days, she did not throw up, but noticed that she could no longer bear the odor of the chicory that they used in place of coffee. The taste of the beans they had put up from summer harvest began to leave her mouth tasting of acid. She might be able to fool her mother for a few weeks, but not much longer. Margaret knew. She wrote about it in her diary, which she had hidden behind a board in her wall. The thought that she might be with child by that monster made her angry. It could not be! But as the time passed and certain things occurred, Margaret knew the horrible truth.

Margaret needed Elizabeth now. She was frightened and knew that no one else could help her. No one else would know what to do. Only Elizabeth would believe that Thad had taken her against her will. Most of their neighbors would not believe that he had forced her. Everyone would simply consider that she had done as all white trash do. Also, she could not bear for Elizabeth and John—her new friends—to imagine that horrid man so close to her. It must be faced. She would have to inform Elizabeth, but she would not tell who had violated her. She would tell Elizabeth that a Yankee deserter had come on her in the woods. Now, she must have a husband, or she would be ruined for life—but it would never,

ever be Thad Ball. Suddenly, she thought of him as a mad dog. He was violent, sick, cowardly, skulking and without regard for decent human feelings. He had stalked her, caught her, and violated her, thinking to make her his own.

"Never," she thought, "never will I be so careless again!" She tore a page from the back of the diary, got her pen and ink pot from the top drawer of her clothes chest and sat down to compose a letter. It had to go to Elizabeth by the very next post. She wrote:

My dear Miss Elizabeth,

I know you are in Charleston until after the baby comes, but please tell me if you can come back for a little while. Something very bad has happened to me, and you are the only one who can tell me what to do. I must speak with you. Please let me know soon if you can come home. I can't tell you in the letter. I have to see you.

Please.
Margaret O' Donnell
'Tally s Nook
December 30, 1864

She folded the paper, melted the sealing wax with her candle, sealed and addressed the letter to Elizabeth. Early the next morning, she walked the two miles to the village to deliver the letter to the post office.

Mrs. Wills now acted as postmistress while her husband was away fighting. Mr. Wills had been one of the few who had not yet been killed or wounded in battle. Each time a new list of "Killed in Action or Missing in Action, or Taken Prisoner" came, Mrs.

Wills waited for someone else to come by the general store and post office to read the names for her. She would not look until she was assured that her Mr. Wills was not on it.

When Margaret opened the door, she saw the stout lady standing on a ladder cleaning an empty shelf. Hearing the door squeak, Mrs. Wills turned to see which of her neighbors had entered. She was ready for a rest and a bit of a gossip. She was both surprised and disappointed to see that it was only Margaret O'Donnell, who, she thought, had begun to act too uppity for her station.

"I have a letter to go to Charleston. Will it go out today?" Margaret asked Mrs. Wills, walking toward her proffering her letter. Mrs. Wills took it and read the addressee.

"Oh, I see it's a note to Miss Elizabeth," she said, turning the note over in her hand inquisitively. Her voice dripped with sarcasm as she continued, "Hope she's well down there in Charleston. Good thing, too, with her baby coming and all. Yes, this should go out before evening. In Charleston they take the mail right up to her house, so she'll likely get it tomorrow. That soon enough for you?"

"Yes, ma'am, Mrs. Wills. That's soon enough, Ma'am," replied Margaret. She gave a little curtsey as Miss Elizabeth had taught her. Turning quietly, she left the store and began the long walk home, with Mrs. Wills staring contemptuously after her.

"Puttin' on airs," Mrs. Wills said to no one in particular. "Puttin' on airs. Just white trash, puttin' on airs."

SIXTEEN

THE THREE YOUNG WIDOWS kept each other company by catching up on news of friends, family, deaths, births and marriages until the afternoon that Margaret's letter arrived. They were having tea with a special blend that had been brought to Charleston by blockade runners when the postman dropped the letter through the slot. Alice ran to get it.

"It's for you, Elizabeth. From Maclin. Maybe it's from your Father?" she asked as she handed the folded note to Elizabeth.

"Maybe," answered Elizabeth. "Let's see." She took the letter, read the address and turned it over. "No, this is not from Father. I know this handwriting. It is from my young friend, Margaret."

"Margaret who?" queried Ellen.

"Margaret O'Donnell," answered Elizabeth.

"O'Donnell? We don't know any O'Donnells. Where did you meet a family of O'Donnells?" asked Ellen. "That sounds Irish. River people?"

Elizabeth smiled and explained, "She is sort of a young protege. She reads to me ... and she reads beautifully."

"What about her parents?" asked Ellen again.

"Her father runs the turpentine operation for Mister Anthony Parish, the overseer at Tally's Nook. She lives on that property."

"Why are you associating with the help, Sister?" asked Ellen.

"Not really associating. Margaret reads to me. Helps me to pass the time and she is showing promise that she may teach when she is of age. Her teacher pointed her out to me as being worthwhile to work with."

"Elizabeth, you were ever the soft-hearted one. But you must be careful of choosing friends," admonished the younger woman. "You know you have to have friends from your class. Just make sure you keep her in her place."

Not wanting to argue with the girls, knowing they would never understand, having been reared in Charleston society, she said nothing more.

"What's in the letter?" asked inquisitive Alice. "Read it out loud. We haven't had a letter in a long while."

"All right," agreed Elizabeth, as she opened the note, smoothed it out and read aloud Margaret's impassioned plea for her to return to Mockingbird Hill.

"But you can't leave. You just came," Alice cried out.

"Something is dreadfully wrong for her to summon me home now," Elizabeth said.

"Nothing can be that bad. You can't travel now. You've just come and you're seven months along," pleaded Alice, running to place her arms around Elizabeth's shoulders.

"I know Margaret," she explained. "She wouldn't ask this of me unless it were absolutely necessary. I fear I will have to go."

"But the roads, they're so dangerous now. There are Yankees, deserters and all sorts of bad men out there. We hear about people being attacked," pleaded Ellen, trying her best to dissuade Elizabeth from taking this journey.

"I'll send a note tomorrow that I will be leave as soon as I can hire a carriage. I must."

"But...," continued Alice, and Elizabeth interrupted.

"I know. I know what you're thinking, and I know the dangers but it might be Father. Something might have happened to him."

"She would have said, wouldn't she?" Ellen demanded to know. "She would have said."

"Maybe. Maybe not. All I know is that I will have to return to see. But don't worry. I'll come back. Just as soon as I take care of whatever it is, I will come back. I promise."

The promise mollified the sisters somewhat. They were not happy to see Elizabeth plan to return but insisted that their houseboy, Malcolm, drive her to Maclin in their coach.

For Margaret, waiting for Elizabeth's return was torture. Two days after she had posted the letter to her friend, she went to the post office again and asked Mrs. Wills if a letter had come for her. She didn't really expect an answer so soon but was hopeful.

"Nothin' yet, girl. Might be tomorrow. Today is only Monday and she ain't hardly had time to get a letter to the post office yet. You in a mighty hurry, ain't you?" pried Mrs. Wills. "Must be somethin' real important."

Margaret replied, "Yes, Ma'am, kind of," and walked away.

Margaret came again on the following day, her heart pounding and her palms sweaty, she asked her question again, "Morning, Mrs. Wills. Did a letter come for me yet?"

"No, Margaret. What are you expecting from Mrs. Perry?" she purred, hoping to find some new gossip. "Mrs. Perry doin' all right? Must be somethin' mighty important for you to expect her to write to you."

Margaret answered as politely as she could, "Yes, Ma'am, I think she's doing all right. I must hurry home now."

Mrs. Wills watched a troubled Margaret turn and walk out of sight.

"Somethin's going on for sure," she mused.

Margaret walked home with her fear growing; becoming more and more afraid that Sylvie would realize her condition. They lived closely together in their little cabin, and Sylvie's eyes were always prying, waiting to see if something like this would happen. As it turned out, as soon as she arrived back at the miserable cabin, Sylvie had something else on her mind about which to complain.

"Ain't got much to eat," she complained, scraping the end of her snuff stick in the bottom of the tin. "Last of my bakkie gone, too."

"We got cornmeal and some flour left. There's lard and grits," said Margaret.

"No more fatback, hocks is gone and here's the last of the chicory."

Sylvie shook the almost empty sack.

"Them two scraggly hens is barely able to give one egg each a week. Seems like they could find 'nough to eat scratching around like they do," Sylvie continued to complain. "You ain't' been huntin' fer days. When you gonna go fishin'?"

"I'll make hoecake tonight and tomorrow I'll go out. I'll bring in something."

Margaret knew that she had to go searching for game but felt afraid to go into the woods alone. Thad had done that to her, also. Once totally confident and unafraid, enjoying being in the woods alone, now she found herself looking over her shoulder in fear of being hurt again. She would have to go past the Ball place to either set her snares or to fish.

Early the next morning, she picked up the old shotgun, got her knapsack and slung it over her shoulder. She pulled her old hat down over her ears and left the house. Keeping her gun ready and scanning the woods on both sides of the road, she walked in the direction of the river. As she came near the mill and stopped to listen, she heard no noise of chopping or sawing. She could see neither Thad nor his father out working. Still, as she warily passed by and continued down the road toward the river, she looked back over her shoulder at every sound. At the clearing, rain had washed away all signs of the struggle, but Margaret shivered, nevertheless.

She walked down the path that went along the river bank, by each place where she had placed her snares and checked them. They were all empty and had to be baited again and set up. Edgy and nervous, she looked over her shoulder at every tiny noise and kept her shot gun in the crook of her arm while she followed the path. If followed far enough, this river path led to Mockingbird Hill. Knowing that, she felt safer and hoped that her friend would return or write to her.

She finished her work, returned to the clearing, and found her fishing pole still propped up in the branches of a young pine where she had left it. She dug for worms in the soft, wet earth and baited her hook with several of the wet squirming creatures, then dropped the others in the old rusty can she kept by her tree. She sat down on the bank close to the edge of the water, her shotgun close by. Slinging out her line, she let the current take it downstream as the cork bobbed gently on the surface of the water. Enjoyment of the quiet and solitude of this place had always soothed her troubled soul and it did so again as she watched the sunshine glistening off the ripples in the water. The soft calls of the whippoorwills and the multitude of songs from the mockingbirds kept her company. Here, in this place she had always felt free of the troubles of her home but no more. Now she carried trouble with her, inside her belly.

When the better part of two hours had passed, she had caught a mess of bream. She would cook these fish over an open fire, saving the small bit of lard remaining for making bread. There would be enough for her mother and herself for today and tomorrow.

The following day Margaret awoke early. She gathered her knapsack and shotgun, then dressed warmly against the December chill and left the cabin without disturbing Sylvie. She checked her snares and brought home two fat rabbits. Then she tried to remain calm while waiting for some word from Miss Elizabeth. Afternoon came before she heard a noise on the road. Rushing to the front door, she saw Toby mounted on the seat of the old buggy, pulled by the mule, slowly coming into the yard. She opened the door and stepped out into the bright cold sunshine, hugging her arms to ward off the December chill.

"Howdy, Miss Margret. How's you?" drawled Toby. He pulled on the old mule's reins to bring him to a stop, which the animal seemed all too willing to do.

"I'm fine, Toby. Miss Elizabeth send you? Is she coming?"

"Yassum, she here a'ready. Dat's what I'se s'pose to tell you. Miss Lizbeth come yestiddy. And she say I's s'posed to fetch you over to de house soon's I can. So, you betta hop on up heah, and we go. Take a while cause dis ole mule, he done seen his young years and he ain't too swift."

"All right, Toby. Let me get my shawl and tell Ma. I'll be right back."

She closed the door, grabbed her wrap off the wooden peg by the door and went to look for her mother. Sylvie was in the back yard, in the now frostbitten garden, digging in the dirt, looking for old potatoes or turnips that may have been missed last week when she had dug this same ground. Under her poke bonnet, the old face was wrinkled and pinched.

Old dark saliva dribbled down her chin from the snuff stick stuck in the corner of her mouth.

"Ma," Margaret called, "Miss Elizabeth's back and she sent Toby to fetch me. It's early, so I suppose I'll be back before too late. If what she needs me for takes a long time, I'll stay overnight and come back tomorrow. There's fish in the cupboard left from this morning and there's enough cornbread left 'til tomorrow. By then, I'll be back."

"Make her give you some money, Girl. I needs snuff."

Without giving a reply, Margaret turned and walked around the cabin to the waiting wagon and Toby. She climbed in alone, because Toby knew he was not allowed to touch her. He did manage to hold the old wagon steady while she climbed aboard, even though the mule—knowing that he was now going home—showed signs of a vigor that he had not shown going away from home.

"He know he goin' home now, Miss Margret," Toby chuckled. "Giddy up, ole mule. Go on home."

They rode in silence. Usually Margaret would have asked after Nellie, Toby's woman, but today she was deep in thought. Toby seemed to sense her troubled mind and with the wisdom of the old he respected her wish for silence. She was wondering how she would find Miss Elizabeth, how she would tell her what had happened, how Elizabeth would respond, and what they could do about her terrible situation. She wrestled with guilt at having to recall her friend from Charleston. At the same time, she knew that there had been nothing else that she could have done. She also felt guilty because she was afraid she would not—could not—tell Elizabeth the whole truth. If she did tell her the true name of the one who violated her, what would be her reaction? Would she really believe her or would she feel disgust? How could she help Margaret to find a willing husband if she knew that Margaret carried a child of that creature, Thad Ball? It would be best for Elizabeth to think that a Yankee deserter had violated her. Telling her the truth was a risk she could not take.

Shadows were lengthening as they approached the front entrance of the house at Mockingbird Hill. Toby didn't have to pull on the reins to stop the tired mule when he drove the wagon up to the front steps. The mule stood still, his head low and long ears turned back to hear any command that Toby might make. Dropping the reins, Toby jumped down from the driver's seat and waited as Margaret climbed down. She thanked Toby for fetching her and looked up to see John Grenville standing at the top of the steps. She was surprised to see him, for she thought that he would have been away in Virginia. As she walked toward the steps, her eyes met his. She thought that she saw a brief smile flicker about his mouth and a new sparkle enter his eyes. Margaret considered that he was still a very handsome man, even if he was so old. He started down the steps and greeted her.

"Afternoon, Margaret. It's good to see you. We've missed you here." He reached out his hand to help her up the steps. "You should have come to visit."

"Thank you, Mister Grenville, but Miss Elizabeth was away, and I thought you were in Virginia with General Lee."

"I didn't go at all. Received a telegram from his command. They wish for me to remain with the barges in the event that they are needed. They must consider me too old. Hope the tide will turn for us. Elizabeth is resting in the parlor. There's a nice fire there. Hurry on in and say hello to her, then warm your hands. I have evening chores to which I must attend, so I will see you both at supper."

Shooing Margaret in toward the parlor, he gave her a warm smile. Much to her surprise, he said, "To have both of you back at the same time is very good. I have missed you. House too quiet since Elizabeth went to Charleston and you stopped coming. Go on in now. She's waiting for you."

When he walked away Margaret stared after him for a moment before turning into the parlor. This was the warmest welcome she had ever received from John Grenville, but she did not believe for a minute his idea of being too old. Older men than he had gone off to fight. She was sure there was some other reason. Maybe the tide would turn and the barges would still convey arms and supplies.

Elizabeth lay on her favorite blue velvet settee, close to the fireplace where a small fire flickered cheerfully. The candles had not yet been lit and shadows of the fire danced across the room. Hearing her father and Margaret at the door, Elizabeth opened her eyes and called out to her.

"In here, Margaret. I am just resting from the journey. Come in and let me see you."

Margaret swiftly went to the settee and grasped Elizabeth's outstretched hand. "Oh, Miss Elizabeth, I'm so glad to see you. I'm so sorry that I had to ask you to come home. I feel so guilty but I need you. I don't know who else can help me." She began to cry as she knelt on the floor beside her friend. She could see immediately, even under the heavy wool throw, that Elizabeth's belly was much bigger with child than before. She repressed a feeling of guilt again for having had to trouble her.

Elizabeth kissed her cheek and said, "Come now, Maggie girl. Let's have a cup of hot tea and then we can talk. Nellie has had a fever, so I sent her to rest. I'll get the tea. She's left a few coals in the stove for us. You wait here by the fire and warm yourself. I'll just be a minute." She started to get up from the settee, but Margaret would not let her.

"No, please, ma'am. I need to talk now, before your father comes back. I don't want any tea and I'm not cold. I just need to talk to you," Margaret pleaded, her face white.

"All right child." For the first time, Elizabeth sensed the extreme mental anguish of the girl and the urgency of her problem. "If that's what you need, then that is what you shall have. Tell me what it is. What has happened that is so bad? Is it about your father? Have you bad news?"

Margaret's hold on Elizabeth's hand tightened and she dropped her head. This was the moment she had waited for and dreaded. She had to tell—yet, how could she? How could she relive that awful scene? The words did not come, but tears began to run down her cheeks.

"Margaret," Elizabeth said with authority. "Tell me. How can I help if you don't tell me? Speak up child." She lowered her legs from the settee and held Margaret in her arms.

"Are we alone?" Margaret quietly asked.

"Yes, totally alone. Father's out, Toby's in the barn, Nellie is in her cabin and I didn't bring a maid with me. I came home alone, so there is no one here but you and me. Now talk," she commanded.

Margaret turned her tear-stained face to Elizabeth and said, "Almost two months ago I was ...," she hesitated before blurting out, "violated."

"Violated?" asked Elizabeth. "What do you mean, violated? How were you violated and by whom?"

"He held me down and did THAT to me," Margaret replied slowly—not wanting to say the awful words.

"Who? Where?" Elizabeth asked, as she gripped Margaret tighter.

Thoughts tumbled in Margaret's mind as she struggled with the truth, knowing she should name Thad Ball. She opened her mouth, but the whole truth failed to come out. "I don't know who he was. I think he was a Yankee deserter."

"And he violated you? You mean he did something to your body?" Elizabeth could not bring herself to say the awful words either, but she thought she knew what Margaret meant. "Did he hurt you?"

"Yes, ma'am. He did hurt me. Hurt me bad," sobbed Margaret.

"Where did he hurt you, child?" she demanded.

"He hurt me down there," came the reply, and with this said—here in the protection of Elizabeth's arms— Margaret began to feel herself lose the tight control she had maintained these nearly two months.

As Elizabeth held her tightly and stroked her hair, she let the last, painful, terrible words out. "I've missed my monthly and I know what that means." She felt Elizabeth's body go rigid and felt herself being held tighter.

"Oh, you poor child. My poor little Maggie. You should have told me sooner. You should have told me right after it happened." Elizabeth held Margaret as she sobbed. She would not ask her the details now— the where and the when. That would come later, when the tears stopped.

"What can I do? What will happen to me?" sobbed Margaret. "I don't know what to do."

"Just cry and let me think." Elizabeth replied. She rocked Margaret back in forth in her arms and continued to stroke her hair, tying hard to comfort her. "Let me think."

As Elizabeth continued to hold Margaret, the sobs began to subside and she became quieter. Shudders went through her body—shudders of relief that the horrible words had been said. Now that Elizabeth knew, she would be here to tell her what to do and to help her think clearly when she herself could think of nothing.

"Have you told anyone else about this? Sylvie, your mother, does she know?" Elizabeth asked.

"No, no one knows. I told no one. Only you," replied Margaret.

"Well, there is only one thing we can do. I will take you with me to Charleston and we will have to find you a husband. We will have to find you a husband," she repeated. Disengaging herself from Margaret, she instructed her, "You lie down here where I was. I'll go to the kitchen and fetch some tea. Even if you don't need it, I certainly do."

"No, ma'am. You shouldn't have to wait on me. It's not fitting. I should get the tea."

"Nonsense, Maggie. I'm not crippled. Do as I say. You rest here and I'll be right back," Elizabeth said. She gently pushed Margaret down on the settee, tucked the soft quilted blanket around her and pulled her handkerchief from her pocket. "Wipe your eyes, child. I'll get the tea and after we drink it, we will talk. We will think of how to go about this." She left Margaret alone with the fire and went to the kitchen.

The wood-burning stove in the large kitchen was one of the modem additions at Mockingbird Hill. John Grenville had brought it home by barge one fine day several years ago from Charleston and told Nellie that she need not cook in the fireplace. Of course, Nellie did not want it. She preferred the familiarity of the fireplace and the wall oven to make her superb dishes, saying that she didn't hold with newfangled things. Eventually, she did use it. A small box holding slivers of fat wood kindling and a bigger box of slower burning hard wood stood beside the stove. Toby kept both full.

Lifting the round, iron lid of the stove, Elizabeth saw a few red coals left inside from the noon cooking. She rummaged through the kindling box and found some small, thin pieces. These she added to the glowing coals and watched as the resin from the pine splinters began to bubble and spit, then catch afire. When the fire was going strongly, before the small pieces of wood burned up, she added larger pieces of hard wood to the flames. Replacing the lid over the fire, she put the kettle of water on to heat. While the water heated, she got cups and saucers from the cupboard and laid them on the table. Her thoughts were concerned with Maggie's situation. Questions bombarded her mind. Who was he? Was he really a deserter, one of the roving ne'er-do-wells? Where did it happen? Why was Margaret out alone? Elizabeth really knew the answer to that. She knew that Margaret had done the hunting and fishing for herself and her mother ever since Charlie had gone off to war. She had constantly worried about Margaret's doing this, so she began to blame herself. She had thought of having Margaret live with them, but there was no way she could have endured coping with Margaret's mother. Because of this dislike of Sylvie, she had not asked Margaret to stay. Suddenly, she remembered something that might do them both a world of good—a small bottle of brandy that she had hidden on the top cupboard shelf, away from Nellie. She pulled a chair over toward the cupboard so that she could stand on it and reach the brandy, which she had pushed to the rear of the cabinet. She felt clumsy and uncomfortable with her large belly, but she lifted one foot and placed it on the seat of the chair. Holding the edge of the countertop, she pulled herself up until she was standing on the chair. She opened the cupboard door and reached in to find the brandy bottle. Not finding it, she groped farther toward the right, realizing that it might have been pushed aside when other jars had been added. Suddenly, she felt herself losing her balance. There was too much weight on the right. Her thigh was pushing on the back of the chair and causing it to tilt over. She was falling and screaming and feeling herself going through the air toward the floor. She grabbed for something to hold on to, but there was nothing. She hit the floor, her head striking the edge of the wood box with considerable force on the way down, and then—blackness.

From the parlor, Margaret heard Elizabeth scream, then heard a loud thud and clatter as the chair and Elizabeth fell. She jumped up from the settee, ran out into the long hallway and back to the kitchen. What she saw as she entered the kitchen paralyzed her. Elizabeth lay sprawled on the floor by the overturned chair, not moving. As Margaret stared, she saw a pool of dark red blood slowly spreading from Elizabeth's head. She broke through her own paralysis to run to Elizabeth.

"Miss Elizabeth," she called. She picked up her hand, then noticed the absolute stillness of her. Elizabeth was unconscious, at the very least. She must get help!

"Mister Grenville!" she screamed. "Toby!"

No one came.

She would have to go out to fetch someone. Her friend was badly hurt. Margaret ran out the kitchen door. From the steps, she could see the barn where old Toby worked. She called to him: "Toby, come quickly! Miss Elizabeth has fallen."

At the panicked sound of her voice Toby came to the barn door and yelled, "What dat you say, Miss Margret? Cain't heah ya so good. What happen?"

"Get Mister John. Miss Elizabeth's had a fall. She's hurt bad. She's not moving," Elizabeth pleaded. "She fell in the kitchen."

"Yassum, I'se comin, I'se comin, I'se comin," he said. Then he called to her. "You go get Nellie. Tell her to come quick," he yelled as he hobbled as quickly as he could toward the kitchen.

Nellie had the yelling and left her bed, throwing on her shawl as Margaret reached her door. Pounding with both small fists, she called to Nellie. "Nellie, come quick. Miss Elizabeth fell." Nellie was through the door before Margaret finished speaking and ran ahead toward the kitchen.

"Come on, chile. Hurry! What happen to Miss Elizabeth?" Nellie asked as they ran.

"She fell, Nellie. She hit her head," Margaret said as she caught her breath. "She won't answer or move." They entered the kitchen and saw Toby kneeling over the still form of Elizabeth and could tell by the look on his face that they were too late. He was shaking his head from side to side and tears were in his eyes. He held Elizabeth's hand and stroked it as an old father might stroke the hand of a beloved daughter. He looked up at Nellie and said, "She gone."

At that instant John Grenville burst into the kitchen. "I heard the commotion. What's happened?" he asked while his eyes stopped on the still form of his daughter on the floor, the pool of blood around her head mixing with the pool of blood that was soaking her skirts. Before they could answer, he whispered, "Elizabeth? The child?"

Toby answered his master. "She gone, Massah. Like I tole Nellie. She gone," Toby shuddered. "Po li'l thing." He rocked back and forth on his knees, still patting the white limp hand.

Suddenly, Nellie, with the wisdom of age, spoke up, "The chile, Massah John, he might be alive, but he gonna die real soon long as he inside."

Seconds passed before John Grenville was able to focus on her words. He stood speechless and motionless while he struggled to comprehend all that had happened and was still happening. Then he stared at Nellie with something akin to horror as the meaning of Nellie's words entered his mind. Elizabeth was about seven months or more along. Many people had babies at seven months, he knew, and many of them lived. This one might live also, if they could get to it before too late. It was then that he realized the extreme urgency facing them all.

"But we would have to ... you'll..." He could not finish.

"Yes, Massah John," Nellie sternly prodded. "You got no time for feelin' sorry now. You got to tell me what you wants. You wants me to take dat chile or not? Ain't no time for cogitatin'. Effen you wants it, say so now," she demanded.

John Grenville went to his daughter and felt for her pulse. There was none. There was no breathing. She had the still, quiet look of death. He knew that she would never open her eyes again. Turning to Nellie he asked, "You can do it? You're sure?"

"Massah, it's a chance. Das all." She was afraid to give him too much assurance. "I cain't say he'll live ... but dis way, we all know he ain't. He yo gran' chile. Tell me quick!"

"Get the child," John Grenville ordered.

"All right, sir. Now y'all go on outa here. All o' ya. Out!" she demanded.

They obeyed. The entire exchange had lasted only a few brief seconds. Toby went out the back door and sat on the steps in the evening cold. John and Margaret left the kitchen — now dark with evening shadows and pungent with the sickening odor of blood — and went into the parlor. They were both in a state of shock, each not able to accept the horror. Moving as though sleep walking, John turned to her and she could see him crumble, the pain on his face almost unbearable to see. She opened her arms and he came into them. She held him and he grasped her tightly as he let his emotions loose. Oddly, at that moment, with all the insane tragedy around her and within her, what came foremost to her mind was her first realization that the great John Grenville was human ... a very human man. This aristocrat who she had admired and worshipped from afar — this blue blood with his great family, his estate, and his background — needed her strength. He needed her.

Huddled together, they waited, trying not to think about what Nellie was doing in the kitchen. Then they heard slaps and waited for the wailing of an infant. Nothing came. There were more slaps but no other sound. John held her tighter fearing that the infant was beyond help, but suddenly there was a noise — not the healthy wailing of a full-term babe, but a sound like the soft cry of a kitten. John held her away from him and listened, then they both went into the hallway to see Nellie emerge from the kitchen, a small bloody, living thing wrapped in her shawl. She walked up to John and held out the bundle.

"He a boy, Massah John. He tiny, but he alive. He gonna need lots o' care."

John took the infant from Nellie's arms and felt how extraordinarily light and tiny he was. Nellie pulled the shawl away from the baby's face and showed John Grenville his grandson. The babe was bloody, covered with a white, pasty goo. He was not a pretty thing. John did not know how to hold it. He turned to Margaret and silently handed her the child. Plainly, he could not speak.

Nellie said softly, "Massah John, now we got to take care of Miss Elizabeth. Leave the babe with Miss Margret. She can take him into the parlor by the fire and keep him warm for a little bit so's we can do what we gotta do. We got to carry up to her room and I'll clean her up. I done tole Toby to tend to the fire and heat up some water. I'll take care of things, but I needs you to take her up the stairs. It ain't pretty, Massah John. It ain't pretty," she repeated, closing her eyes and shaking her head wearily.

While Nellie and John took care of Elizabeth, Toby cleaned the kitchen floor. Margaret sat on the settee by the fire and held the babe. He made no noise. He did not squirm or even move. He was helpless and she loved him. Loving him caused her to begin to love her own unborn babe. Babies were the most helpless creatures of all and there were so many harmful things in the world. Those harmful things came in more shapes than she had ever dreamed.

After that horrible day, Margaret stayed at Mockingbird Hill to help Nellie care for the family and the baby boy who had not yet been named. Tiny and weak, he was kept alive by sucking on a rag dipped in goat's milk mixed with molasses. There was no sugar to be had. It was offered to him every time he awakened or stirred. He sometimes sucked on the molasses tit without ever opening his eyes, as though he knew he must conserve all his energy just to live. He was a most tenacious child.

John remained in a daze, hardly able to function. He depended on Toby and Nellie for care and on Margaret to make his daughter's funeral arrangements. The funeral was a pitiful affair. The service took place during morning church on the following Sunday. The minister read the words and when the service was over, the few neighbors who had been able to come, gathered for Elizabeth's burial in the small cemetery yard behind the ancient Episcopal church. A biting, cold drizzle fell from gray skies. Margaret sat under an umbrella holding the babe. It was difficult for her to believe that they were here to bury her best friend in the world. She sat beside the grave holding the baby, who was holding onto life by the barest of threads. Here in her arms, he was still and quiet as they laid his mother to rest in an open grave, already muddy from the rain. There were few men at the grave side — an old grandfather and two young crippled boys back from war. Most of the neighboring women had come to the service but departed before the burial, fearing illness from the cold rain..

Toby and Nellie stood together at the back of the crowd, holding on to each other, both crying as the young woman, whom they had help to rear, was laid to rest. As the coffin was lowered into the grave, Nellie turned to Toby.

"I knows why she was up on dat chair," she whispered between sobs. "She lookin' fo' dat bottle o' brandy I put back on de shelf. When I come down wid de fever, I took some o' dat brandy. Den I puts it back, but I must of pushed it too far. 'Cause sho' as anything, Miss Elizabeth was lookin' for dat bottle. What I cain't figure out is, why?" Her voice was changing from sadness to perplexity. "Why she in de kitchen makin' tea and huntin' dat brandy? Why Miss Margaret ain't in dere doin' dat?"

Toby softly punched Nellie in the shoulder. "Hush up woman. Don't go aksin' no questions. We don' know and ain't no way we gonna know. It's done and over. Leave sleepin' dogs lie."

Toby had gotten word to Sylvie as soon as possible about the tragedy, telling her that her daughter would remain to care for the child and that Mister Grenville would send money to compensate for Margaret's absence. The old woman walked to church to witness the burial. Seeing her daughter seated by John Grenville with the brand-new infant in her arms caused her to see Margaret in a new light. She spoke to Margaret and to Grenville, but did not linger with them, preferring to remain in the background. In her own mind, Margaret had crossed the line. Her daughter had gone into another world where Sylvie could never go, had never been accepted, and would never be accepted. Margaret had gotten what Sylvie had always wanted and had never realized. Never having achieved her dream had been the cause of all her pain in life. After the coffin had been lowered into the ground, she followed the small crowd—now soaking wet and

142

cold—as they quickly left the churchyard for their homes.

John and Margaret, holding the quiet babe, rode back to Mockingbird Hill inside the buggy with Nellie sitting on the driver's seat with Toby, his big Mackintosh draped over them both. No one spoke. The quiet was heavy and nothing broke it except the sound of buggy wheels and mule's hooves squishing the soft, wet earth and the patter of rain on the buggy top. When the sad ride ended, Toby cared for the mule and put the buggy away. Nellie, her fever now a forgotten thing, went into the kitchen to cook the midday meal. Margaret prepared the milk and molasses for the child and took him into the kitchen by the fire to feed him.

John silently went into his study, closed the door and stayed there throughout the remainder of the day, until evening when the household slept. For several days this is where he went each evening until his candle burned down. No one disturbed him. They left him to his grief and private thoughts. A few nights after the funeral, John left the study door open. Margaret saw him retrieve the big family Bible from the bookshelf in his study and write in it. She supposed that he was finally able to record the sad event and the happy one, the death and birth ... the continuation of life.

Days later he would tell them that he had written the baby's name in the Good Book. He would be called Andrew Grenville Perry.

SEVENTEEN

NELLIE RUMMAGED THROUGH TRUNKS in the attic and found infant garments from years past. Toby brought down the cradle and placed it a safe distance from the stove in the kitchen where it remained all day. At night he took it to Elizabeth's room where Margaret now slept with the babe. She did not know how long she would be needed to care for the boy but vowed to stay if John wished. Her own problem seemed small compared to the death and birth.

Late on a cold Sunday afternoon John had Toby build a fire in the parlor. When the room had warmed, he bade Margaret bring the babe in with them. In the warm glow from the fire Margaret sat on the settee and waited. John stood by the fireplace, his back to her. Minutes passed with no words between them and Margaret wondered why he had called her. Was she to leave now? Who would care for the babe to whom she had become attached?

While she wondered silently John turned and said to her, "I want you to stay here with me. I need you. Will you stay?"

Margaret did not understand. Did he want her to remain as a nanny to the boy?

Seeing her questioning expression, he explained, "Maggie, I am proposing marriage to you. Will you accept me?"

He misread her shocked expression. Thinking that he had offended her, he quickly apologized, "I'm so sorry. You must think me horrid to ask you this way. A young girl wants beautiful words at a time like this, and I have blurted this out like a young fool. I am old enough that I should know better. Please accept my apology. For an old man like me to ask a young girl like you to be my wife, I should at least be gentle about it," he said.

With a pained look, he came closer to her. Taking her hand, he knelt on one knee beside her, turned his face up to look directly into her eyes and said, "Margaret, I know this isn't the best of circumstances for a young girl to be married, even though I do need you mightily, now above all times. It is true that I have admired you these past years as I watched you grow into a lovely young woman. I do care for you and if you think you could tolerate an old man and forsake the thought of finding a young husband, I would be honored if you would become my wife."

His dark blue eyes peered into hers. Shadows flickered across the room from the flames in the fireplace. The room whirled around her. Thoughts too fast for her to sort out sped through her mind. As though she were outside, looking in on this scene, she heard herself accept John Grenville's proposal. She heard herself agree to be his wife.

One week later, on Christmas day, Margaret stood in the same little church where they had said their farewells to Elizabeth, only this time she was there to become Mrs. John Grenville. The same group of friends and neighbors who had come for the funeral gathered again for the wedding. In another time and under other conditions, they may have been scandalized over the haste of this marriage and over the social beginnings of his bride but by December of 1864, in this place, these things seemed to have lost the importance they would have had in happier, less chaotic times. People now did what they had to do to survive. A few, like the Wills, may have still felt that the marriage was not proper, but were compelled to come out of curiosity.

Margaret had taken no time to consider the fact that she was bringing to this marriage a child already conceived. She had not—and would not—inform John Grenville. His proposal seemed to be a blessed gift from heaven. She even allowed herself to believe that her dear friend Elizabeth had willed this as the perfect solution—that the union had her heavenly blessing. John had seen his own grandson survive a violent, premature birth. Therefore, he would likely blame another early birth on the stress through which she had gone.

Dressed in Elizabeth's wedding dress, which John had bidden Nellie find and prepare, Margaret said her vows and listened to John as he declared that he "would keep her only unto himself, so long as they both should live." It was only then, as they were pronounced man and wife, as he turned to plant a kiss on her cheek, that she realized she would have wifely duties. The sudden memory of the afternoon of Thad Ball caused her face to blanch and her knees to grow week. She felt herself begin to grow faint. Her head whirled with dizziness and nausea. Had John not held her tightly, she would have fallen to the floor. John picked up his bride in his arms and quickly carried her out of the church into the bright Christmas day sunshine.

146

Someone placed a robe on the ground and John laid her on it, saying to everyone: "This has been all too much for Margaret. I fear that she is overworked and exhausted. I must take her home. I thank you all for having come. When she is well, we will welcome you to our home."

Mrs. Wills, standing back from the crowd said to her husband, "Humph, that might be a while if I know a thing or two!"

Nellie took the babe to her cabin for the wedding night so that her Master and his new Mistress could have a peaceful evening alone. John Grenville allowed his new bride to see to her evening toilet and to get into bed before him. When he went to his bedroom and found her tucked into the large four-poster, he felt safe and content for the first time in many months. This was right and natural. A man should have a woman in his bed and in his life. He knew he needed her. He needed a wife and he would not condemn himself for it. Aware that she was frightened and trying awfully hard not to show it, he walked up to the bed and spoke softly.

"Margaret, my dear, it has been a terrible time for you. You are exhausted and need more than anything to rest," he said as he took her small hand in his and stroked it.

She did not mind his touch and did not flinch. She was afraid, terribly afraid of the coming act, but even more afraid that she would do something or show something that would cause him not to take her in his arms and consummate the marriage. Not only must

147

this be endured, it must be welcomed, for it would be the only way she could convince her husband, seven months hence, that he was the father of her child. She took his hand in hers, slowly drew him down toward her, then smiled a welcoming smile to him.

"I am your wife now, John. We will both rest later." She threw back the covers to invite him to come to her.

There remained one thing to be done. Early the next morning, Margaret went into the room where Elizabeth's travel trunk had been placed. She looked for Elizabeth's writing box, her stationery, pens and other writing things. She did not see them lying about the room, so she unlocked the small trunk with the key from Elizabeth's key holder. There were only a few things inside—another dress, night clothes, underwear and some toilet articles. Elizabeth had not planned to stay long at Mockingbird Hill, just long enough attend to Margaret's emergency and then return to Charleston. Margaret rummaged through the items looking for the letter she had sent to Elizabeth. Finding it quickly, she removed it and placed it her pocket, later to be tucked into her diary. This, if found, could spoil everything. She would continue writing in the diary, but both it and the letter must be well hidden. She would search the house for a proper hiding place.

EIGHTEEN

ELLEN ACCEPTED THE LETTER from the postman and listened while he told her the latest news about the war, which he did with a sad countenance, there being no good news to share. When he had told her all he could recall, knowing that the two sisters lived alone and seldom ventured out, he shared the latest bits of gossip he had gleaned on his route. He hoped he would hear more from Ellen Perry that he might share with others, but she disappointed him, closing the door and shutting him out.

She looked at the envelope. From Mockingbird Hill. It must be from Elizabeth. Without waiting for Alice, who lounged in her room upstairs, Ellen felt too impatient to wait for her sister to open the letter with her. Elizabeth had left more than two weeks ago and both sisters had become anxious. Ellen tore the letter open with a feeling of anxiety, fearing that their sister-in-law considered herself too far along in her pregnancy to return to Charleston or that the roads might be unsafe. Feeling slightly guilty that she had not waited for her sister, she silently read the words on the paper but did not really comprehend the message. Elizabeth dead? A child? John married? It was too much for her.

"Alice," she said, hardly above a whisper even though she felt that she had shouted. "Alice! Come quickly!" Her knees buckled and she found herself sitting on the bottom step of the staircase.

"What is it, Ellen?" Alice asked, as she came to the top of the stairs, seeing Ellen's face as white as a sheet, with a letter in her hands. "What's wrong? Is it from Elizabeth? She's not coming back?"

Ellen could not answer her sister. Wordlessly, she handed the letter to her to read for herself.

"No!" Alice screamed, the letter flying as the younger sister fell to the floor to grab onto Ellen. "It can't be! No! No! I won't let it be true. No one else can die! No one."

Once more, as they had when news had come of their young husbands' deaths, they held each other and sobbed endlessly. Almost an hour passed before they were able to pick up the hated letter and read it again. In doing so, they read to the end and discovered that Elizabeth's son had survived. Alice was the first one to speak.

"I want him to come here. We should rear him. He is a Perry, not a Grenville. Ellen, promise me that when the war is over, we will go and bring him home to Charleston. We deserve that child. He will be the son we never had. Brother Andrew would want it. Promise me, please."

"I promise we will do what we can," Ellen answered, trying again to sooth and console her sister. "But it won't be easy taking the child from John Grenville. After all, he is John's grandson."

"He is our brother's son. He is a Perry." She reached for the letter that Ellen held crumpled in her hand. "Did John say what he is named?"

"No, he did not."

"He is the continuation of our family, our name, Ellen. He should be named for our brother, his father.

150

Surely John will do that?" Then she begged, "May we go soon? To see him, I mean?"

"No, Alice," replied her sister. "The postman said that Union soldiers are close now. They will be in Charleston within days. He said General Sherman's army is also near. Travel will be out of the question for a while. That's what I thought John was going to say; that travel was not safe for Elizabeth now. I knew she should not have gone back. That woman, whoever she is — that Margaret! And now this letter says that she is married to John? She is now a Grenville!"

"Ellen, how could John do such a thing?"

Ellen did not answer. She knew that wresting his only grandson away from John Grenville would be a formidable task, but she vowed that they would do all that they could. Maybe John would be able to give the lad much more than they could in the way of male guidance, but the child was, after all, a Perry.

Quietly she said to Alice, "We have as much right to him as they do."

"We don't know the O'Donnells," voiced Ellen. "We don't know this woman John married while he is in such grief."

"You're right, sister," agreed Alice, and then continued matter-of-factly with her innocent, Charleston-bred logic. "Like we said to Elizabeth — if we never knew or met her, she can't possibly be good enough to be a wife to John Grenville or to rear our nephew."

"They aren't in our class. We know everyone here, even in Maclin, who is," reasoned Ellen. "I can't believe that John Grenville would marry someone not proper."

"How could he have allowed Elizabeth to become friends with her? Maybe he could have allowed her to help her — maybe even teach her--but friends? How could he allow Elizabeth to befriend a person of the serving class?"

"Her attitude was always too egalitarian. I remember once I had to remind her of her position in society as a Perry. She just smiled. Didn't even answer me."

"Maybe John will explain later," said Alice with encouragement. "I dislike a mystery."

** **

Ellen made it her occupation to ferret the details of Margaret's social background through letters to friends in and near Maclin and when these details filtered back to her, she vowed to do whatever it took to claim the Perry child back to his kind, regardless of John Grenville's claim on him. Ellen felt that John had betrayed his class. She and Alice would take the boy away from that situation as soon as the war was over and they would bring him up in the genteel atmosphere of Charleston.

NINETEEN

MARGARET'S DAILY ROUTINE AT HER NEW HOME revolved around caring for the tiny baby. She spent many hours sitting in a rocking chair close to the fire, keeping him warm during the bone-piercing, damp chill of January. Everyone feared that he would develop the lung sickness, the illness that took many an infant during the winters. John had Toby and Nellie move from their cabin to Elisabeth's room at night and little Andy slept in his cradle in that room so that the newly-weds would have time to themselves.

With loving care of everyone in the small family, the babe survived his first month but had not gained as much weight as he should. A search went out for a wet nurse who could give him the much-needed mother's milk. When he had survived to five weeks, one of the few slave women who yet remained on the plantation gave birth to a daughter. Nellie had been waiting for this and as soon as she heard about the birthing, the woman was brought in, with her babe, to help nurse the young Master.

Life for everyone became a struggle for survival. They had almost become primitive hunter/gatherers once more, with either John or Toby going almost every morning into the woods to hunt or in the boat to fish or gather oysters. Game and fish had completely taken the place of pork, chicken and beef on the Grenville table. The evening supper pot was full of squirrel or rabbit stew instead of roasts of beef and cured ham. Some evenings there was only 'possum or 'coon. Margaret had dined on this fare all her life, but not John Grenville. When he saw these in the serving bowl he often ate his cornbread and greens and left the stew to the others.

On one of these evenings, after supper, Margaret asked, "John, will you please take me hunting with you? The babe is quite fine here with Nellie and the nurse. I know how to hunt. Maybe I can help. I can bag a turkey."

John looked up from his cup of hot chicory and frowned.

"No, my dear. I will do the hunting in this house. I can provide for you and the babe."

Margaret would not argue with him. She knew that he meant it. He countered her disappointment by asking, "How would you like your mother to come and stay here at The Hill? There's room a'plenty."

Margaret hesitated briefly before replying.

"I don't think she would like to live with us. She is used to her own ways and stays many evenings with Mrs. Tally."

"She could always take one of the empty cottages out back. It would be close enough, and heaven knows there are enough empty ones, since all the slaves have run away."

She knew that John was trying to please her. She was afraid, however, that Sylvie would notice her waist, which was beginning to thicken noticeably, but what could she say? Nothing.

"I'll ask her."

"Very good. I want you to be happy and with her here, you won't have to worry so much."

She knew that she would have to at least ask her mother and next morning Toby drove Margaret to Sylvie's cabin. As usual, they found Sylvie out in the kitchen garden, digging for missed sweet potatoes in the cold, damp air. Margaret bade Toby wait in the buggy while she spoke with Sylvie.

"Ma," Margaret called, walking toward the garden.

Sylvie raised up and shaded her eyes from the morning sun.

"Oh, it's you," Sylvie stated matter-of-factly. "I been
wonderin' how you doin'."

"I'm just fine, Ma."

"How's dat young'un? Still alive, is he?"

"Yes, Ma. He's growing fast now that he's got a wet nurse."

"What did ya come for?"

There was never any softness, any welcome in Sylvie's voice. No invitation.

"John wants you to come to The Hill to stay. Sent me to ask."

"John, huh? So Mr. Grenville wants me to his house? To live?"

"Yes, ma'am, he does."

"That what he said?"

"He said he wants to make me happy."

"That's a laugh, ain't it? Me there make you happy? I don't think so. I'd rather stay here. Miz Tally, she needs me now. We sort of takes care of each other. I sleeps there most nights in her room, cause she ain't got nobody else. Aunt Leah she dead and Flossie gone God knows where. You tell your fancy husband that I'm busy." She turned her back to Margaret and bent down to her digging.

"Ma, how many times you plan to dig there? Didn't you get all the potatoes already?"

"Might have missed one or two. Don't hurt to try. You better go on home. Miz Tally and me — we doin' a'right."

Margaret was relieved — terribly so. She had not let herself think about what it would be like if Sylvie took John's invitation. She returned to the buggy and climbed in, motioning to Toby to drive on.

"We'll go into Maclin, Toby. I'll check to see if any new supplies came in."

"All right. Giddyap, mule. Miz Margret, if anything did come in, it would come up river and Massah John, he'd know."

"You're right, of course, Toby. But let's go anyway. I can at least check to see if a new list came out. Maybe I can find news of my Pa."

Toby stopped the buggy in front of the general store.

As Margaret got down from the buggy, she saw Thad Ball standing across the road from the store, staring at her. She quickly turned from his gaze and entered the store. Toby was right. There were no new supplies on the shelves and Mrs. Wills stared at her belly. Margaret felt strongly that the harridan knew

another man whose back was to her. She could not quickly determine his identity. His scrawny back was covered only in a thin coat against the cold. John spoke angrily to him. She heard the other man raise his voice also, speaking above John's.

"Don't care what you say, mister high and mighty. She might be your wife, but she ought 'a be mine. I done fixed it so's she'd be. I done it to her and looks to me like she's carrying. I won't be cheated outta what's mine. I can see she's got a belly, and it's too soon for y..."

His voice abruptly stopped, replaced with the sound of Margaret's shotgun blast that tore the air as she fired off one barrel. Thad Ball fell to the ground. John's shocked face turned to look toward the edge of the clearing in the direction of the blast. He saw Margaret. His face showed his disbelief at what he had witnessed.

"Margaret?" he called. "Margaret? What are you doing? What have you done?" He stood still, in shock at what he had seen happen. "Who is that, Margaret? Why did you shoot him? What he said, Margaret." John was unable to move, not able to take in all of this quickly enough to understand what she had done. "Have you killed him?"

Then looking at the still form lying on the ground, blood coming from Thad's open mouth, he broke through his paralysis and ran over to the body lying on the frosty leaves. John looked up at her with shock and bewilderment on his face. "Did he speak the truth?"

Margaret remained silent, not understanding any better than John what had caused her to pull the trigger. It had happened so suddenly. Seeing Thad and hearing him shout those awful words ... she just could not bear for them to be said aloud for John to hear. But he had heard. She watched his face as all of it slowly entered his mind—as disbelief changed to belief, understanding and horror. Seeing this, and suddenly seeing her future, Margaret raised her gun once more, pointed it at John Grenville and shot him dead.

PART II

LOS ANGELES, CALIFORNIA
1996

TWENTY

ELIZABETH PERRY WILSON SAT ON THE FLOOR by her mother's old, large leather trunk. Only a few short weeks had gone by since her mother's funeral, but the time had come to open the trunk and go through the bits and pieces; the many keepsakes that represented the physical evidence of her mother's life. The teakettle whistled. Leaving papers and letters scattered about her on the floor, she went into the kitchen and reached into the cupboard for her favorite mug. Methodically reaching for the container of tea bags, she opened it, took a bag, dropped it into the mug and covered it with boiling water. She stood by the kitchen counter and waited, dipping the tea bag up and down while her mind was in another place.

How many late evenings and early mornings had she and her mother spent in this kitchen, sipping tea from these mugs, the two of them exchanging the latest gossip? She felt her tears start again and angrily wiped them away.

"I'm a mature woman," she chided herself aloud, "and shouldn't miss my mother so much."

Taking her cup of tea back into the living room, she placed it on the flat seat of her mother's walnut chair by the trunk. Remembering her mother's pride over the antique chairs, she folded a napkin and placed it under the teacup. She took a cushion from the sofa, put it on the floor by the trunk and lowered herself, knowing that this task would be both sad and pleasant.

She unlatched the large brass fasteners and remembered that polishing those fasteners — seeing them change from dull brown to gleaming brass so that she could see her reflection — had been one of her favorite childhood tasks. Now putting her shoulders into the effort, she pushed up the heavy trunk lid. There before her, neatly arranged, were the bits and pieces that her mother had so cherished: letters, news clippings, scraps of this and that, souvenirs, dance cards, certificates of various achievements, diplomas, memorabilia from her husband's army career. Here were hundreds of mementos that spelled out a life enjoyed over many years.

As a little girl, Elizabeth had often watched her mother carefully tie up little bundles, place tiny items in small boxes, before putting them in the trunk, saying to her daughter, "Someday you will have these to remember me by. These are my treasures, my past. And they will be for you to give to your children along with the things of yours that you add as you grow up."

Elizabeth selected a Chinese box lacquered in black and red, opened it, and saw that it held several pairs of wrinkled, formal men's gloves. Originally white, the gloves had aged to the color of old ivory. When she was a little girl her mother showed her these gloves and had told her how she came to have them. In her mother's time, those gloves were always worn by the young girls' escorts to formal dances that were held at The Citadel, Charleston's famous, or infamous, military college. Before the dances, the young ladies were given both garters made of blue satin and lace and corsages of gardenias by their beaux. When the elegant evenings were over, the young gentlemen handed their gloves over to their ladies as keepsakes. Her mother had told her of girls who made a game of collecting dozens of pairs of gloves, all from different young men.

In the lacquered box were also four dance cards from which small pencils tied to silk cords still dangled. On the cards were written the names of the lucky dance partners. Julia Adams had been a lovely young girl, a belle of the ball on many occasions. Many thought that young Lieutenant Andrew Perry was a lucky young man when he met his bride at the alter after graduation. Those others, young ladies and their mothers, who had failed to capture the most eligible graduate of The Citadel, had enviously remarked that Andy had married down, implying that the common Julia had married up. They had been referring to the family name and social position of the Perrys, one of the earliest families of Charleston. Of course, there were also those who said it was Andrew who had married up. Those astute people were aware of Julia Adam's many qualities — how her gracious charm, her delightful personality and her quiet beauty would be a great help to Lieutenant Perry in his military career.

Elizabeth laid the gloves aside and reached for another box — very old and of great beauty — fashioned from intricately hand-carved mahogany. She remembered what was kept inside. Inside the box, in one tiny brown bag was a lock of hair from her mother's very first haircut. In another was a lock from

Elizabeth's first haircut. These locks were the same: a vibrant and dark chestnut color.

Spying what looked like an old letter under a stack of old lace scarves, she reached in and pulled it out. There was no envelope...just a folded piece of paper. Not remembering ever having seen it before and noticing how brown with age it had become, she carefully unfolded it. The writing looked like a schoolgirl's work, the lines slightly going up toward the end of the lines. Beneath the old signatures was the date—1864, on the last day of November. She began to read an urgent plea of someone named Margaret O'Donnell, to someone named Elizabeth, just like her. Could this be the Elizabeth for whom her mother had named her? The letter was short; merely a plea for this Elizabeth to return in haste because something had happened that could not be written. Margaret mentioned that she had written about it in her book.

"Curious," mused Elizabeth aloud as she placed the letter on the floor. "I wonder what little book she was referring to. A diary, perhaps?" She turned again to the trunk and saw four old Bibles nestled down in the bottom next to where the letters had been hidden. She carefully took them out, selecting what seemed to be the newest one. She placed the others on the floor beside the letters. Even the newer one was old. Turning to the inside cover, she saw names and dates of births, deaths and marriages—some from as early as the beginning of the century. Putting it down, she quickly picked up another and opened it. There were earlier dates from the turn of the century. She then found, upon inspection of the others, that the oldest of them contained information from the nineteenth century. Like her mother, she had never been much interested in names and dates and was about to put the Bibles away when she saw the edges of papers sticking out from the middle of the oldest one. Turning the thin, brittle pages of the old Bible, she removed the folded papers. There were several pages, quite large, that had been folded over and over. Opening them very carefully, lest they tear, she was intrigued to see that they were diagrams of family trees with different pages showing the various generations and family lines. Elizabeth remembered that her old Grandmother Perry had been involved in trying to continue determining the family history. More than once, as a little girl, she had listened to old tales about the family having descended from Welsh nobility. Grandmother Perry had seemed obsessed and had wanted her daughter- in-law, Julia, to continue the records.

Elizabeth remembered hearing her grandmother tell her mother about her theory of family history. "Julia, my dear," she had said, "it's not about the past. It's about how the past created the present, so that you will know how your present is creating the future. Family history is just the same as history of a country — or a culture, or a whole civilization, for that matter. It's just as important. The past lives with us. It is a major part of us. We all are not just born yesterday and are here today for some unseen tomorrow. We were all born long ago in the actions and reactions of our ancestors. Deprive us of that and we would not be who we are."

Julia had politely listened to her mother-in-law; however, it all sounded like make believe and it simply had not interested her. She explained to Grandmother Perry, "I can't see the issue of family history as being the same as history of a country or civilization. I only see that everyone in the South would like to have everyone else believe that they were descended from nobility." She had not added, but genuinely believed, that the entire issue was a waste of time. "This country," Julia continued, "is America, a classless society where what matters is nobility of spirit, rather than nobility of blood."

"Yes, dear. You are quite right. But just as you cannot understand your country and civilization as it is now without knowing how it was in the past and what made it how it is in the present, you cannot understand your personal present without knowing how it got this way." Grandmother Perry's relentless words seemed to be a plea for understanding from Julia.

Her grandmother had been quite serious and had tried her best to bring Julia to her own understanding of these things but had no success. Instead of continuing her mother-in-law's work, Julia had simply packed it away in the trunk and had forgotten it. She had not understood the motivation of those who she referred to as "old ladies, all caught up in family glory."

"Perhaps," thought Elizabeth now, "there had been the tiniest bit of insecurity and jealousy hidden in Mother's mind that kept her from considering Grandmother Perry's request." It was difficult for Elizabeth to ever find fault with her mother, but she was experienced enough to know that no one was perfect.

Elizabeth glanced through the pages briefly and was about to refold them and replace them in the Bible when she saw, on the last page, scribbling in a hand that looked like her grandmother's. Had she hurriedly written a note to herself?

Her grandmother had written, "Find the diary! Find out about John Charles Grenville, Jr." And then she had written clearly in large letters, "If the dates are correct, something is wrong!"

This was intriguing! What was wrong. What dates? Elizabeth got up from the floor and cleared off a side of the dining table. She placed the three pages there and smoothed them out to examine them more closely. There was the entry seeming to be written in a dainty woman's hand for John Charles Grenville, with his birth date in 1810. Beside it, in a bolder hand, was the name of Margaret O'Donnell, her birth date in 1849, and their marriage date, December 25, 1864, and then in the next line was the name of her son— John Charles Grenville II, his birth date given as July 29, 1865. Beside that date Grandmother Perry or someone in the past had made a large question mark. With a bit of counting Elizabeth realized that a full nine months had not passed between the date of the marriage and the birth of baby John. Her first thought was that there is nothing strange about premature births. It happens all the time. But then her glance went on to the line in the record; the date of John Grenville's death, February 20, 1865, with a tiny note that read, *accidentally shot while hunting*. John's death had occurred less than a month after their marriage.

That someone had underlined these few words only served to heighten her curiosity.

Picking up the old letter once again, Elizabeth thought of that book. Was it a diary? She wondered what else might be written in it. What had occurred ack in that dim and almost forgotten time concerning her ancestors that her grandmother had been working so hard to find out. What about John Charles, the son who was born too soon? Was her grandmother questioning the date of the boy's birth? If so, why was it so important. It was well over a century ago. Even though it must have been frowned on in that day and age for a man and a woman to be together before they were married, it did happen. Customs are often overlooked in times of chaos and stress, even in 1864. Wherever men and women were close together, this sort of thing happens. Why the fuss? Was her grandmother that much of a prude?

Knowing her mother's attitude about this research, Elizabeth understood why Julia had not been so keen on digging up the past and possibly uncovering an ugly little mistake made by an unfortunate young girl and an older man. She probably would have simply said, "He was old enough to know better, but at least he married her." And that would have been the end of it.

"I'll spend no more time on it tonight," she said aloud. The trunk and its contents had exhausted her. Putting the mystery of the letters and little book, bibles and dates from her mind, Elizabeth gathered everything she had removed from the trunk and replaced them all as neatly as she could. Taking her now cold tea to the kitchen, she nuked it in the microwave and took it upstairs to sip while she prepared for bed. She found it difficult to put the things that she had just learned out of her mine — the strange happenings that took place so long ago, back in the old home place in South Carolina.

Elizabeth knew she would have to go back to the small town of Maclin very soon. She had to settle the question of what to do with Mockingbird Hill, the estate that had come to her upon her mother's death. Originally the plantation had been the Grenville home and it was still called the Old Grenville Place by locals. When her maternal great-great-grandfather, John Charles Grenville I, had written his will, he had named his daughter, Elizabeth Grenville Perry, his sole heir. Family tradition told that she had died suddenly in a tragic accident, her own son, Andrew Perry, being taken from her still warm body. Obviously Old John had never changed his will, so the estate went to the boy, Andrew, who when grown, followed the family tradition to a military career. The Perrys became the owners of the estate; however, it fell to Harriet and Jake, the descendants of John Charles Grenville Jr., to reside on the property and to maintain it while the Perrys travelled the world fighting one enemy after another, until her own father became heir to Mockingbird Hill. Julia could not bear the thought of returning to the small town of Maclin to live and felt gratitude that their Grenville cousins, Harriet and Jake, were willing to remain.

With her father passed on and now her mother gone, The Hill now had come to Elizabeth. She knew that she must return and decide once and for all what she would do about it. Her first thought had been to sell outright to her cousins if they had the desire to purchase the place, but memories held her back from an act so final. She and her mother had spoken about it during the final days of her illness.

Julia had said to her, "Elizabeth, it is still a beautiful place. Your father loved his time there on his leaves. He said it was a wonderful way to get away from everything. He hunted, he fished, he sailed and always wanted one of us, someday, to live there. You might really like it. You haven't stayed there long enough as an adult to learn and to appreciate all of its charms."

Elizabeth had perhaps unkindly reminded her, "Mother, you never did either. You seemed happy for the Grenvilles to stay."

"I know. You are quite right. But it never suited me. Too remote. "She had grasped her daughter's hand as she said, "You loved it like your father loved it. Ever since you were a tiny little girl you loved going there and you always cried when you had to come away."

"Until you made me stop going there for my summer holidays," Elizabeth had reminded her mother. "Why did you, anyway? Why did you say I could no longer spend my summers there?"

"I had my reasons," Julia replied softly and quickly changed the subject. "Besides, childhood pleasures are nothing like what you would discover as an adult. You love to paint and the coast offers so much opportunity for that. You could sell in galleries in Charleston."

Elizabeth had sat quiet and pensive for a moment, holding her mother's hand, remembering and wondering what those reasons might have been. Had they had anything to do with Jake? What she had loved about going to visit The Hill, but had never told her mother, was seeing cousin, Jake. That was the pleasure she had always looked forward to all through the interminable school year. It was leaving Jake at the end of August that she had always dreaded when vacation time was over. This was not the time to upset her mother, so again she had remained silent. Instead, she had given her mother a kiss and had promised, "Yes, Mom, I will go there, spend a while getting reacquainted with the place, talk with Harriet and Jake, and ask if they want to buy. Maybe after a couple of weeks I'll know if I really want to sell." She had smiled at Julia and said, "I'm a bit surprised at you, Mother. I didn't think you would care so much about what happened to the place."

Tired from conversation and drowsy from the morphine drip, Julia had replied quietly, but also mysteriously, "I care about and think about many more things than you might know, my dear."

Elizabeth lay in bed, the light still on, thinking that tomorrow she must call and plan to go to The Hill. No more delays. She turned off the light and slept.

TWENTY-ONE

ELIZABETH WOKE WITH A START. She had been dreaming. As she struggled to remember it and to make sense of it, the dream faded into the never, never land where dreams live and die. Fully awake, the next thing to cross her mind was coffee. First things first. She left her bed, pulled on her robe, put her feet into her slippers and descended the stairs. In the kitchen she inserted the filter, spooned Sumatra, poured water and pushed the button. Only then did she go to the bathroom. When she returned to the kitchen her coffee was ready. She filled her favorite cup, added Half and Half and, taking the phone off the cradle, she went out to the patio. She sipped the delicious brew and planned her morning. First, she must call her cousins to find a time convenient time to visit them. She would not presume to go without this, even if the place were hers.

Only hesitating momentarily, Elizabeth reached for the phone. No time like the present, she thought. She remembered the number and dialed. One ring. Two. Was Harriet outside, she wondered? Away? Almost hoping for that and feeling relieved, she was disappointed when on the third ring she had success.

"Hello," came Harriet's thin, rather nasal voice in a Charlestonian's unique accent. "Who's calling?" she instantly inquired.

"It's Elizabeth, Harriet."

"Elizabeth who?" came the voice again.

"Your cousin." Heavens, she thought, Harriet's going to be difficult.

"Oh, well, yes. Where are you?"

"I'm here at home in Los Angeles. How are you all?"

"We are all just fine." There was a brief, tight silence, then, "We were sorry to hear about your mother. We would have come to the funeral, but you know how I simply hate to fly. Just makes me ill thinking about it. And Jake was away in the hills. He didn't get word 'til the funeral was over."

"Of course. Don't concern yourself. Jake sent a lovely card with flowers for Mom's grave. He called, but I was out. He left a sweet message on the recorder."

"Well, then," replied Harriet in her distinct low country accent, "what can we do for you?"

Oh, she was making this difficult, Elizabeth thought again. Why hadn't Jake been the one who answered.

"I want to plan a trip to The Hill," she began, "and, of course, I want to come when it is convenient with you and Jake."

Harriet's voice became cold and polite as she answered, "I'm always here. I never leave. You may come when you wish. I don't know about Jake, but perhaps he can tell you. He's here, in the kitchen. I'll get him."

Elizabeth could hear the phone being laid on a table. It was like Harriet that she would go to fetch Jake, not call. She waited and then heard the phone being picked up.

"Elizabeth, that you? My God, woman, it's been a while," came Jake's strong, deep voice over the miles. "Get my card? And flowers? I tried to call, but you were out."

"Yes, Jake, I did. Thank you. It was a lovely message."

"You're coming, aren't you," he stated as a matter of fact, then asked, "When? I'll meet the plane."

"Wait. I don't have the flight booked yet. I wanted to make sure the timing was good for Harriet."

"Won't ever be a good time for Harriet. Just come."

They were speaking with each other as though they had been apart a fortnight, not more than twenty years.

"It's good to hear you," he continued. "I've wanted to see you. I called a few times, but were you were never in."

"Sorry, I didn't know. California is that kind of a place. I seldom stay inside. And mother was ill for so long. She spent the final weeks in the hospital and I had to be there."

"I'm glad you're coming. You don't know how glad I am. Make the reservations, then call me right back. I'll pick you up at the airport and drive you up to The Hill."

After they hung up, Elizabeth sat quietly for a moment and reflected on the conversations with her two cousins. Harriet must be anxious about the disposition of her home—knowing the possibility that Elizabeth may wish to live there. As for Jake, it seemed as though no time at all had passed since they

175

had last spoken. He remained, as ever, her cousin and best friend — the same as when they were children.

TWENTY-TWO

ELIZABETH'S FLIGHT WAS SCHEDULED TO DEPART from LAX at 7:10 A.M. She hardly slept all night and climbed out of her bed quite early. She skipped making coffee, knowing that she could hit the Starbucks at the airport. Dressed, luggage packed with final items, she waited impatiently for the airport shuttle which she had scheduled the previous night. Afraid that he would be late and she would miss this flight, she breathed a sigh of relief when the van approached as scheduled. She took her luggage, shut the door and locked it behind her. The friendly young driver loaded her luggage, asked what airline she was taking and, before driving away, reminded her to check to see if she had her ticket. Shortly after 5 A.M., they were on the 405-freeway traveling south in greatly reduced Saturday morning traffic.

Not in the mood to chat with the young man, Elizabeth quietly gazed through the window as they passed by familiar landmarks. The Los Angeles skyline had become quite imposing with its new skyscrapers. Now, in the brilliant glow of the new sunrise, the glass-walled buildings glowed with breathtaking reflections of gigantic slabs of sunlight. In just a few weeks, with the arrival of June Gloom, those same buildings would rise from a shrouding mist of the early morning marine layer drifting in from the ocean. It would look like a fairy city.

"More beautiful than New York," she said quietly.

"You say something, Ma'am?" queried the young driver in broken English.

"Just talking out loud to myself," Elizabeth answered. "Thinking how beautiful the downtown skyline is."

"I like it, too," commented the young driver. Anxious to make his boring job a little more interesting with conversation, he continued. "This your home?"

"Well, yes, I suppose it is now. But I didn't always live here," she answered, finding herself chatting after all.

"Who did?" he laughingly bantered. "I came here to go to school."

"Which college?"

"Not real college. Not like UCLA or one of those. I go to beauty college. I'm gonna be a movie make-up man," he explained excitedly.

"That's nice," Elizabeth commented, wondering what had brought this young man from halfway across the world to attend make-up school in LA. Then she realized that, more than anything else, the youth of other worlds watched movies and videos made about America in Hollywood.

She said, "I've finally come to love this place. It's crazy sometimes, but there's so much energy. All kinds. People, ideas, life happening wildly every day."

"Yeah, it's a real crazy place. You got that right."

"Your parents here with you?"

"Nah! Have no parents. Both killed in fighting long time ago. My Grandma raised me. She's still over in Lebanon. Too old to make the change, she said."

"This is what LA is made of," said Elizabeth. "People from all nations coming here for all kinds of reasons. This is what makes it such a strange place."

Some people could not deal with the mix of cultures and intensely disliked the place. Not Elizabeth. An International at heart, she enjoyed the freedom and the energy that seemed to radiate from the hills which bounded the city on three sides and the vastness of the great salty ocean that lay peacefully to the west. This was not at all like the quiet, staid, predictable atmosphere of Carolina — full of tradition and family expectations — where everyone knew what you did or did not do and judged you for it. There was no freedom for her there and the energy was of a totally different sort. One's energy in Maclin, South Carolina, came from knowing who you were and where you came from, not from following one's muse.

Elizabeth wondered if she could make the change. Could she adapt to life there after Los Angeles? Should she even contemplate leaving this place and living back east again. These questions remained in her mind and she hoped this short visit would give her a hint or a warning to tell her how to plan her future.

The driver stopped the van in front of the Delta terminal. He jumped out and took the bags to the baggage check-in counter in front of the building.

"Going for a long time, looks like?" he inquired.

"Maybe two weeks, more or less." She handed him a generous tip and said, "You have a nice day, now. Maybe I'll see a movie someday that you worked on. Good luck!"

Traffic had been so light and the driver had no other passengers to gather that they had arrived at the airport earlier than necessary. No matter, she would check in, find the gate and settle down with her book for a good read. She left her luggage with the skycap on the sidewalk and carried only her handbag along with her small carry-on case that held her book, a few magazines and her reading glasses. After checking in and getting her boarding pass, she found a seat in the waiting section facing the wall-sized windows with a full view of the tarmac. Here, the early morning sunlight glowed on the waiting plane parked beside the covered walkway while being readied for flight. Baggage carts pulled up under the belly of the plane. Attendants loaded boxes and luggage in the baggage hold. She pulled out her book, opened it, and tried to read but her gaze kept drifting upward to the sky where the sun was now a huge red ball. In Charleston, a world away, the sun already was far up on the horizon. She found that her mind too easily drifted from the book and put it away to simply stare out the window and think until they called her flight for boarding.

Elizabeth had not been to visit The Hill in a long time. Twenty years ago she had attended a Perry family reunion but had only stayed the weekend in town and had not visited The Hill at all. As she sat on the airliner, listening to the hum of the engines running the air conditioner, she tried to remember what the old plantation looked like and wondered how much it had changed. The house was a large, three-story dwelling out in the country — about a mile off the main highway — close to the land between the three rivers that flowed down to the sea. A wide veranda on the lower floor followed two sides and front of the house, on the lower floor, arranged to catch any breath of cool air that might be moving during the long, hot summer. On the top floor small balconies extended off the bedrooms. When she was a child and came to visit in the summer, that veranda had been their favorite place to sit and play when rain came, which happened quite often. They had even slept there under mosquito netting on hot, sultry summer nights. From the third-floor balconies one could see the river — wide and gently flowing to the sea. If she closed her eyes now and thought of those long-ago days, she could see her Grenville cousins, Jake, Harry, and Simon in the mornings at the farm. After gobbling heaping bowls of cold cornbread and milk, they would all dash outside to play tag. After much rough and tumble, when they were hot and sweaty and smelled like the worst of outdoors, Cook would not allow them back into the house. She would hand them their favorite treats through the doorway; slabs of freshly baked bread slathered with homemade butter and topped with a generous sprinkling of sugar. Then they would all pile into the little rowboat and row out to the best fishing spots. After jumping over the side of the boat for a swim — in lieu of a bath — they fished for bream and perch. There were old cane poles with heavy white cord, rusty hooks, and little balls of lead tied to the cord. Her elder cousin, Jake, would always put the worm on the hook for her. He never teased her for being

181

squeamish, as did Simon and Harry. Five years older—twelve to her seven—Jake, in his wisdom, seemed to think that this squeamish aspect of females was the way God had ordered the universe. If they used chunks of bacon for bait, they caught glistening, squirming blue crabs instead of fish. When his two brothers had tried to get her to pick up the crabs from the bottom of the boat, he had shooed them away and did the frightful task himself.

Elizabeth remembered that their sister, Harriet, would not go out in the little row boat at all. She considered fishing too tacky, a task best left to the help. Refusing to play with them because they smelled of river mud from digging for the tiny fiddler crabs on the river banks, Harriet had always been aloof and critical of her brothers. Elizabeth had struggled with the resentment she felt from Harriet, especially since she and Harriet's brothers were such good playmates.

Families on the river celebrated summer's end with neighborhood get-togethers, peanut boilings, fish fries and expeditions to the forest to gather hickory nuts to store for cracking on cold, winter nights. Relatives and close friends would come to The Hill bringing their huge cast iron skillets to set over outdoor fires. The delicious odor of fresh caught perch, blue gills and hush puppies frying filled the air. Peanuts ripened in late July and after harvesting and washing the green peanuts went into galvanized tubs, covered with salted water and placed to boil over fires until they were soft and tender inside. Many an evening, she and all her cousins had gone to bed with bellyaches from eating too many boiled peanuts.

Her seat in first class was comfortable, the champagne chilled and food palatable. After eating and watching a film, Elizabeth slept soundly and awoke to the pilot's announcement that they would be landing in little more than half an hour. As the plane slowly circled for a landing, she was amused to find that she felt excitement; like a child going on summer holiday.

The pilot brought the plane in for a smooth landing and passengers took their usual time unloading the overhead bins of their packages and carry-on luggage. By the time the line began to move, Elizabeth was beginning to feel the effects of the heat and a bit of claustrophobia. Finally, she walked down the narrow aisle and out into the passenger terminal. Glancing around quickly to find Jake, she caught his image and recognized him immediately. He stood back from the crowd, leaning against a wall. At middle age, he was still trim and fit, looking very distinguished with splashes of gray at his temples. His piercing blue eyes met hers. They smiled and began to walk toward each other. He took her bag at the same instant that he enveloped her in a bear hug with his free arm, planting a kiss on her cheek.

"Hi, Cuz. Long time, no see," he said. "How are you?"

"It's good to see you, too, Jake," she said when he released her. "I'm doing all right. I miss Mom, but you know her illness kept her down for quite a while. I'm almost happy that she's gone and no longer suffering. You know her. She'd rather laugh than eat and didn't like anything that mucked up the world. I think she's happy now. I'll get over missing her ... I suppose ... with time ... or get used to it. But you, please tell me about you. It's been so long."

"Not much to tell. I retired from lawyering and do some consulting work when I feel like it. Mostly, I keep busy out in the hills backpacking." After a brief pause, he asked, "Why did we stay apart for so long? Seeing you coming through that door was like going back decades to when we were kids. We can't let that happen again. We've got to stay in touch."

She held his arm and gave it a squeeze. "We did grow up and apart, didn't we?" she acknowledged. "We shouldn't have done that."

"Had to," he said quietly.

She dropped her gaze quickly. Did he mean what she thought he meant? That it was wiser for them to be apart? Is that why he had always avoided her since they grew up? For all those years?

They continued catching up on old and new happenings as they made their way toward the baggage room to collect her luggage.

"You still go fishing?"

"Yeah, sometimes. I take a rod with me when I go camping and sometimes find a few trout. Will you have time to go with me while you're here?"

"Don't know. I'm not quite sure how long I'll stay. Just have a few loose ends to tie up. Must decide what I want to do with The Hill, now that Mom is gone. Doesn't seem quite right that it stayed in my side of the family for so long when we didn't really use it or do all the work. Seems like it should belong to you and Harriet. It's the Old Grenville Place and you are the Grenvilles."

"Don't feel that way. No need. We enjoyed it and took care of it because we were doing the most living in it. Your dad and mom understood that the old house was loved. The place has been the Perry place since the War."

"Yes, technically, I know," replied Elizabeth. "But it began as the Grenville place."

"S'pose so, but Old John Grenville willed it to his daughter, your great-great-grandmother. The one you are named for. She had married a Perry—that's when it changed. His will gave it to her and her children and he died before he knew he would have a son of his own. I descend from his second wife, Margaret. She was quite young when they married and he only lived long enough to sire a son, but never knew him and he never changed his will. He was old by our standards when he married my great-grandmother, who was quite young. I've always figured he wouldn't have been too upset knowing how we worked it all out."

"How do you know all this?" she asked in good humor, having just learned these facts herself.

"Harriet. Harriet knows all about every ancestor we ever had and she is very defensive when people ask her anything about the place."

"It's too complicated for me," she laughed. "But maybe I've come to the right place for some other answers. Speaking of Harriet, how is she?" Elizabeth inquired as they came to the baggage room where they could see the carousel revolving and a few scattered bags going 'round. "It was difficult for me to tell over the phone."

"Well, you know Harriet. She hasn't changed much over the years. Still stuck up and overbearing. She mostly keeps herself busy with her genealogy clubs and historical societies, Junior League and all that."

"She's very much involved in researching the family history?"

"Yeah, most of her time is spent with the DAR, the Colonial Daughters, the Daughters of the Confederacy, or the Daughters of Wright's Creek ... or some such," he jokingly replied, making a face. "You know our mother belonged to those organizations and Harriet kept on with the family tradition. I used to think they were a bit crazy, but one day Mom told me some mumbo jumbo about good southern families losing everything in the war but their background ... or some such like that." He stopped for a moment as one of the bags came into view, then continued in a more serious way. "She said that the women lost their men, their sons and sometimes their homes and land. Most lost what money they had and were left with nothing to hold onto but their heritage, their background. Those who were "quality" ... meaning those who were true blue bloods ... used that knowledge for their own emotional survival and sometimes for more than that... you know ... ego boosting. They used it to make business or military connections. Anyway, after Mom explained it to me, I never faulted Harriet so much for getting too involved. I figured that it kept her off the streets," he laughed.

"Maybe Harriet can help me with a mystery," responded Elizabeth. "I found an old letter and a few old Bibles in Mom's trunk, along with a family history chart. Whoever made it up was quite excited about something having to do with John II and a little book. Don't know what they were referring to, but there was some question about dates and marriages and births with little notes in the margins, you know? You ever hear Harriet say anything about this? I thought I'd ask her about it just to satisfy my curiosity."

Jake was quiet for a moment, thoughtful, and Elizabeth wondered if she had upset her cousin with her innocent question.

"We've all heard rumors and old aunts' gossip," he responded finally. "Nothing I ever gave much thought to." His voice became soft. With a quiet finality, he let her know that he did not wish to discuss the matter.

Well, she would take it up with Harriet. This was not the sort of subject that concerned most men anyway. She had probably exhausted his interest. With Elizabeth's bags in tow, they went out into the bright Carolina sunshine and found his truck in the parking lot.

"You didn't bring much with you," he said, changing the subject. "Not planning to stay long?" indicating the two pieces of luggage that he carried.

"I brought enough for a couple of weeks. Need to come to a decision about The Hill soon. It is something we should talk about and I suppose I thought that we could decide in a fortnight. How is The Hill?" she asked. "As lovely as ever?"

"Yep, it is. Harriet has done well by it and it shows her pride in it. She couldn't love it and care for it more if she owned it herself."

"Well, that may happen," Elizabeth replied. "I haven't decided yet. I don't even know if I could live in it. It's been Harriet's home for so long that...," her voice trailed off, the sentence unfinished. "Does she still live there alone? All by herself?"

"Cook and maid and butler and her. So, yes, she is there all alone. I drop in a few times a week to see about things."

They both remained silent as Jake drove the truck from the small airport, entered Interstate 26 and sped out on the highway. The drive to The Hill required less than an hour. Several times during the drive, her eyes and Jake's met as they passed some familiar landmark which they remembered from their youth. Most of the old places were gone—torn down to make way for new development. She saw billboards, neon signs and automobile junk yards instead of the small roadside stands that used to be run by local craftsmen and women selling vegetables, peanuts, sugar cane, hand woven baskets and other homemade souvenirs.

Jake turned off the freeway and drove for a few miles on a narrow, two-lane gravel road before turning into the driveway at The Hill.

The Hill was not laid out like many of the old southern plantation houses that had been built just before the war, with long drives lined with moss covered trees. The front of this house was quite close to the road, with the expanse of lawn going all the way down to the river. It was spring time and

188

camellia bushes were in full bloom. Azaleas grew around the house in neat, ordered patches. Where the woods met the lawn, they had gone wild and mingled with wild berry bushes among tall pines. The air smelled warm, fragrant and damp. Sweet perfume of wisteria wafted from pines and oak trees where the vines, struggling with moss for control, grew all the way to the treetops, their purple and lavender blossoms hanging like soft, velvety bunches of grapes. In all her travels over the world with her parents, then with her husband, she had never found any other place quite like South Carolina. There was something mystical about it; quiet, pungent, waiting, almost as if something were going to happen, yet never quite did.

A culture and heritage, both violent and dramatic, yet filled with quiet charm, made up this state. It seemed to Elizabeth that this place, Mockingbird Hill, personified it all. Not a fancy antebellum mansion built from the proceeds of King Cotton, the house at The Hill had begun as a small house made from logs hewn from the surrounding pocosin — the swampy forests — in a raw, new land. It had grown along with generations of people who carved it out of the swamps — at first, a mere livelihood, then a thriving culture based on agriculture and stock raising. The swamps had been drained and had become vast productive areas where cattle and hogs roamed and fattened themselves. The country saw some of the first cowboys in this Carolina low country as young men rounded up stock, loaded the animals barges, and shipped them to ports in Charleston, Georgetown and Beaufort.

As years passed, the house had been added onto—first one wing, then another, then another floor. Sometime in the dim past a Grenville had built another house, much larger and a bit fancier for the growing family. When the family had recovered from the Civil War, the house had been covered with fine lumber and painted a glistening white.

"Harriet has done a few things inside," stated Jake as he parked the truck. "She has the inside decorated with new rugs and carpets. She got new furniture for almost all the rooms. A few pieces even came from England. I hope you like what she did."

"I am sure I will. Harriet always had excellent taste," replied Elizabeth as she got out of the truck and stood looking at the imposing structure—a working plantation home.

"Painted not too long ago?" she asked.

"What with the weather and mildew, paint has to be kept up," replied Jake. "Don't worry though. Funds come out of the trust."

Elizabeth noted the freshly trimmed border hedges that kept the wilderness, the bugs and woods from encroaching onto the lawn. The grass lawns were carefully mowed.

Jack could see Elizabeth taking it all in. After a moment he said, "Harriet takes care of it."

"I see. Her love of it shows in the work. No mean task taking care of a place like this."

"Remember when we were kids? No lawn. Just dirt yard with pigs and chickens running around. Yard men didn't cut grass, they raked the yards clean."

"I remember stepping in chicken doo," laughed Elizabeth. "Getting it between my toes and hobbling to the pump to wash my foot."

"I'll leave you here at The Hill and head on back to my place." Seeing the look of consternation on her face, he quickly added, "I'll be back in time for dinner. This'll let you get settled and allow time for you to have a chat with Harriet. And you look tired. Maybe a nap?" Jake suggested with a smile.

"All right," Elizabeth responded. "Maybe I will take a short nap. I am more tired than I thought I would be. Getting old, I suppose," she laughed.

"We're not old yet, but not young either. Guess we're really middle aged."

"Jason!" called Jake loudly, then turned to Elizabeth to explain. "Jason is Harriet's new butler," he said with a smile. "Butler! Can you believe that? Nobody has butlers nowadays—anyway, not out here in the piney-woods. But that's my sister," he concluded.

A tall, imposing man opened the front door and came down the steps to help Jake with the luggage. "'Lo, Jason. How's the lady of the house today?"

"Miss Harriet, she doin' fine, suh," replied Jason. "I thinks she knows y'all are heah and I thinks she'll be waitin' in the parlor. She had me lay a fire in the fireplace a little while ago, suh."

"Jason, this is Miss Elizbeth. Elizabeth, meet Jason."

"Glad to meet you Miss "Lisbeth. We been spectin' you."

"I'm happy to meet you, Jason," she replied, holding out her hand.

Jason hesitated only a second or two before reaching out to take the offered hand, his smile getting wider and showing a gleam in his eye. It seemed to Elizabeth that this butler spoke the way he thought people wanted him to speak, but he did it with a twinkle in his eye. Elizabeth had no doubt that he could speak perfectly correct Charleston English, if he so chose.

"I'll take these on up to yo' room," Jason continued. "You go on into the parlor. I thinks you'll will find Miss Harriet waitin'. She has Sally fixin' tea."

"Yes, thank you, Jason," she said as she and Jake followed him into the house.

She knew exactly where Jason would take her luggage. It would be the room on the second floor in the front with a view of the river. Harriet would not have forgotten that when they were little girls she had kept the door to her bedroom locked, insisting that they play in Elizabeth's room. Harriet kept her room tidy with every small thing in its place; disturbed if her room got messy. Elizabeth knew that even though she had not visited in years, Harriet would have kept her cousin's room ready for her — at any time.

They found Harriet seated on an antique settee in the parlor arranging tea things. Seeing Elizabeth, she arose, smiled politely and spoke. "Hello, Elizabeth. It's good to see you again."

She spoke as though only a few months had passed since they met. There was no warmth in her voice; no more than when they were children. Her expression showed thinly disguised displeasure. This was not going to be as easy as she had hoped, but she had to say something to put Harriet at ease. What could she say or do? She walked around the tea table and held out her arms to her cousin.

"It is so very good to see you, too. It's been much too long," she said, mustering as much warmth as she could find to put into her voice.

Jake stood quietly by and watched as his sister allowed Elizabeth to give her a cousinly embrace but saw that she remained stiff and unyielding and did not return the gesture.

"Harriet, the room is beautiful!" exclaimed Elizabeth as she stepped away from the light embrace. "When did you re-do it?"

The parlor had been redecorated since Elizabeth had seen it last. The old-fashioned wall paper had been replaced with a lovely pattern of soft lavender wisteria blossoms on a background the color of ivory magnolia blossoms. The furniture had been covered in matching cream. A muted green carpet gave her the feeling of being outdoors. The outside wall had been cut to place a huge picture window that showed a large expanse of lawn. It was not the same room they had played in as children, where they hammered hickory nuts on the brick hearth. Only the fireplace and that ancient brick hearth hinted at the age of the room. It was the original room—in the beginning, the only room of Mockingbird Hill.

"You have such wonderful taste! You did do it yourself, didn't you?" asked Elizabeth.

"Why, yes, I did do it myself," Harriet answered, seemingly caught a bit off balance with the compliment. "I accepted some suggestion from a decorator in town. He suggested the green carpet. At first, I didn't think it would go but it did, didn't it, Jake?" She looked over to her brother as though to get his approval. He smiled and nodded his head in assent.

Harriet seemed to catch herself and continued with a less enthusiastic tone. "How was your flight? Pleasant, I hope?"

Why did she feel that Harriet suddenly wished that the plane had crashed?

"Yes, quite comfortable and having Jake there to meet me was simply great."

"Yes, he was always willing to give you a hand." Hostility was now creeping into her voice.

"How jealous she must be," thought Elizabeth. "How unfortunate." She realized that Harriet must feel like a guest—or worse, a caretaker—in this house, knowing that Elizabeth was the real mistress of the place. They were the only two girl cousins. All through their young lives, they could not be friends. Now both were middle aged and should have outgrown the childhood pettiness, yet friendship still seemed impossible.

"I've made tea for you and there are some sandwiches and scones. I didn't know if you would eat that horrible food on the plane or not."

Harriet's voice sounded as though to be friendly, or at least trying to be civil and Elizabeth suspected that Jake had given his sister the evil eye as he did when he caught his little sister losing her manners.

Jake boldly confirmed her suspicion when he said, "You'd better eat something, hungry or not, or Harriet will never get over the insult."

This earned him a glare of anger from Harriet and Elizabeth tried to sooth the situation.

"Yes, thanks, a cup of hot tea would go very well now. I see you've taken down the old tea service. Do you use it often, or is this a special treat?"

As soon as the words were out of her mouth she wished she could put them back in. She meant the comment as a compliment and felt surprised when Harriet took it negatively.

"I do use it now and again. We are not totally in a backwater here at The Hill." Her voice barely held in her anger.

"I'm sure you have many occasions to entertain," Elizabeth hurriedly said. "Jake told me how much you've become involved in local historical societies. They must be so demanding and exciting," she added, trying to pour soothing oil on troubled waters.

"It's good that at least one of us has kept in touch with our roots," replied Harriet. "Someone has to do it or else we would forget our heritage."

"I've never been very good at that sort of thing," said Elizabeth. "I'm sure it must keep you busy all the time. Maybe later this evening we can discuss some of the fami..."

Before she could finish her sentence, Jake, who had been standing and quietly observing the reunion, cut her off with a curt, "I'm off now, ladies. Be back in time for dinner. Harriet, dinner as usual?"

"Of course, Brother dear. Dressed and at eight." Harriet answered Jake with a strained attempt at a smile.

"Dressed?" Jake asked with a frown.

"To the nines," replied his sister.

"Harriet, I didn't pack anything special. I only brought casual things," said Elizabeth.

"Then I'll dress casually as well," said Jake, bringing a frown to Harriet's face.

Before she could complain, he walked away, out of the house, got in his truck and drove away, spinning gravel in the drive.

The quiet between two women as they sat sipping tea continued as it had always been; perhaps, even more so. Elizabeth had thought that maybe on this trip she could pry into Harriet's mind a bit, try to understand her life and her pleasures. After all, they were women and cousins—albeit distant ones—and they must have something in common. Since neither had a sister, it would have been good if they could behave like sisters. She knew she had to try harder, but now, exhausted from the long flight, a wall of exhaustion hit her.

"Thank you so much, Harriet. This was all delicious and welcomed but I think I'll go up now and have a rest and a good hot bath before dinner. We can talk more then."

"As you wish," Harriet replied. "Jason has taken your things up to your old room already. Come down whenever you like. Jake will probably be here at seven—in time for his julep. I'm sure you will want to join him."

Harriet remained seated as Elizabeth awkwardly took her leave, fighting anger. Why did Harriet insist on making her feel uncomfortable?

Elizabeth opened the door to her old room and saw that Harriet had indeed been busy. The ancient four-poster with the pink ruffled canopy was still there, although the pink ruffles were made from new fabric. New scatter rugs showed off the gleam of polished oak floors. The small, maple writing desk was just as she remembered it, but she could tell that her grandmother's vanity had recently been refinished. The bathroom was completely modern with gold-plated fixtures. Jake was right. Harriet had taken care of the house as well as if she had owned it. Having lived here most of her life, she probably considered it as much hers as anyone's. A double glass door opened onto the little balcony where one could go to catch a breeze off the river in summer. There was enough space on the balcony for a small, white wrought-iron tea table and two matching iron chairs. Here, as a little girl, she had played at having tea with her first set of fine china. How sad, she thought, that little girls no longer received miniature china tea sets—a young girls first treasure. Handling china tea cups and saucers taught little girls how to take care of good things. She learned how to be a lady while serving imaginary tea and cakes to either her dolls or play friends. She mimicked her mother and her mother's friends, so by the time that she became a young lady, serving tea with an elegant tea service came easily.

She opened the glass doors to the little balcony and stepped out. A glowing red sun hung low in the sky and a spring chill was in the air. She could see the river clearly over the treetops from this height. She wanted to stand and gaze at it, but she needed to rest.

Returning to the room and closing the doors, she opened one of her bags. She unpacked a skirt and sweater and hung them so that the wrinkles would fall out. She left the rest until tomorrow. With that small task finished, Elizabeth undressed, turned back the covers from the high bed and climbed in.

As she lay there drowsy and close to sleep, she began to contemplate seriously whether she could ever live here permanently. She'd have to leave the nomadic life she'd always lived with her military husband and settle in one place for the rest of her days. Could she do it? Already middle aged, one more move would be the final one. The question was, how happy would she be here? Her thoughts then went to Jake. She remembered one time when she was a little girl, after an especially fun day of playing with her cousins at The Hill, she had asked her mother if, when she grew up, she would marry Jake. Feigning horror, her mother declared that it certainly would not happen, reminding her that they were cousins. Her mother had declared that enough cousins in their family had married and that had to look elsewhere for a husband. At that time Elizabeth had not understood that at all, but her mother's absolute "No!" was reason enough, so she had given up on marrying Jake.

They had become the best of friends — much closer than most cousins — and had remained so until they began to grow up. Her father was often transferred. Elizabeth and her mother followed him as often as they were allowed. After she and Jake grew up, she seldom saw him. He went to the university law school and then went away for his military service.

He married Laurel Clark, a university homecoming queen, just after completing law school. After his stint in the army, they had settled in Charleston where Jake had quite a lucrative law practice. Elizabeth had looked elsewhere and found Alexander Wilson, a bright young lieutenant in her father's company — a Yankee from upstate New York. They'd married within a year of meeting each other. It had been a very happy marriage until Vietnam. Alex was killed and Elizabeth did not marry again.

"What was that Jake had said at the airport?" she said aloud and tried to remember. It was something to the effect that we had to. Suddenly, she realized what he must have known all along — that they had been deliberately kept apart and that he had been a willing ally. It had always seemed strange to her that after they had been so close as children, as adults, they seldom met. Often, he knew that she was coming to visit and would not be there when she came. He would be off on a trip or something.

She realized that her mother was afraid for them to be close and had deliberately kept them apart. Elizabeth was stunned to realize this and to realize that her mother had believed that something unhealthy would develop between them. She tried not to think about it, determined to sleep. Her body was exhausted and now her mind was leading her into paths it had better not go. She drowsily lay in bed, her eyes closed, then let her drifting thoughts go to Harriet. She thought she heard a tiny sound beside her bed. When she turned to look, she saw an enraged, horrifying Harriet poised over her with a knife. Flinging herself up in bed, she reached to catch the arm and suddenly woke to find that she had been asleep, and it had been a brief dream. Shivering now, cold with sweat, she pulled the goose down comforter up under her chin and tried to calm her rapidly beating heart. She scolded herself. How could she have dreamed such a horrid dream? Being disliked is one thing, being murdered is another. Elizabeth felt certain that she had become morbidly paranoid where Harriet was concerned. She lay back down and fell asleep again.

The tinkling of the phone on the bedside table woke her. Her mind was fuzzy with sleep and she struggled to regain focus as she reached for the receiver with a sleepy, "Hello?" It was Jake on the line.

"Have a good nap?" he asked.

"I think so. I might still be asleep," she laughed. "I have that feeling of where am I?"

"Weird, huh? You know, I once had that kind of waking up, but I couldn't even figure out what I was! That's weird!" laughed Jake.

"You'll have to run that by me again when I'm awake."

His voice changed from a jocular tone to a more serious one, as he quietly asked, "You haven't said anything to Harriet about the family history stuff yet, have you?"

"Barely. I only mentioned her activities. Why?"

The mention of Harriet caused her to remember her brief dream in its short, horrid totality.

"Then don't. At least not until you and I have had time for a long, private talk. This is important," he said, his voice full of urgency. "You've noticed about

Harriet, haven't you? She's a little 'round the bend, you know, and stuff like talking about family history can really set her off."

"Are you serious?"

"I am. Quite serious. We'll talk later."

"All right," Elizabeth answered, more than slightly puzzled, "I won't say anything."

"Good," he said. "Don't mention it 'til you and I have had a chance to talk privately.

"About Harriet being 'round the bend. I noticed a few oddities, but Harriet's always been odd. I just thought I'm being paranoid."

"I'll explain everything after we talk. I must hang up now. See you in a bit for a julep. I'm on my way."

She heard a click and was left holding a quiet receiver. The clock on the bedside table indicated that she had slept almost two hours. The bad dream of Harriet trying to knife her must have come in just those first nanoseconds that she had drifted off — that brief instant between being awake and falling asleep. The dream had not disturbed her subsequent sleep, but now, after Jake's phone call and the dream, she found herself uneasy.

Pulling on her robe, she went into the bathroom to run a deep, hot bath. Negative feelings must be thrust away if this visit was going to be successful at all. To redirect her thoughts, she went to the closet where she had hung her clothes and took down the navy pleated skirt and the soft ivory sweater to wear with it. No wonder I'm dreaming wild dreams, she thought. Jake is being so serious and mysterious about something so simple as family history. What's gotten into everybody?

The hot, sudsy water was refreshing and twenty minutes of soaking in the tub washed away her drowsiness. Drying off with a gigantic pink towel, she went back into the bedroom to dress. Around her neck, she placed her favorite necklace, a gift from her Alex on their last Christmas together.

Dark had fallen. The spring evening had settled in around her. She opened her suitcase and took out a light cardigan to throw around her shoulders and went downstairs to meet Harriet and Jake. When she entered the parlor, she was startled to see Harriet dressed in a long, elegant dinner dress and wearing a lovely diamond necklace, in all probability, an heirloom. Just then Jason opened the front door and she heard Jake's voice.

"Evenin', Jason," Jake said, slipping very easily into the local patois.

"Evenin', Mistah Jake," he replied, taking Jake's overcoat. "The ladies, they's in the parlor. Them juleps is a-waitin'. Y'all hurry up now."

As Jake came into the parlor, Elizabeth saw that he had kept his word and wore casual slacks and jacket.

Seeing Harriet's attire Jake said, "Harriet, aren't you overdoing it a bit seeing as how we're just a family at supper. Thought we agreed on casual."

Harriet spoke quickly and defensively, "We haven't forgotten how to be genteel here at The Hill. If I didn't insist on it, everyone would come in jeans and T-shirts to the dining room—like Californians. Someone has to maintain appearances," she said haughtily with a deliberate insult to Elizabeth. "Unfortunately, someone has to remind ..."

Jake cut her off and exchanged a quick glance with Elizabeth. He smiled at Harriet. "Yes, Sis. We know that we need you to remind us who we are and where we came from. If you didn't, we'd forget we're Grenvilles."

Although Jake smiled his words carried a smidgen of sting and Elizabeth felt sure that he was both mocking Harriet and humoring her, yet Harriet took no offense. She reacted as though he only said what she was going to say, in all seriousness. For the first time, Elizabeth began to wonder if Harriet was all right, or if maybe she had indeed gone over the edge—or, as Jake had put it, "round the bend!" Jake handled her with a kind of gentle mocking and still coddled her as though he were dealing with someone quite reasonable, though she was not reasonable.

Harriet continued, "Jake can take you shopping tomorrow and you can purchase a decent dress, since you didn't bring any."

Elizabeth felt quite reprimanded and looked to Jake for help.

"Yes," he said with a twinkle in his eye. "Tomorrow we'll go shopping."

Dinner was a strange affair with Jake doing his utmost to keep Elizabeth at ease. The food was excellent. Harriet had chosen the menu to show off some of the best recipes of old Charleston. Served by Jason and the maid, the steaming bowls of she-crab soup were delicious, the cress salad crisp and cold, and the shrimp pie was melt-in-your-mouth quality. Harriet talked mostly of activities with her various organizations and it soon became obvious that she was totally compulsive about them. She went to all the meetings and held office in most of them. Her only friends were those ladies who also belonged. Church activities took second place to the other. Religion was not as important to Harriet as family history—or maybe that was her religion—Elizabeth observed silently.

All through dinner, Jake allowed Harriet to talk on and on about activities, events and people who were alive. Not once did either of them mention a family member who had passed on. Harriet did not even bring up Julia's recent passing. Remembering Jake's caution and taking his lead, Elizabeth remained silent, preferring to be a listener. She also noticed that neither Jake nor Harriet mentioned the reason for her visit—The Hill and what she might decide to do with it.

Desert consisted of ripe pears served with a soft, melted brie, covered with roasted, buttered pecans. Jason brought out an old bottle of port which created a just finale to the sumptuous meal. Elizabeth had eaten so much that she could hardly move.

"Certainly not California cuisine," she remarked. "Do you eat like this every night at The Hill?"

"I don't know about Harriet," Jake answered, "but when she invites me out, the spread is just about as lavish. She knows shrimp pie is one of my favorites. You remember when we used to be able to get it down at the Francis Marion at lunch? Well, they stopped serving it when the old chef died and Harriet started making it for me. I'm sure she does as well for her friends," he continued. "If I came here often, I'd have to go hiking every day instead of weekends."

Elizabeth hoped she and Jake could soon excuse themselves and take a walk out by the river so that they could have that private conversation Jake promised. Jake suggested exactly that.

"Harriet why don't you and Elizabeth come and take a walk with me down by the river. It's chilly outside, but after this meal, I need the walk. Do you both a lot of good," he coaxed. "It'll put some color in your cheeks."

"Not for me," answered Harriet. "You go ahead, and I'll stay here with Elizabeth."

"I think I'll go with you, Jake, that is, if you don't mind too much, Harriet? I really need to walk off this dinner and it's not too cold. I did bring my outdoor jacket. I'll just run up and fetch it." Elizabeth pushed away from the table without looking at Harriet's face. Somehow she knew that she would see displeasure there. Running upstairs to fetch her coat and change to walking shoes, she was back down and ready to go in a jiffy.

"I keep an old pair of shoes here in the porch closet," Jake said, "because I'm always walking off Harriet's dinners. I'll get them and we can go all the way down to the water."

They left Harriet in the dining room while Jason and Sally were clearing the table. Elizabeth felt so relieved to be away from her, yet she felt guilty that she had abandoned the cleanup. Yet, there was Sally to help. Harriet could be so exasperating! She always seemed to be able to get inside one's head. She was what her mother had called an emotional manipulator. She could make you feel sorry for her, angry with her, or pity her — and then she could make you admire her for having that special skill of being able to do all these things to you. Always difficult, Harriet now seemed even worse, or maybe she was imagining it. Maybe it was only that Elizabeth had been away for so long and was having trouble adjusting, but Jake even said she was difficult. As they walked down the back steps and out onto the lawn, she turned and glanced back at the house. She could see Harriet's torso through the glass panel at the back door. She was staring after them and Elizabeth felt a sudden chill.

Jake reached over and buckled the top of her coat around her throat, pulling the hood up over her head. His hands lingered a few seconds on the hood, then he took them away and jammed them down into his coat pockets.

"You don't want to catch a cold while you are here."

Good old Jake, ever the big brother, she thought. The moon was up, the stars out, the night clear. The old familiar odor of the river assailed her nostrils. They were not far from the sea. Here, ocean water blended with fresh water as the latter flowed down from up-country. This smell of pluff mud and brackish water, mixed with the smells of the reeds that lined the banks, was something that she remembered from childhood. It was probably the one thing about the coastal low country that she loved most—this odor, this pungent, musty, swampy smell that was present all year long, even in winter, but much more so in the heat of summer. Tonight, the birds were silent except for an occasional sound of scrapping as one bird fell off his perch onto another in his sleep. Sounds of croaking frogs came from the shallows.

Jake interrupted the soft night sounds. "You've noticed that she's worse?" he asked.

"Well, yes. I did think that, but then I thought that maybe it was just me. It's been a long time that I've been away. You've been here with her and you know her much better. What's happening to her?" she asked.

"Well, lots of things. You know she never married. She's alone here—for all her clubs and associations. She is alone. Only me and Jason and Sally really know her. Maybe I know her best of all." He was quiet for a moment, then continued, "It's not obvious to most people, but I see her being obsessive with this place, with the family, with those damn fool clubs. I think she's going over the edge. Sometimes when she is going on about the place, her expression comes close to showing hysteria."

Elizabeth interrupted, "When did she get Jason? A butler? And dressing for dinner?"

"Yeah. How about that! That's kind of what I mean. She hired Jason about two years ago and, of course, Sally's been here a coon's age." Jake paused before going on. "Nothing is really sick, but it is just too much ... you know? I've talked with Doc Baggett, but he just says it's the old spinster in her. He thinks it's because she never married ... that's what's wrong with her. I asked if she should get some counseling and he just laughed and asked me, 'Who's she hurtin'?' All I could say was, 'Nobody.' Then he said, "well then, what's your problem? Leave her be. If she's got the money for a butler and if you're fool enough to get all dressed up for dinner, then hurrah for Harriet.' That's what he said. What could I say to that?"

"I see what you mean."

"She thinks you came to tell her that you're goin' to move back to The Hill. She thinks you're gonna take her home away," Jake said abruptly.

Elizabeth looked at him, startled to hear him say it bluntly, to put into such harsh words what had been in the back of her mind all along. He had done it on purpose, to let her feel the heaviness of it, so that she might know how it must be making Harriet feel.

"Yes, I think you're right. The way she looks at me sometimes makes me shiver."

"Are you?" he asked. "Will you come back to The Hill?"

"I don't know. Really. I haven't made up my mind. That is why I came back. I've never really lived here for any length of time. This house has always been Harriet's home. And yours. I was here only at summer vacation and Christmas holidays. I was the visitor. It was her home. I think I've been wondering if the two of us could live here together ... to share."

Jake looked at her quickly. "I doubt it," was his reply. "She'd never allow it. She could never share this place with you. It would have to be all hers or she would leave."

"But where would she go?"

"I don't know. Certainly not with me. She'd drive me nuts having her around every day. Besides, I think she'd just go crazy. Crazier," he said.

"That puts me in a very difficult position, doesn't it? If I want to stay, I'll be responsible for completely ruining her life. If I decide to give it up, even if I might want to stay, I ..."

"Don't think that way! If you want the place, why, it's yours. Always has been. Doesn't matter what she thinks or wants. Don't let her manipulate you that way." Jake's voice was firm and he was frowning. Suddenly, he stopped and turned to her. "Do you think you might want to stay? Do you?" He reached down and took her hands in his, facing her.

"Sometimes I do. Sometimes I want to come back. When I stand here by the river and listen and smell, it does something to me. Sort of reaches back inside me and touches memories. Those things we used to do as kids. The boat rides, the fishing, the worms you used to put on the hook for me. Christmas and Santa Claus in the parlor. Our stockings hanging on the mantle. Those were times I felt at home here. I don't know if I could ever recapture that feeling again, but sometimes I think I'd like to try."

"Do you miss Alex?" Jake suddenly changed the subject.

"Well, yes, in a way. But he's been gone for a long time. Seems like Vietnam was a hundred years ago."

"Why did you stay in California when he was killed?" Jake asked. "Why didn't you come home then. Mom and Pop were still alive, and they wouldn't have minded if you wanted The Hill then. They would have taken Harriet with them and now you wouldn't have this problem."

Jake took care of thirty years with one fell swoop.

"California was the last place Alex and I lived together and Mother loved living there. It seemed like the thing to do, the place to be. Besides, I like

California. Part of me is a real LA-LA," Elizabeth answered jokingly. Then she asked, "Do you miss Laurel?"

"Hell, no! We were wrong for each other right from the start. She was a sexy little thing and I fell for her like a ton of bricks. Boy did she take me for a ride!" Jake was laughing now. "Bein' married to her for eleven years just about killed me. We had no kids so when she took off with that damned fool Ralph Jackson, it was the best thing that ever happened to me. Boy, I pity him. Hear she leads him around by the ... well, hear she wears the pants in that family," Jake laughed out loud.

"We'd better go back," he said, suddenly serious, "but before we do, I want to warn you. Be careful of Harriet. Just be careful," he stumbled around for the right words. "If she thinks you're goin' to take away The Hill, I don't know how she will react. I want to be here as much as I can while you're here and if you decide to stay, tell me and let me be with you all the time. Don't talk about it with her — even if she asks — and don't ask her about the family or that little book you mentioned to me. That above all!

"You are scaring me, Jake. You need to explain."

"I'm sorry, but I know what drives her. I know the name of the devil she fights and I think the time has come for me to tell you, too. I will soon and it will help you decide what to do. But not now. We've been out long enough. I'll come out tomorrow, carry you to town and tell you the big secret."

Jake ended the conversation on this very mysterious, but final note. She knew not to nag him to tell her now. He would tell her tomorrow.

As they turned and walked slowly back to the house, they could see Harriet's shadow, still framed in the glass panel of the back door. Had she been watching them the entire time? It wasn't jealousy, was it, she wondered? Was Harriet jealous of Jake and her? Her brother and her cousin? Was that the big secret Jake was going to tell her?

They went in through the mud porch, left their wet shoes, and hung the jackets. By the time they went into the kitchen Harriet was nowhere to be seen.

Sally had finished in the kitchen and said, "Miss Harriet, she done gone up to bed. She say she tired and to tell y'all she'll see y'all in de mo'nin'. Dat all she say."

Now there would be no way Elizabeth could give her a proper thank you for the lovely dinner. Jake went around to Sally's backside and gave her ample shoulders a squeeze, at which the maid emitted a delighted squeal.

"I do declare, Mistah Jake, iffen you ain't a piss ant! A reg'lar li'l piss ant!"

"That was a great shrimp pie, Sally. I know you made it, not Miss Harriet."

"Go on now," she laughed coyly at the welcome praise. "Thanks to you Mistah Jake. You always knows what to say to make my day!" They left her mumbling to herself, grinning and shaking her head, "That Mistah Jake, ah swear, he a li'l piss ant sho!"

At the front door, Jake gave Elizabeth's cheek a kiss and said, "Get a good night's sleep. I'll be here bright and early and we'll go to town."

She stood by the window and watched the tiny red glow of the truck's tail-lights fade into the night.

She smiled. It was so like Jake. Driving a pick-up truck and an old one at that. Suddenly, she felt lonely — she who had not felt lonely in years.

"Strange," she said as she turned and climbed the stairs to go to her bedroom.

That night Elizabeth's sleep was troubled. Twice she awoke from bad dreams. In the first, she dreamed that something seemed to be in the river, something that beckoned to her ... and when she went to it, it disappeared just beyond her grasp, but almost within it. It was something she should have or needed to find but could not. She tossed and turned, trying to fathom just what it was. Next, she dreamed that she heard crying, or so she thought. But it was rather more like a pitiful wail than a cry. Was it from Harriet's room? Or was it the sound of a night bird out on the river? When she woke she did not know if it had been real or a dream, but an uneasy feeling stayed with her the rest of the night and she slept fitfully.

Before daybreak she awoke — not well rested but too restless to sleep any longer. The dreams and noises in the night had left her with a mood. The strange bed, the strange room, strange house ... this was not her home. The complete strangeness of it all hit her and suddenly she was homesick. "Homesick for L A?" she asked herself as she climbed out of bed. She reprimanded her reflection in the mirror as she combed her hair. "This is home. This is really home!" She tried to laugh at herself and to shake off the feeling of the dreams. I felt lonely when Jake drove away and now I feel homesick, she thought. What is happening to me? What do I really want? I'm too old for all this. What I need is a brisk walk ... right now ... before sun up — or, as the Gullahs would say, 'fo' day clear.

Digging into her suitcase, she pulled out a pair of corduroy trousers and a bulky, warm sweater and changed from nightgown to her outdoor clothes. She put on her hat and warm gloves. Except for her shoes and jacket, which were out on the porch, she was ready for her walk. She tiptoed down the hallway past Harriet's room and down the stairs. She thought to find the kitchen empty, but Sally was already up and the kitchen was redolent with the aroma of fresh coffee brewing.

"Momin', Miz Elizabeth. "You up early." she remarked.

"Yes, Sally. I'm going for a walk."

"It still dark out there. How you gonna fin' yo' way?" Then she smiled a big smile and continued, "Mistah Jake, he done called this mo'nin'. I'se wonderin, him up so early too? Don' you white folks sleep a'tall?" She asked with a hearty laugh.

"What did Jake want, Sally. Did he say?"

"He done axed if you wuz still 'sleep or if you wuz up. I tol' him you wuz still 'sleep. He said he wuz comin' out real soon. So I puts on the coffee. Why don' you wait fo' him?"

"I'm just going down to the river and walk along the bank for a way. I want to see the sun come up. When he comes, tell him where I went and that he can come find me."

"All right, miss. Then why don't you take a cup a' coffee wit' you. It's good an' hot."

"Later, Sally, when I get back. I'll have some with Mr. Jake. It does smell good."

"Well, Miss Harriet, she usually down early, too, so's I always has a pot ready fo' her. Spec she be down terekly. I'll tell her you done gone out. I'm gonna go down to the pantry and fetch up some of them home made plum preserves for y'all breakfast, if I can find a jar. Then I'm gonna make y'all some fresh hot biscuits. My, my, out o' bed 'fo day clear!" Sally sat shaking her head in bewilderment at the strange ways of white folk who didn't really have to rise so early.

"Very well, then. See you in a bit." Elizabeth left Sally talking to herself. Grabbing her coat off the hook where she had hung it the previous evening, she went through the back door out into the brisk morning dampness. The sunrise sent rays of light through the trees, enough that she could see to make her way down to the river. Walking across the damp expanse of lawn, she reached the river and tramped along the bank through brambles, wild berry bushes and weeds. The bottoms of her trousers were wet with dew. Birds awakened and stirred, chirping sleepily. A few early frogs—or a few late ones—croaked intermittently, calling to each other from one place to another, and she could make out the silhouette of a water bird standing on the edge of the dock that jutted out into the blackness. Somewhere out there on the river, the surface broke as a fish jumped and splashed. She continued and neared the woods just as a glow began on the eastern horizon. Here, the remains of the old pine and oak forest came down to the river's edge. There used to be an old, narrow path winding along the bank. She looked for it now and in the soft beginning daylight she found it. When they were little, Jake had led her along this path to the place where it left the river, went through the woods and broke out onto an old road so overgrown that one could barely to see the old wagon ruts. In olden times that road had led to a lumber yard and sawmill, but by the time they were kids, the road no longer led anywhere. Farther along, the path widened and opened onto a grassy clearing. A very old oak grew up close to the bank, close enough that one could sit on the old gnarled roots and put a fishing line in the water if one was of a mind to. Elizabeth turned to look toward the heightening glow in the east. The sun peeked over the tree-tops. Darkness faded away fast. Silhouettes took shape and color. She stood still, taking in the surroundings — the sunlight, the birds, the oak trees draped with Spanish moss and the forest floor covered with brown needles from the pine trees. She determined that she would stand there and make up her mind one way or the other — this very morning — about whether she would keep this place.

Suddenly, the world exploded around her. She felt as though a cannon had hit her and spun her around, flinging her down close to the river bank. She felt no pain, just the intense force of the thing that had hit her from behind. She tried to grab onto something — anything — to stop falling, but she fell and fell deep into blackness, her fingernails clawing deep into the soft earth until she saw nothing, heard nothing and felt nothing.

She did not see Harriet come out from behind the large oak and stand over her, still holding the gun. She did not see the look on Harriet's face as she stood looking down at her. She did not hear as Harriet said to her, in a voice filled with hatred and venom, "You'll never take my home from me. You and your high and mighty people. No one will ever take The Hill from me. I have as much a right to it as you. More right than you. You don't love it! You don't care for it!"

Harriet did not hear or see Jake as he quietly came up behind her and slammed his fist into the side of her face, knocking her to the ground, unconscious. He had no time to fight or struggle with her now. He only wanted her out of the way. He must see to Elizabeth. He would take care of Harriet later, so he left her where she lay.

Quickly kneeling by Elizabeth, he felt for a pulse and found it, thankful that she was not dead, just unconscious. He needed to see how badly she had been shot and where. He opened her coat gently and just below her left shoulder her sweater was wet and warm and sticky. He felt underneath her back and his hand came away with blood. He knew that the bullet had come through and had not lodged somewhere inside, but it had come close to her heart. She was losing blood fast. Taking his handkerchief from his back pocket, he placed it over the wound. Harriet had shot her in the back! Had she shot to kill or did she only intend to warn and frighten Elizabeth? If the sun had not been in her face, would she have missed her aim, and would Elizabeth now be dead? What was Harriet thinking? These questions pounded at his mind as he lay Elizabeth gently on her side and went to look for the gun. He had seen it fly from Harriet's hand when he sent her sprawling and did not want to leave it where she could get it and come after them both while he carried Elizabeth back to the house. This he had to do, because if he left Elizabeth here, she would lose too much blood. Also, he could not leave her with Harriet. In the early morning shadows, it took longer than he wished to locate the gun, but finally he saw a glint of sun on the barrel and ran to it. Picking it up, he saw that it was a Colt .45 automatic. Where had she gotten it? How long had she had it? It seemed that there were things he did not know about Harriet and he thought he knew all. After resetting the safety, he carefully placed the gun in the deep pocket of his down jacket and went back to Elizabeth. She stirred and struggled to regain consciousness.

"Be quiet." he gently demanded when she tried to speak. "Don't talk." He knelt and began to lift her. As he did, she tried to sit up, so he again told her, "Don't try to help. Just go limp. Don't try to use your left arm. I can pick you up and carry you."

At his insistence, she tried to relax.

"You've been shot," he told her simply. "Harriet." Elizabeth's face showed her sudden alarm and she tried to turn to look behind her, but Jake had her safely in his arms and, with a bit of struggle, stood up. "If you want to and if you can, put your right arm up over my shoulder to help steady yourself. I'll carry you back to the house. Have to phone the hospital."

"I am sure I can walk," she replied. "Put me down and let me try."

"No," came his quick reply. "You are losing blood. I think you're only wounded in the left shoulder but I'm not sure how much damage there is. If you walk, you'll lose more blood."

She did as he said and felt that she helped a little by steadying herself with her right arm. She had felt no pain when she first regained consciousness, but now the pain began and with each step that he took, it shot through her torso.

"It's so far to the house. I walked a long time on the path," she said.

"I won't keep to the path, though. I'll take the straight line through the woods. It'll be closer." Jake left the path and began to walk through the woods. "Remember how we used to run through here when we heard the dinner bell ring? To see who could get home the fastest?" he asked, trying to take her mind off the pain.

"Harriet?" she asked. "Where is Harriet? I didn't see her."

"Back there," he replied. "Think I knocked her out. We'll see about her later."

Elizabeth stiffened in his arms as she began to fully comprehend what had happened to her. Harriet had shot her!

"Why?" she whimpered.

"Not now," came his firm reply. "Later. We'll talk about all that later. I'll phone from the house and tell them we're on our way. It'll be quicker and easier if you just don't talk now." He continued walking through the woods. From over the next small rise, he could see the lights from the kitchen. What had taken her a half hour as she had slowly walked along the river path—stopping to watch and to listen to the early morning sounds—took him less than twenty minutes. As they reached the steps to the mud porch behind the kitchen, he had to put her down. He could not climb them with her in his arms. Smiling and trying to make a joke, he teased her and made fun of himself. "Of all the things a man imagines himself doing, the best is rescuing a damsel in distress and I can't even carry you up the steps."

With that, he called loudly to Sally.

Sally opened the back door. "That you, Mistah Jake? You find Miss Elizabeth? Coffee's hot and waitin'..."

He cut her off short. "Miss Elizabeth's been hurt. I want you to do two things. First go inside and call 911 and tell them to send an ambulance to The Hill."

"Aww, Mistah Jake. What you mean hurt?" Sally moaned.

"Sally do what I asked. Then call Jason and tell him to come here."

"All right, Mistah Jake, I'll go call the am'lance now." Sally went back into the kitchen shaking her head and mumbling to herself, "911, 911."

Jake heard her on the phone as she shouted to the 911 operator, "Miss Elizabeth she been hurt, and Mistah Jake, he say for you to send the am'lance out here to The Hill." After a brief silence he heard her say, "What you mean, what hill? You knows what Hill I'm talkin' 'bout. Out here to Mockin'bud Hill. Yeah, When? Right now! OK, I'll tell 'im."

Sally came out to tell Jake and he reminded her, "Good girl, now get Jason."

"Yassuh!" Sally slammed the door and he heard her run through the house calling, "Jason, Jason, where you, Jason? Mistah Jake he say come here! Now!"

Elizabeth had begun to shiver. Jake took off his jacket and placed it around her shoulders. Her face had gone quite pale. "I can't sit up any more, Jake. Feel ... going to ..." she tried to say as she fainted in his arms.

Jake laid her down on the ground and placed his jacket over her just as Jason came out of the kitchen door.

"What wrong, Mistah Jake?"

"Miss Elizabeth's had an accident. I'll tell you about it later. "Harriet's had an accident, too."

"Where she?"

"At the clearing on the river path. That is where I left her. She may not be there now. Might be on her way back here but the sheriffs got to see to her, not us."

"What's she done, Mistah Jake?"

Jake thought it wise to tell Jason. He would know soon enough anyway. He would need Jason to handle things with the sheriff when he arrived. Besides, he found that suddenly he needed Jason's quiet strength, because he was beginning to have a reaction to the shock also.

"Harriet shot Miss Elizabeth, Jason. I knocked her out and carried Miss Elizabeth back here. Walked through the woods."

"Lawdy, Mistah Jake!"

"Miss Elizabeth needs to get into the house 'til the ambulance gets here. It's too cold for her out here and

I'm so tuckered that I can't take her up the steps alone. Help me get her in."

"Yessuh," said Jason. He helped an exhausted Jake lift Elizabeth. Together, they took her up the steps. Sally opened the door and followed them as they went through the kitchen.

"Y'all carry her into the downstairs bedroom," instructed Sally. "Let me run ahead and turn down them covers."

They did as she ordered. Sally turned the covers down and they laid Elizabeth on the bed. She was regaining consciousness but continued to shiver with shock and loss of blood. Jake pulled the covers up to her chin. He could see that the wound had stained through her jacket.

Before he could say anything, Sally appeared carrying clean towels, which she gave to Jake. "You needs me to heat some wawta?"

"No, Sally. The ambulance will be here soon. We just need to keep her warm 'til it gets here."

Jake placed a towel on the wound, trying not to cause her too much pain. He tried to stop the bleeding with gentle pressure. When Elizabeth tried to speak, he placed his fingers softly on her lips and shook his head.

"Later, my love. Later."

The ambulance came and while the medics attended to Elizabeth and readied her for transport to the hospital, Jake telephoned the sheriff. Sheriff Otts could not be reached and Jake left instructions for the sheriff to return his call. Jake followed the ambulance in his car and while Elizabeth received emergency care, Jake waited for a telephone call from the sheriff. Otts knew Jake well, having dealt with him often over court cases. They weren't exactly friends, coming from different places in society, but mutual respect existed between them. The duty nurse came to fetch Jake to the phone at the nurses' station.

"Mr. Grenville?" she inquired. "There's a phone call for you. Come take it out at the desk. It's the sheriff."

"Right," replied Jake as he picked up the receiver from the desk and spoke. "Jake Grenville here."

"This Sheriff Otts. What's going on Mister Jake? I called your house and your man, Jason, said I'd find y'all at the hospital. He said Miss Harriet shot somebody."

"Yes, she did. I came here with Elizabeth. She's in emergency now. I suppose you want to know what happened?"

"Rather talk in person. I'll come over to the hospital and we can talk there, or out in the car. Have to speak with my men first. You be there?"

"Not going anywhere Sheriff. But you might want to send a deputy to the house and talk with Jason. I hit Miss Harriet and she fell down. Down at the river clearing. You need to find her."

"I'll send a man out now and I'll come on to the hospital. Need to get some details."

"I'll be right out here in the waiting room or in Elizabeth's room as soon as they let me in. Ask for me at the nurses' station."

"Will do. See you when I get there."

Jake put the phone in the cradle and turned to see the emergency room doctor standing behind him with a smile on his face.

"You can go in to see her now, Mr. Grenville. She is asking for you, but please don't talk much. She's going to be all right, but she's lost a lot of blood and needs to sleep. Just down the hall to that first room on the right. By the way, that bullet missed her heart by an inch. Somebody did a good job of shooting. Should I ask who?"

"My sister, Harriet, Doc. My sister, Harriet. I didn't even know she knew how to hold a pistol."

Jake stood beside Elizabeth's hospital bed and held her small, cold right hand as she slept. Her face had little color. She had needed a transfusion. A needle in her vein pumped fluids to nourish and sustain her until she recovered from shock. The doctor told him that aside from the heavy loss of blood, she was not in critical condition. She would recover from the bullet wound. With rest and care she would gain strength quickly.

He looked up to see Sheriff Otts poke his head in the door.

"I'll be right with you, Sheriff," Jake said softly.

The sheriff withdrew to the corridor to wait. Jake checked to see that the IV solution still dripped and tucked the blanket gently around Elizabeth. He went out into the corridor to speak with the law officer.

Sheriff Otts, a small man in stature, not over five feet seven inches in his stocking feet, had been sheriff of the county for over twenty years and was admired by all. He was a quiet and competent man, also a consummate actor, respectfully deferring to gentry, tradesmen and tenant farmers alike. The gentry made sure he continued to be elected and the rest of the population, both black and white, admired him and called him "Cap'n" or "Boss." When Jake came out of Elizabeth's room, Otts stood holding his hat in his hand while rubbing his shiny scalp with plump fingers.

"Mr. Jake, what's goin' on?" he began. I told one of my deputies go out to talk with Jason and he called me and said him and one other deputy went to the river where you said. They looked all over but ain't seen no Miss Harriet or anyone else down there. We went right where Jason said to go. Found nobody. Do you know where she might be now? Where she might have gone? What was her condition when you left her?"

"I don't really know, Sheriff Otts. I've been so concerned about Elizabeth that I almost forgot about Harriet. I am pretty sure I knocked her out cold. After I hit her and she fell, she didn't move. Then I just had to get Elizabeth back up to the house."

"You know she shot Elizabeth? You see that?"

"I did, Sheriff Otts. Saw the whole thing. She got one shot off and then I hit her and that knocked the gun out of her hand."

"How's Miss Elizabeth doin'? She gonna make it? Jason didn't say how bad hurt she was."

"The doctor said she's going to be all right. The shot went through the shoulder. Lost a lot of blood, but no vitals."

"Good. That's good. Jake, we didn't find a gun."

"Yes, I know. I have it. I picked it up and put it in my pocket." Jake reached into his pocket, pulled out the weapon and handed it to Otts, who held it gingerly with thumb and forefinger. "I forgot I had it. Couldn't leave it there for Harriet to get ahold of and come after us again, now could I?"

"Well, you got a point, but you did remove evidence from the scene. That ain't good." Sheriff Otts stood quiet, his head lowered, then looked up and asked, "Why'd Miss Harriet shoot Miss Elizabeth? Do you know?"

"Maybe," replied Jake. "It's a long story."

"I got time," answered the sheriff. "Well, maybe I'll have time later, but I guess we better go find Miss Harriet and ask her."

"Sheriff, I wasn't thinking about evidence and legalities when I came on what I saw happening. I just did what I had to do. I'm just glad I came up on them in time."

"I understand," Sheriff Otts replied. "I just wanted you to know that those things will come up. If there's a trial up ahead, I mean."

"First we have to find Harriet. Then find out why ... what was going on in her head. I don't even know if Elizabeth will want to press charges, seeing as how Harriet is family and all that."

"Don't think she has a choice. You know it's against the law to try to kill somebody. It's called attempted murder. There'll be a hearing at least," Sheriff Otts explained sympathetically. "First, though, you're right. We gotta find her."

"How far did your men look down river?" asked Jake.

"'Bout a mile or so they said. I called back down to the station. Told them to get the dogs out and track her. She can't have gone far. You said you knocked her hard and she was out when you left? Well, if she got up, she might have been dazed and walked into those woods and got lost. We'll find her though, you can be sure of that!"

"Now that 1 know Elizabeth is going to be all right, I'll go on out to The Hill. The doctor said she just needs to rest now and she's asleep."

"OK. You can be a big help, 'specially if we find Miss Harriet." After a moment he said, "Shoot Miss Elizabeth?" His voice expressed his shock. "Miss Harriet ... well, I've known her more than twenty years ... ever since I came down to the low country from up Orangeburg way. I mean ... shootin' family? That's crazy!" exclaimed Otts. "Course, it happens a lot, don't it? He saw the look on Jake's face and stopped. "Sorry, Mistah Jake. Don't mean to pry. Didn't mean no harm. Let's go." Otts turned and walked down the hospital corridor, shaking his head and muttering to himself.

Jake peeked into Elizabeth's room and saw that she still slept. He motioned to the desk nurse.

"I'll be leaving now. I'll call in an hour or so, but if Miss Elizabeth wakes up, you take good care of her and tell her I'll be back as soon as I can. Don't you try to explain any of this to her."

With that final admonition, Jake left the hospital with Otts, got into his car and followed the sheriff out to The Hill. When they arrived at the house, Sheriff Otts called his deputy. Jake heard him speak.

"Otts here. Go ahead. Say you got a footprint?" he questioned his caller, looking sideways at Jake, then back to the road. "Where?" He listened while the caller spoke again, then repeated what he had heard. "By the river? Down close to the edge? Right ... well, all right... you call... we'll be there in ten or fifteen minutes. I got Jake, er ... Mr. Grenville with me. Yes, the lady is gonna be awright. She just got it in the shoulder ... right."

Sheriff Otts finished the cryptic conversation and said to Jake, "Deputy Jarvis. They think she went into the river. They's a footprint down there close by the water's edge. Dog's led 'em. No signs that she might have slipped either. I think we'd better look in that river a bit downstream."

Jake said nothing as he attempted to fathom Harriet's possible actions. Had she gone into the river? Harriet hated the river. However, the inevitable questions stared at him. Had Harriet stumbled into the river or had she tried to drown herself? Had she succeeded?

Jason and Sally came out into the yard waiting for news. Sally's eyes were red and puffy from crying.

Jason walked over to meet Jake and asked, "They find Miss Harriet yet, Mistah Jake?"

"Not yet, Jason. They're still looking. I came out here to see if I can help."

"How's Miss Elizabeth?" Jason asked.

She'll be OK, Jason. A shoulder wound," Jake answered.

"Lawdy, what happened out there, Mistah Jake?" Jason asked again.

"We're not sure of that either, Jason," Jake said, trying to comfort them both, but not knowing how to do it. "You told Sally?"

"Yessuh, I did. Thought she might as well know. I hope I didn't do wrong, Mistah Jake?" Jason asked. He placed his arm around Sally's shoulders and she started to cry again.

"No, Jason. She'll have to know anyway. What matters now is that Sheriff Otts and his men find Miss Harriet as soon as possible," he continued. "We're going down to the river now. I think they're looking in it."

Hearing that, Sally began to wail loudly and Jake motioned for Jason to take her into the house.

"I'll let you all know as soon as we find something." Jake turned and followed Sheriff Otts, who had started to walk toward the woods. Again they remained silent, each not knowing quite what to say to the other. Upon arriving at the clearing, Sheriff Otts directed one of the deputies to return to the house and remain there until the river crew arrived with the scuba gear and dragging rig. They would need to be shown the way.

The crew arrived within a quarter of an hour and immediately went to work. The had two inflatable boats manned with two men each, one to dive and one to row. Both went downstream. The boatmen rowed while the divers swam back and forth underwater, from the middle of the river to the banks. They had not gone far downstream when those remaining on the bank saw one diver motion to his oarsman. They saw the boat go over toward the bank and stop. The boatmen motioned to Sheriff Otts and called out. Jason and the sheriff walked along the bank until they came to the divers. They were pointing toward the body of Harriet, which had caught on a submerged tree limb just under the waterline where the bank hung over the water.

Jake watched as they brought Harriet's body out of the water and placed it on the stretcher. He remained aware that Sheriff Otts watched him closely, but he felt nothing but relief that it was not Elizabeth they had pulled from the river. He knew he would feel for Harriet later. He would deal with it at another time. For now, he felt numb. For the second time that day an ambulance came to The Hill.

Before they took Harriet's body to the morgue Sheriff Otts asked, "Jake you want to ride in the ambulance with the body?"

Jake replied, "No, Sheriff. I've got some things to do. You carrying her to the morgue?"

"Yes. There'll be an autopsy. You understand, don't you?"

"Of course," replied Jake. "I understand."

"As I said before, there'll be an inquest," continued the sheriff. "We have to talk with Miss Elizabeth, as soon as she's able. I'm afraid the department will want a full investigation of what happened this morning out by the river between Miss Elizabeth and Miss Harriet and you. Sorry about all this, Jake, but it has to be done," Sheriff Otts explained. "I'm gonna take your word for what part you had in it for now."

"I know, Sheriff. Don't worry about it. We— Elizabeth and I—have nothing to hide."

"OK, then, I'll call in and tell the coroner we're bringin' her in. They just need to verify if she died from drowning or not. To me, it looks like she just went in the river and drowned herself. No sign of anything that I could see except that little bruise on her face where you said you hit her and she fell. But we'll know for sure soon. I'll keep in touch. You gonna be home or at the hospital?"

"After I run my errands, I'll be either home or at the hospital — one or the other. If you don't get me one place, call the other. I think Elizabeth will be there for a day or two, then I'll carry her back to The Hill. Call me anytime you need to and as soon as you find out about Harriet."

"Sure will. You take care now. I'll be in touch."

"I'll go up to the house first and tell Sally and Jason the sad news. Sally's gonna fall to pieces. Don't know why but she was fond of my sister. I also have an errand in town that I need to do. Can you give me a couple of hours before you call?"

"I can do that."

"Better get that over with," he said aloud as the sheriff drove away.

On his walk back up to the house, Jake thought long and hard about what Harriet had done and asked himself many questions. Was this his own fault? Should he have brought deeply buried secrets out into the open long ago? Should he have encouraged Harried to see a therapist about her obsessions? He had not because to have done so would have deeply hurt Harriet or his mother and father, so it had finally been Elizabeth, the one person he had never wanted to hurt, that felt the brunt of his silence. Knowing painful secrets at a youthful age, when he had not been mature enough to know the right thing to do, he had done nothing except continue to keep the secrets.

Harriet knew the secrets, too. He had watched, as she grew from a child into a woman, and had seen what that knowledge had done to her. He had not known how to help her. Harriet had not known that he knew. Had that been a mistake? They could have talked together and he may have been able to help her accept the truth. He never told her about the nights he heard her crying, the one night when they were still children. He had climbed the chinaberry tree outside their parent's bedroom. He had seen her curled up on the big four-poster clutching a small book to her chest and sobbing as though her heart were broken. She did not know that he had watched as she replaced the book in its hiding place in the back of the big, ancient oak desk. She did not know, when she went to find it again, that Jake had seen and heard all, had found the book and discovered that it was a diary. He read it and then found a new hiding place where Harriet could never find it.

Harriet had been thirteen years old that year. How could he tell their parents about the diary, or did they know? If not, learning the truth would only cause problems. So much damage could be done with the information the diary contained. At the time it had seemed unwise to the boy, Jake, to hurt so many innocent people. He had hoped that taking the little book away from The Hill so that Harriet could not read it again would somehow protect her from the sordid facts it contained, but he had been wrong. He had been able to take away the book, but not to take away Harriet's knowledge of what it contained. That knowledge had eaten away at her and turned her into the caricature of southern womanhood that she had become.

He had watched her grow through her early teens and had been her escort at the Charleston debutante ball. He had watched her develop into an attractive and genteel young woman. He had waited for her to land one of the eligible young men of Charleston, but she had not. She had not sought dates. When her mother tried to arrange one for her, she had expressed the desire not to have to go again. She never married. She chose to attend the College of Charleston instead of going away to a more prestigious girls' school. By staying close to The Hill, she could come home each weekend. Finishing college, she came back to The Hill and there she remained. How convenient it had been for her. The Perrys traveled the world with the Army and she remained to live in and take care of The Hill.

Jake knew now that Harriet never forgot. Neither had he. Keeping their secret, they knew that they had no right to be there; no right to the hallowed Grenville name. They had been Grenvilles for so long—how could it suddenly not be? Jake realized that this knowledge had slowly driven Harriet mad and caused her to hate Elizabeth so much that she had tried to kill her. He knew that he should have told his parents and they should have dealt with Harriet's emotions. Now it was too late. Jake knew that when he could feel again, he would feel overwhelming guilt and grief, not only for Harriet, but for himself as well, for to keep the dark secrets and protect his family, he had given up the one girl he had ever loved.

When Jake reached the house the morning was gone. He had eaten nothing, not even had a cup of coffee. Sally and Jason sat together in the kitchen, Jason's arm around the woman's plump shoulders. She had been crying.

"Suh, y'all find Miss Harriet?" asked Jason.

"Divers found her down river a piece," replied Jake quietly and immediately Sally began again to wail.

"I have an errand in town. You watch after Sally?"

"Yessuh, I take care of Sally. She be all right soon."

Jake's errands in town included a trip to the bank to retrieve the diary from his safety deposit box, where it had been kept since he grew old enough to know about banks and private boxes. Time had come for Elizabeth to know. The secret had to be shared. He had to help her understand why this thing with Harriet had happened. He had wanted more time to prepare her for this, to talk with her and tell her gently, to try and help her understand why he had made the decisions that he had made. He had waited too long and could wait no longer.

By the time he made the drive to Charleston, found a parking place on busy King Street close to the main office of the bank where he had his box, fetched the diary and drove back to the little hospital in Maclin, several hours had passed. He tiptoed into

Elizabeth's room and found her asleep; her complexion pale. He left the room and found the duty nurse, her name badge pinned to her uniform.

"Good evening, Nurse Sullivan. I'm here to see Mrs. Wilson. Elizabeth Wilson. How has she been? Did she awake at all? She looks too pale."

"I just came on duty at three o'clock." She looked down at her wrist and checked her watch. "It's almost five. Her chart says she had a transfusion earlier. She must have lost lots of blood. I've checked her several times and found her asleep. If she did wake up, it must've been only briefly. The doctor gave her a powerful sedative, so I expect she'll sleep most of the evening."

"Thank you," said Jake, suddenly feeling extremely tired. "I'll go stay with her."

Nurse Sullivan took a long look at Jake and said, "Mister Grenville, you look like you're ready to drop. You've run on adrenaline all day and now you're crashing. You better go sit quiet. If you need something ring the buzzer. I'll come."

"You are correct about the adrenaline," agreed Jake. "My knees are shaking."

He went back into Elizabeth's room and sat down beside the bed to keep watch. The chair had a deep, soft cushion and a high back—just the sort of chair needed for bedside vigils. Before long, in the quiet of the hospital room, exhaustion and the stress of the whole day found him and he drifted off to sleep.

He slept until just before nine o'clock when Nurse Sullivan again came in to check her patient. She took Elizabeth's pulse and checked to see that the intravenous fluid dripped. Seeing that everything was in order, she turned to Jake.

"Can I get you something, Mr. Grenville?" she whispered. "Maybe some hot chocolate or some pudding? I noticed that you haven't eaten all evening. I know I can get something up from the kitchen."

Waking from his deep sleep, Jake hadn't realized his hunger until then.

"Thank you, Nurse Sullivan. I think maybe hot chocolate would be good right now. I'd appreciate that, thanks."

"You don't have to call me Nurse Sullivan. Just Janet will do."

"Right, again. I forgot to eat supper earlier."

"You wait right there. I'll go out and order you something." Janet Sullivan went to her desk and telephoned the kitchen.

While he waited, he thought over his state of mind from early morning. He had hurried out to The Hill early in the morning, skipping even his morning coffee because he had that awful sense of dread that something was going to happen. He had ridiculed himself for being unduly dramatic. He still had no idea that Harriet's mind had deteriorated so far as to make her do the thing she had done. When he got to The Hill and found both women gone, Sally told him where Elizabeth had gone. He feared something would happen between them — an argument or worse. He had gone to find them and had gotten there just in time.

Nurse Sullivan slipped in the room noiselessly, bearing a full supper tray and a huge mug of hot chocolate. She placed it on the bedside table next to his chair.

"Eat as much as you can, Mr. Grenville. It's not so bad for hospital food."

Later, after he had picked at the hospital supper, he sat beside Elizabeth's bed in the dim light of a small lamp with a blanket over his lap. Janet Sullivan had quietly placed it on the back of the chair for him when she brought the supper tray. He stared at Elizabeth, trying to decide how he would break the news to her; that they had found Harriet's body in the river and by all the evidence, it seemed that she had simply awakened and walked into the river and drowned. There were no signs that she had slipped at the edge of the water. Her footprints in the mud were firm and sure and pointed away from the safety of the bank. Jake felt sure that she had drowned herself deliberately.

At eleven fifteen, the night nurse came on her rounds and found Jake asleep in the chair beside Elizabeth's bed. When she pulled the blanket up over his chest, he stirred and opened his eyes. He recognized the nurse as Frances Evans, an old schoolmate of one of his younger brothers, but he couldn't remember which one.

"Mr. Jake, why don't you go on home and get some rest," she whispered. "Elizabeth's going to be fine. You can come back in the morning," she suggested.

"No, Frances. I'd rather stay here. I checked with her doctor and he said it would be all right if I stayed. I want to be here when she wakes," Jake replied.

"All right. Guess she will be glad to see you're here when she wakes in the morning. I'll be off duty at seven. If she sleeps beyond that, give her our best. We heard what happened, Jake, and we're all sorry."

"Thanks." Almost as soon as she left the room sleep overtook him.

When morning came, Elizabeth awoke before Jake and saw him asleep in the chair beside her bed. She remembered only part of what had happened the previous day — the part about being in the clearing by the river — and only flashes of the time that Jake carried her in his arms to the house. She remembered nothing of the ambulance ride or of the time in the emergency room. Now she experienced feelings of confusion and trouble. Sensing her eyes on him, Jake opened his. They smiled at each other. Happy to see her alive, he arose from the chair, went to her bedside and took her free hand in his.

"I'm sorry. I'm sorry for all this. It's my fault," he began.

Her frown showed her lack of understanding.

"How much do you remember about yesterday?" he asked.

"Not much," she whispered hoarsely, trying to recall all the details that were still escaping her. "I just feel scared. I'm in a hospital, I know. Did I have an accident? Something bad?" Trying to shift her weight in bed, she suddenly felt the stab of pain in her left shoulder. She turned her questioning eyes to Jake and her expression asked him to explain.

First Jake took the water pitcher and poured a small amount of water in her glass.

"Here," he said, as he lifted her head and placed the glass to her lips. "Drink some of this." He dabbed her chin with a tissue where the water dribbled from the corner of her mouth and continued softly, "You were shot. You have a gunshot wound in your left shoulder. The bullet missed your heart and you're going to be OK."

"Who," she began, but did not finish the question. Suddenly she remembered the explosive sound as the early morning had been shattered. "Harriet shot me? Was it Harriet?" Her memory of the incident at the river slowly came back. "I remember you taking me to the house and Harriet wasn't there. Only Jason and Sally."

"Yes, Harriet shot you, but I am probably to blame. Looks like I've made a mess of things."

She patiently waited for him to continue. She could see the pain and the confusion on his face and could only wonder as to what he alluded. Jake knew that she would never guess the truth and would understand nothing without knowing the whole of it — the ancient past, the tragedy, the deceptions, both then and now. How could he begin to tell her — to explain so much. What words could he choose to say what had to be said? Here was the precipice he had imagined in front of him for years. It was now or never. He might fall to the bottom or he might sprout wings and fly but jump he must.

He plunged. "Elizabeth, I'm not your cousin. Neither Harriet, nor Simon, nor Harry."

Her expression showed nothing at first, then he saw a look of surprise, shock, and lack of understanding, as his words penetrated through the fog of the sedative. She said nothing, waiting for him to continue.

"I have a book for you to read. It's a diary that Harriet found years and years ago. I took it away from her and hid it and never told anybody about it and now you have to read it."

"Whose diary, Jake?" The sedative had made her thinking very fuzzy and difficult to focus on what he said.

"It's the one you asked me about on the way from the airport. It does exist and you have to read it."

"It's real?" she asked. "Can't you just tell me what this is all about?" Elizabeth's hand squeezed Jake's. "What's the big secret of the diary? Just tell me!"

"My God, how can I tell you what happened? I'd have to start so long ago. I can't say it with just a few words. It would take all day and all night."

"All right, Jake, we do have the time, don't we? I don't think I'm going anywhere soon." She smiled up at him and tried to reassure him.

"I think...," he paused, "I'll tell you what I know about yesterday, first. Then we'll talk about the other. OK?"

"Yes. Just talk."

"I'm sure that Harriet thought you had come back to The Hill to reclaim the place as your own. She thought she would lose the only thing she had ever loved and all it meant to her. It had become the foundation for her life in a way that you don't yet understand. She couldn't bear it, so she shot you. I didn't know that she would," he continued. "Had no idea that she had gotten that bad, but I did have a feeling of dread—especially yesterday morning when I came out."

"And you followed? How did you know where to find me?"

"Sally. I got to the house early and Sally told me that you had gone out to walk by the river and then Harriet had followed you. I came out to find you and arrived just in time. I don't like to think what might have happened if I hadn't gotten there just when I did. I saw you standing there in that clearing, looking out over the water at the sunrise, then I saw a glint of the sun on the barrel of Harriet's gun just as she pulled the trigger. The bullet hit you, you went down and I lunged out of the trees for Harriet, knocked her down and sent the gun flying away out of her reach. I didn't even know she had a gun. Had no idea. She never mentioned it. I don't know where she got it or how long she had it. But we'll find out. Like I said, there is more to this than I can tell you in a few minutes," he paused again to catch his breath. "Remember, I just said that Harried wasn't your cousin and neither am I."

"Wasn't? You said wasn't? Is Harriet dead?" Elizabeth tried to raise up in bed but gave a sudden moan as the pain again shot through her shoulder.

"Don't move. Keep still. Don't hurt yourself anymore," pleaded Jake. "Yes, Elizabeth, Harriet is dead."

"How ..." began Elizabeth. She fell back onto the pillows.

"Don't know yet," Jake told her. "Sheriff Otts thinks she just went in the river and drowned herself. That's what I think, too." Jake released her hand and placed it down on the bed.

"I don't really understand you. About you not being my cousin. How? Why?"

"No more now. It's all too much for you. Too much to take in. All you need now is rest, not more stirring up." One precipice at a time, he thought. One at a time.

"You look tired, too," remarked Elizabeth. "Were you here all night?"

"Yes, I stayed here with you. I wanted to be here when you woke up."

"You should go home now and get some rest. I know you have things to attend to now. I'll be all right." Elizabeth felt weak and her shoulder hurt. She felt overwhelmed. She wanted the nurse to come back and give her another shot so that she could sleep again. Sleep was merciful and learning secrets was exhausting. She encouraged him to go.

"All right. I'll go and take care of things, but I'll be back later this afternoon. I'll bring the book for you to read. It's time you knew all of it." Jake planted a kiss on her cheek, then he tucked the blanket around her chin. "See you later. Eat a big breakfast and then go back to sleep," he ordered. "We have a lot of talking to do."

Jake went out into a bright, warm April morning. A blue sky and puffy clouds hung low on the ocean horizon and the smell of salt marsh permeated in the air. He found the truck and climbed inside sitting there for a few minutes, quietly contemplating where

241

he must go next. While he sat, the activity of a mockingbird caught his glance as it hopped up and down on its perch atop a telephone pole, singing at the top of its voice, announcing to the world of other mockingbirds that he had successfully staked out his territory.

Jake said aloud to the bird, "You've got your territory. Wonder where mine is? Where do I belong? Where does she belong?"

He started the truck, backed it out of the lot and drove slowly along the side streets toward the Sheriff's office, less than a mile from the hospital. He parked in the lot in front of the police station and sat quietly for a moment. He dreaded going in and hearing the coroner's report, already knowing what it would be.

"Better get this over with." He smiled at himself. "And better stop talking to myself. People will begin to think I'm getting daffy."

Dropping his keys into his pocket, he walked with determined steps to the front door. Deputy Gary Felder sat at the front desk.

"Good morning, Mr. Grenville." He started to get up from behind the desk.

"Morning, Gary. No, don't get up. Just wanted to ask if Sheriff Otts is in?"

"Yes, sir. He's in the back. You can go on back there. I think he's expecting you." As Jake began to walk away, Larry called after him. "Sorry to hear about your..." he stumbled for the right word, "... your sister's accident, sir."

"Thank you, Gary. I'll just go on back to his office."

Deputy Felder sat back down and tried to busy himself. He liked Mr. Grenville very much. The Grenvilles were quality and should not be involved in anything sordid like a shooting and a drowning.

Sheriff Otts saw Jake through the window of his office. He arose to greet him, hand outstretched. The two shook hands.

"Morning, Sheriff. You got the reports back yet from the Coroner's office?" Jake asked.

"Yep, came in 'bout a half hour ago. I was gonna call you at the hospital if you didn't show up soon, but I figured you'd be on by."

"What'd it say?"

"Just what we all figured. Suicide. Body didn't show any signs of struggle. The only bruises found were the ones she sustained from the blow you gave her and her fall. Lungs full of river water. She walked in for sure." He sat down on the edge of his desk and fiddled with a pen. "Sure am sorry 'bout all this Mr. Grenville. Real sorry."

"Will there be an inquest?"

"Naw. Miss Harriet's fingerprints were all over that gun. We'll just have to get all the happenings straight. Have to put on record how you found the two women, what they were doing, what you did and why. No one's pointing fingers at you for anything wrong. Just did what you had to. I'll set up the meeting and let you know when and where."

They were both silent briefly, then started speaking at the same time. Jake stopped to let the sheriff speak and Sheriff Otts continued.

"Mr. Grenville, I know it might be none of my personal business, but why'd she do it? I mean, go in that river?"

"I'll put it in the record, the motive I mean, and soon everyone will know. But there's someone else I'll tell before anybody else. Soon as I tell her, then I'll tell everybody."

"Good enough," he answered, offering his hand again. They shook hands. As Jake turned away, the sheriff called after him, "Y'all take care.

Hungry and tired, Jake stopped at a Piggy Park for an early brunch of a Charleston barbeque sandwich. Then he went home to sprawl across the bed and fall into a fitful, troubled sleep.

He woke about two o'clock, showered, shaved and dressed. He picked up the diary from his desk and drove back to the hospital where he found Elizabeth awake.

"Hi, Jake," she greeted with a smile. "You get some rest?"

"I did. Ate a Piggy Park and went right to sleep. You seem to be in good spirits. Feeling stronger?"

"You had Piggy Park for breakfast?"

"An early brunch. You eat?"

"I did. Ate some eggs for breakfast and soup for lunch," she replied. "They took out the drip," she said pointing to her free arm. "Said as long as I can eat, I won't need that anymore."

"Good. You don't know how glad I am that you weren't hurt any more than you were."

"I think I know," she answered, then asked, "Harriet? Did you find out any more about Harriet?"

244

"Went to talk with the sheriff this morning. They had the coroner's report back and it said everything pointed to her just walking into the river. It's what I thought, too."

"Poor, poor Harriet." Elizabeth turned her head away for a moment, then turned again and looked up at Jake. "You going to tell me about it now?"

As an answer, he pulled the diary out of his jacket pocket and handed it to her.

"Here it is," he said, "the cause of it all."

She took the book, looked at it, turned it over and stared at the back. "This little book? It looks so old. Whose diary was it?"

"My great-grandmother Margaret wrote it," he answered. "I want you to take your time and read it when you feel like it, but the sooner the better. It explains all the mystery, all the things that no one knew but Harriet and me. After you read it, you'll know why Harriet became the way she was— why she never married, why The Hill became so important to her, why she wrapped herself up in her confounded societies, and why she shot you. There's no excuse for that and I'm not trying to excuse her, but when you read it, you'll understand."

"I'll read it," she replied. "After what you told me this morning I've been wondering a lot. Where was the diary? How did you get it?" Elizabeth asked.

"Harriet found it first," he continued. "She found it and read it. One night I heard her crying from Momma and Daddy's room. I knocked on the door, but she wouldn't let me in. I worried about her, so I went out to that old chinaberry tree that grows up by the bedroom window. I climbed it and looked in the window. She sat on the big bed holding this little book. Just sitting there. I watched her a few minutes. Her crying had stopped, but her eyes were all red and puffy and she didn't see me. Then she got up and walked over to that big old desk on the other side of the room. You know the one. She opened the top and pulled out one of the drawers. All the way out. I saw her reach in the back and open another little door behind the drawer. She put the book in it, then shut it up again. She left Momma and Daddy's room and went on over to hers. I climbed down from the tree, went inside and up to the bedroom, opened the desk and found the book where it had been hidden. I took it to my room. Curious and wanted to know what made her cry so hard. I saw it was an old diary and noticed that it had been started right about the time of the War. That really caught my interest. I thought maybe there'd be something exciting about the war in it, so I started to read. And I didn't stop 'til I'd finished reading the whole thing. Then I read it again. I sat up most of that night reading it and thinking about what I'd read." Jake held her hand as he spoke. "When I finished it, I thought about giving it to Momma and I almost did but then I didn't. I'd found out more than I wanted to know. I could tell you now but I would rather you find out the exact same way I did. I want you to read it. After you finish, we'll talk."

"Very well, I'll begin reading it this afternoon."

"Don't push yourself. Just read as much as you feel like. I'll go now, let you read a little bit and come back later tonight. Can I bring you anything for dinner? The hospital food isn't the worst, but the doctor said you can have anything you want. We want to get you out of here. It's no place to spend a vacation. The more you eat, the faster you'll get your strength back. Maybe a big thick steak? Sound good?"

"Sounds great. I'll skip the dinner tray and wait for that steak. Medium rare and potato with lots of sour cream," she said with a smile. Seeing the strain beginning to show on his face, she squeezed his hand and said, "Jake, I don't know what is in the book, but nothing I read is going to change how I feel about you. You've always been my best friend and you always will be. Nothing can change that."

Jake smiled in return and said to her, "You're right. Nothing can take that away."

He knew that he wanted more than friendship. Would it be possible?

"I know you're doing all you can to make this easy on me and I also know that, whatever it is, it's a much greater strain on you than you want me to know. I know when you're trying to hide yourself from me."

She knew when he tried his best to hide his feelings—his anger, his grief, his fear, his bewilderment, even his guilt.

"You know me too well," he said, then kissed her cheek. "Bye, now. I'll be back a little later with that steak." He turned and left her staring after him, the diary in her lap.

After he left, she took the little book—the seemingly innocent little item, the cause of it all—and turned it over and over. It looked old and worn, the edges of the pages brown with age. Opening the front cover, she saw the handwriting of a young girl, written in ink, probably with a quill pen, a slightly familiar, awkward schoolgirl's hand, the same handwriting she had seen in the ancient letter she had found in the trunk. Impatient to begin reading, something stopped her. Somehow she knew that she wanted to read this diary while sitting on the veranda at The Hill, looking out at the river across the broad lawn. It needed to be read there—in the country where it had been written—not here in a hospital bed. With great discipline, she resisted the temptation to scan through it, to look for the parts that had so upset Harriet and that had caused Jake to hide it from everyone. It would be better to begin at the beginning and read it through. She wanted to have the contents revealed to her in the same way that they happened. She would wait.

TWENTY-THREE

ELIZABETH SAT ON THE VERANDAH, relaxing comfortably in a lawn chair with a light throw across her legs. The sun shone brightly and she could see sparkling reflection dancing on the surface of the river as it went out to sea. Sally brought a steaming cup of tea and placed it on the small, white wrought-iron table beside her chair. On the table beside the teacup rested the diary. When she had told Jake of her desire to read it after she returned to The Hill, he had understood immediately and had easily acquiesced. They both knew that the diary would tell of things that had happened close by; of people who had lived and died here. The voice of Jake's great-grandmother, Margaret, would talk to her now and tell her secret things from long ago. She picked up the book from the table and opened it. The writing at the beginning was awkward — little more than printing, not as good as the letter that Elizabeth had found in her mother's trunk. Undated, the first entry began:

Miss Elizabeth gave me this litte book today and I asked her why the pages were empty. She said it will be the book I write in and she said I could write in it every time I think about it. It is a present, she said. It is the first present I ever got from anybody except Pa. And Mister Anthony. He gave me a pig. I like Miss Elizabeth. She is my friend. I guess she is my only friend. She said if I write here all the time, my writing will get better. Now my hand is tired and I got to quit. Bye.

Elizabeth closed her eyes and tried to visualize this young country girl as she might have been over a century and a half ago, sitting by lamplight or candlelight, laboriously writing in her new diary. Ink had smeared on some of the lines. She must have been using a quill pen with difficulty. By the spelling, she could tell that the girl's education had not been completed, but it was difficult to guess her age. Not a little girl, but not yet a woman.

She had dated the second entry.

July 1864.

Miss Elizabeth said I should put down the date I am writing so later I can know when it was that I wrote it. I don't know what the number of today is, but it's Thursday. Next time I go to her house I'll ask her if I can see the calendar and find the date.

Miss Elizabeth is still very sad about her husband getting killed. I see her trying to hide her crying sometimes. She's got a baby coming and now she needs me more than ever. In a way I'm sorry for her, but in a way I'm glad she needs me. That way I can go over to her house more and read to her. I like that because we get hot tea and sometimes little cornbread cakes with real sugar in them. We don't have no sugar here at home. Just blackstrap. I asked Miss Elizabeth if she wanted to read what I wrote and she said, "Oh no." She said that what I write in here is my secret. Nobody ever should read it. I asked her how I was going to know if I got the spelling right and the other stuff I'm learnin' and she said I would just have to make sure myself. She said that reading lots and lots of books and listening to her talk would fix that. I reckon this tittle book is a direy and that it is where I can write down all the things I think and want and dream about. My hurts and fun times too. It can be my second friend. Something I can talk to. Said it's something like a confeshanal. I don't know what that is. I think it is something to do with religion, but the church down in Maclin don't have any. Maybe that is only for quality folks. My hand is tired again.

July 23,1864
Today I know what date it is. Yestiddy I was over reading to Miss Elizabeth and she told me war news. Some of the soldiers from around here got killed down in Atlanta. I think she said the Matthews boys and about ten others got killed and some got wounded. I guess they'll be coming home to the hospital. She gets sad when that kind of news comes. I don't know much about the war. It seems like it's been going on ever since I can remember. Sometimes I see soldiers walking down the road. Some of them is crippled and Ma told me that when I see one coming I am to run and hide. No telling who they are. I'm scared of them. They might be Yankees. I can tell if they are. They wear dark coats. Wonder where my Pa is. I hope he ain't got killed. I miss him a lot. Ma don't but I do. She don't never talk about him and sometimes I want to. It makes him not seem so gone away, if we could talk about him, but it makes her mad and so I don't any more.

Elizabeth placed the diary in her lap with a corner of the throw tucked in to mark her place. She reached for her tea and took a sip, holding the warm cup in both hands. A clearer picture of young Margaret formed in her mind. This struggling child's intelligence was obvious and she could well see why the other Elizabeth had taken her under her wing. There was something so innocent, so charming here — like a lovely bud that would eventually flower.

August 26,1864.
I got a lot to write tonight. Today I went out early in the woods to check my traps. I had just come to the river and I heard

251

somebody talking. I walked slow and quiet like till I got to the clearing and then I saw Flossie sittin under that big tree just lookin at the water. Saw a book on her tap. I stopped and watched her take it up again and start reading out loud. It surprised me because I didn't know she could read. Slaves ain't supposed to read. It's against the law. But she read good as me. She saw me and got scared. Tried to hide the book in her apron pocket but I already saw it. Told her so. She started cryin and beggin me not to tell nobody. I asked her who taught her to read and she said she can't tell. I know why. She thinks she'd get somebody in trouble. Then she kept on cryin and sayin that she knows she used to be mean to me when we was little and she won't be mean to me no more if I won't tell nobody. I feel sorry for her and I told her so. She said she used to feel sorry for me back then and she was some spoiled by Aunt Leah. She didn't know she was a child slave. Then she found out and don't feel sorry for me no more. I told her I ain't plannin on tellin on her. She don't have to worry none about me. 'Then she hightailed it out of there. I went on to see to the traps and found four rabbits still alive. I took them home and put them in the pen and pulled grass for them to eat. Now Ma can cook some meat. She get tired of biscuits and blackstrap and cornbread and fish. Then after that I went to Mockingbird Hill to read to Miss Elizabeth. Only we didn't read much. We just talked a lot. She said my grammar is gettin better and my writin is too, but I need to not drop the last letters. She had out some of her dresses that she can't wear no more and she gave me two of them. One is blue muslin and the other is yellow. I don't know what kind of cloth it is, but it's thin like for hot weather. She told me but I forgot. When I put the yellow one on I wore it out in the parlor when Nellie made tea. Mister John, that's Miss Elizabeth's Pa, he came in for tea and I think he saw me for the first time. Always before he just booked away from me like he didn't even see me. I thought he didn't like me comin over, but today he looked like he might smile. I waited, but he didn't. Only thinking about it. He's

252

an old man but he books good, not fat or flabby yet. But he's got gray hair. Wonder how old he is? Is that why he didn't go fight in the war? I wonder if he knows that Miss Elizabeth pays my Ma to let me come to read to her. That's the only way Ma would let me. Funny how it is that I saw Flossie today and did her a favor and then got these dresses from Miss Elizabeth. When we was little she got the dresses. I wonder if she remembers. Bet she does. I wonder why Flossie is still here. Most all the slaves has run away. Maybe she will soon.

September 24, 1864.
Some more men got killed in fightin down at a railroad station somewhere. Seems like there aren't many more left to get killed. All the men from around here are gone and us women are left to look after things. Miss Elizabeth said I ought to try to write in this diary every day, but I don't have time. I still go to school and then go two or three times a week to hunt birds, or to fish, or get the rabbits out of the traps. If I don't Ma starts bein mean and says if I don't take care of my chores she won't let me go no more. She don't really like me to go. Oh, she likes the money she gets. She takes it and don't give me any of it. So Miss Elizabeth gives me a little bit more than she promised Ma, and I leave it at her house. That way I will have somethin for myself. This morning when I came home from fishin and went by the mill that boy Thad watched me. I could see his big ole red head sticking out from the end of the shed. When I passed him and looked back, he had run up to the other end of the shed and still watched me. Then he ran out in the road and said he wanted to murry me! I don't like him. He scares me and he's ugly. He didn't go to school and everybody says he's not right in the head. That's why he didn't go to the war. Some said a tree fell on him and he ain't been right since. I reckon nobody trusts him and nobody wants him fightin by them. But that don't seem to bother Ma. She said his Pa has land 10 acres of it and I know that makes her think he's somebody worth havin.

October 1864

I don't know what the date is today, but it's early in the month. The leaves are starting to turn red and yellow. Today I went out to the clearin on the river to fish. I keep a cane pole out there and I go out there and dig some worms and sit on the bank and fish. I caught three porgies. Enough for Ma and me. I sat there under that big old oak and listened to that granddaddy whippoorwill sing and sing. Birds are nice. Out there in the woods the whippoorwills live, and down at Mockingbird Hill there are so many mockingbirds. They sing anything they want to. In the springtime they forget to go to sleep and sing almost all night long. I don't know which one I like better. The whippoorwills or the mockingbirds. Today I miss Pa again. He used to talk about the birds a lot and he knew how to sound like most of them, but he did turkeys best. Wonder where he is? Sometimes I get tired waitin.

Elizabeth paused again as she wondered if the clearing Margaret wrote about could be the same one she had walked to the day she had been shot; the same one she and the boys had played in and fished from when they were children. She wondered how many years, how many generations had that clearing played a part in the lives of the family.

October 22, 1864.

Today something awful happened to me. It's so bad I don't think I can even write it in here. But maybe this is what Miss Elizabeth meant when she said it was a confeshunal. I don't think I can ever tell a soul. I went down to the clearin to fish and that Thad Ball he came down there and he did something bad to me. He got on me and he tore my clothes and he hurt me. Then he said I'll have to marry him. But it's not gonna happen. I don't care what happens, I am not gonna marry the likes of him. I am better than him. I can read and write and I am gonna be a teacher. I'll leave here as soon as I can. Miss Elizabeth can get me a place to teach after the war. She said I'm almost ready. I know I've got to hide this diary so nobody can find it. I can't let Ma find it. I can't let her know about this. She would call me trash and say she knew I was bad all the time. She won't believe that boy hurt me. She'd say I wanted him to and I didn't.

Tears had smeared the ink on the paper. Elizabeth dropped the diary into her lap and closed her eyes. She wasn't sure if the diary took her back to a bygone age into the tragic life of this child, Margaret, or whether it brought the past into the present. It did not really matter. The past and the present were co-mingling. She could no longer think about one without thinking of the other. They were part of a bigger whole. Opening her eyes, she looked around her. Just as the land was the same, the river the same, the smells the same, so was time. She took the cup of tea, now cold, and sipped it, then picked up the diary to read on.

November 18, 1864

I can't write too often now. I hid this diary down in the hollow log off in the woods by one of my traps. Came down here today to get away from Ma.

And I'm not feeling too good. Feel like I want to heave up all the time. Ma saw me this morning and started nagging me wanting to know what's wrong. Told her I don't know. Just feeling peaked. Came down here to check the traps thinking some fresh air would be good even though it's getting cold. Soon it will be Christmas. Miss Elizabeth went to her husband's sisters in

Charleston and she's going to stay until after her baby's born. Wonder what it will be. A girl or a boy. She's starting to be a little bit happier now from what she was right after Major Perry got killed. She's got the little one to plan for. Something to love. Maybe she'll let me hold it when she brings it back. I'm gonna talk with her then about helping me to get away from here. Can't tell her about what happened, but I can tell her how much I want to go somewhere to teach. When this old war is over they'll need teachers somewhere. Got to go now.

November 25, 1984
I've got to write to Miss Elizabeth and tell her that I think I'm in trouble. Every morning I get sick and now I've gone and missed my monthly. I know what that means. Ma doesn't know I know, but I do, and I can't hide it from her much longer. She knows every time when I am supposed to have a monthly and she checks. Now she's gonna know and I don't know what to do. I've got to ask Miss Elizabeth. There is no one else can help me. If Ma finds out she'll beat it out of me Thad did it, and then she'll fetch him and make me marry him. I'd rather die if she made me marry Thad Ball and I'd kill him before he'd touch me again. I got to send a letter.

December 1, 1864
I sent the letter yesterday. That old lady Mills in the post office is so nosey. She wants to know every body's business and I think she reads the letters we send to people. She knows so much gossip and the old women come in the store and she stands there and talks to them. I bet she tells them everything she finds out when she reads all the letters.

December 7, 1864

I got afraid that my letter was not going to be strong enough to get Miss Elizabeth to come back home. Yesterday morning Ma found out that I missed my monthly and she asked me about it. I put her off because I said I had been feeling peaked but felt like it was coming soon. Soon she is gonna know. If Miss Elizabeth comes back maybe she will take me back with her to Charleston. I hear the Yankees are getting close and soon no one will be able to go anywhere. Wish this war was over.

December 8
Miss Elizabeth answered my letter and I got it from Mrs. Mills today. She said she will be here in seven days. That is only four more days. I can wait that long. I convinced Ma that I had my monthly. Wasn't hard. Sometimes it seems that Ma isn't here anymore. She spends almost all day sitting in that rocking chair on the front porch sucking on that snuff stick, that awful brown spit dribbling down her chin. Makes me sicker just to look at it. I can't tell her how bad it makes me feel and how bad it looks because she'd slap me from here to yonder for sassing. I know I'm supposed to love your Ma, but I just can't. I can't find anything to love. I'm not a good daughter. But now I think I've got a baby inside me, and I'm gonna be a Ma too. I got to think about what I can do to be good to this baby. I'll find a way to raise it without living like an animal. I should hate it because I didn't want it, and it got put on me in a bad way, but ain't nothing I can do about it now but figure out a way to bring it up good. Miss Elizabeth will help me. She'll be here soon.

The next entry had no date.

I don't hardly know how to write all this. So much happened since I had a chance to write. Miss Elizabeth fell off the chair in the kitchen and hit her head on the wood box the same day she came home to help me. She is dead and buried now, but we got her

257

Little baby boy. He wasn't ready to be born and Nellie took him. Nellie and I are taking care of him. And then before I knew what was going to happen to me, Mister John, Elizabeth's Pa asked me to marry him. He said he just couldn't take care of things and said that he needed me there at The Hill. All this time I thought he didn't even see me. But he did. We got married. Toby and Nellie, they watched from up in the top rows upstairs in the church. When we got back to Mockingbird Hill, Mister Grenville got the big bible down again and he wrote my name in it and the date we got married, January 25,1865. He showed me. He wrote it right there under the name of his other wife who died. Beside it someone had wrote "died of fever."

I didn't tell him about me being in the family way already. Can't do that. No one knew but Miss Elizabeth, and now she can't tell a soul. Now I have a real home and I'll have a good life with Mister Grenville. I'll be a good wife. Won't have to be a teacher. I'll take care of Miss Elizabeth's little baby and mine too when it comes. Mister Grenville will think he is a Pa again and if it's a boy I will name him John after Mister Grenville. It will make him proud to have a son named after him.

I am not that far along that he noticed. Got to be careful now about how I talk and use the words that Miss Elizabeth taught me. There's family in Charleston and before the war they came out here to The Hill a lot. When they come next time, I'll make Mister Grenville real proud of me. We got a message to those Perry women down in Charleston about what happened. But they can't come here now. The war is too close and they can't travel. When things quiet down and the war is over, then maybe they can come and see the baby.

Mister Grenville said he would take care of Ma out at the cabin because she didn't want to come here and live. I have a chance to make something out of myself now. I don't have to be white trash any more. I am one of the quality folk. I am a Grenville. My baby will be a Grenville and not a Ball.

The secret had finally been revealed. Elizabeth closed the diary and placed it in her lap. She breathed deeply. Aching all over from the tension that had been building in her shoulders, she had to stop and rest for a while.

"Miss Lizbeth?" Sally was behind her. "You want some mo' hot tea? I got you a new cup, right heah. It's time for yo' pain medicine now, too. Heah, you take dis little pill," commanded Sally, offering the pill in the palm of her outstretched hand.

"Yes, thank you so much, Sally," said Elizabeth. She reached for the pill and placed it in her mouth. She needed it now, badly. Her shoulder throbbed with pain.

Sally placed the new cup of tea on the table and said, "Let me straighten that pillow behind yo' back. You just lean up a little." Elizabeth did as Sally asked.

"Da's right. Now you be mo' comf'tuble." She came around in front of Elizabeth, leaned down and tucked the blanket tightly under her feet. "I know sun's out but pain, it makes us cold."

"You're a jewel, Sally."

"Yessum," replied Sally, taking up the cold, empty cup. "Bad goin's on, Miss Lizbeth. I'm glad you ain't hurt bad."

"So am I, Sally, but I'm so very sorry about Miss Harriet."

"Me, too, Ma'am. Lawdy mercy."

Sally went away shaking her head and sniffling.

Elizabeth wanted to rest from the diary but found that she could not. She felt compelled to finish, she was so close to the end. She picked up the book again and it felt as though it were burning her hands.

25 February 1865.

Let no one in my lifetime know what I have done lest I be hunted down and destroyed like the mad dog I have become. Here is my confession. Maybe by writing this down I can wash away some of this from my soul. Mr. Grenville has been buried alongside Miss Elizabeth out in the graveyard down at the church yard. And Thad's old daddy dug a grave out behind the sawmill and laid Thad in it. Folks think they killed each other in a bad accident while they were hunting. That's what the paper said. Everybody knows that Thad Ball wasn't quite right anyway, and folks said they must have come on each other by surprise and taken each other for Yankees. Some speculate that just hearing a noise in the woods can make you think you got a turkey. But they didn't. I killed them. I killed them both. I can't say that I don't know why because I do. And I can't say I would do it different if it happened all over again like it did. Because I wouldn't. I know I'll go to hellfire and damnation when I die, but my little baby will have a name and a place in life. It is a high price to pay but I'll pay it.

It was Thad caused it. He came around to the store after he found out I married Mr. Grenville, nosing around, letting me see him. I could tell he was mad. Then last Saturday morning real early, Mister Grenville, went out to try to get a turkey. After he left I went outside too. The weather was so pretty and I was just happy that Miss Elizabeth's baby boy was still living and getting fatter, so I went out and I went into the woods looking for Mister Grenville. I took my gun just in case of coming on a turkey. Nellie was upstairs cleaning and didn't see me go. Nobody saw me go.

I went out and when I found him he was standing there listening to Thad Ball talking to him about what he done to me. I could hear him telling Mister Grenville that I belonged to him because I was carrying his baby. I shot him. I shot him before he could finish saying what he was saying. Then I looked at Mister Grenville and he was staring at me like I was crazy. He must have heard enough and believed what Thad said. He said something to me, but I don't know what. Then he just stood there looking at me, not moving and I could see his face showing disgust. I wanted to say something but I knew it wouldn't matter none. I could see it in his face. White trash. He would never believe anything I said. I still had the gun up and before I knew what I was doing I pulled the trigger again. I don't know whether I meant to hit him or not. I was looking at him, had the gun in my hand, and it was up, and I just pulled the trigger and the other barrel went off. I killed him. I killed my husband, John Grenville and Thad Ball, my baby's real Pa.

After I did it, I just stood there and looked at them lying there not moving. They had their shot guns and after I could think again, I went over and lifted first one gun and then the other and pointed them out to the woods and shot them off. Then I put the guns down bike they fell and I walked out of the woods. It happened deep down by the river and nobody heard. I walked back to the house, went in through the kitchen and took my gun up to my room. Nellie was still doing her chores and little Andy was asleep. I wiped the gun clean and put it back on the rack in the cabinet. I didn't feel anything. I wasn't shaking, wasn't scared, wasn't sorry, just nothing. I know I should have been, but I wasn't and that is why I know I'm bad. I felt like a rabbit in a trap and everybody could do anything they wanted to me and I couldn't do nothing about it. I felt trapped with Ma, trapped with that old lady down at the Post Office, with Thad, and with everybody who called me trash. I know I'm just like a mad dog. There's something in me that went mad.

Maybe everybody is like that, good most of the time, but something can make them mad like the sickness can make dogs *mad. Well, they kill mad dogs, and I recon if anybody ever finds out what I did, they'd kill me. I confessed here in this book but now I've got to hide it so no one will ever find it.*

I'll soon have my own child to raise and I have a name to give him. He's got to be a boy and he'll be John Charles Grenville, Jr. and he'll grow up here at Mockingbird Hill and he'll be somebody. Just so I can live long enough to see to that, I don't care what happens to me. I'll get what I deserve I reckon.

Elizabeth sat almost in a state of shock trying to absorb all that the girl, Margaret, had written. That this young woman, Jake's and Harriet's flesh and blood, had done all this and just wrote it down in a book. It was like reading a gothic novel but this was not a novel. It had happened. It was real. These tragedies had taken place. These things that Margaret had done were still affecting all their lives. She read on, unable to stop now.

March 1865.

'The Perry sisters down in Charleston heard about Mister Grenville's accident and that he was dead and they sent someone to take Miss Elizabeth's baby son away. It was dangerous to take him like that down to Charleston because the Yankees were everywhere. They should have him here. The war is getting worse if that's possible. Yankees crossed the river up by the ferry and burned everything they could. Soon they'll get here. We kept hearing news all last month and this one that the Yankees are coming to Charleston but that's not the worst of it. The Yankees are bad enough but the soldiers who deserted, the slaves that ran away, and that kind are ganging up in bands and they're roaming everywhere and raiding everything they can find. The riffraff and thieves welcome the runaways because they know the hiding

262

places of silver and china and gold coins. They butchered all the cows and sheep and horses and mules what was left. They are raiding houses and burning them, tearing up books looking for hidden money, and setting fire to the other stuff just to see it burn. I wonder sometimes if the Yankees are as bad as these hooligans. Maybe Yankee soldiers are civilized. Ma is staying up in the big house at Tally's Nook with old Grandma Tally. They both don't hear so good and don't see good either. They both are scared to be alone. Aunt Leah died and then that Flossie girl ran off, so Ma stays in Grandma Tally's room with her, sleeping on a little trundle. I heard most of their slaves ran away all except Old Ned and his son. They were afraid of the Yankees coming. Seems strange, the Yankees were going to free them, but lots of blacks here are scared of them, and many away before they get here.

Seems like I remember something about Old Ned being special to Squire Tally somehow. 'Don't know what it was. I remember the first time I saw Old Ned though. When I was little. He was coming down the road with that hoe looking for the mad dog.

April 1865
General Lee surrendered to the Yankees on April the 9th. The war is over but the real trouble is just started. We used to have food to eat, now there isn't any. Everything we had in the cellar got raided and it's too early for the garden to have anything. Anyway Toby said there's no collard seed nor nothing else to plant. I found some old money that Mister Grenville hid away, some real money, not the Confederate money that's not worth anything now. But if I use it, the neighbors will think I am not loyal. And I don't know where to go to use it anyway. I'll keep it hid where nobody will look. Now there's nobody here at Mockingbird Hill but Nellie and Toby and me. I wonder if they'll run off like the others.

It's still April I think but it might be May. Two nights ago about midnight Nellie came running into the house shouting at me to wake up. She was yelling fire, fire! When I got up and ran to the window I could see the sky all lit up over in the direction of Tally's Nook, just a couple of miles away. I got dressed fast and me and Nellie and Toby got in the buggy and went over there quick as that old mule could trot but by the time we got there the house was all in flames. All the out buildings and those beautiful smoke houses. Everything. The smoke was bad. Ashes blowing all around us getting in our hair and eyes. Old Ned standing there crying his eyes out. The mule wouldn't go close and we had to get out of the buggy. Couldn't breathe unless we covered our noses with our clothes. My eyes stung and still do. We ran to Ma's cabin but she wasn't there. She was in that house with Grandma Tally and they both burned up. Next morning when the fire was finished we found 'em. Looked like they were hugging each other when they died. Old Ned is building boxes for them and we'll bury them tomorrow down in the churchyard. Guess Ma went to Heaven because she only killed chickens and such. Now I guess she knows what I did. And if she finds out God don't know, she'll tell Him. We don't know who set fire to Tally's Nook. Maybe it was Yankees, maybe it was slaves or maybe hooligans.'

Yesterday afternoon Old Ned and Young Ned came up to Mockingbird Mill and told Toby they wanted to talk to me. Said they had a secret they had to tell me about. Toby brought them up on the porch where I was sitting and resting. Old Ned took off his beat-up old hat and stood there one foot on the top step. Took him a long time to say anything. He just looked at me strong like.

"Miz Grenville, Ma 'am, I got something to tell you and it's just to you." Then he looked over at Toby. I told him it was all right to say anything in front of Toby. So he started talking.

He said that before Squire Tally died he had them build a pen way out deep in the swamp and he and Uncle Ned took two of his prize hogs out there and hid them from the Yankees. They took care of them since then, feeding them acorns. He said the woods were full of acorns and that the sow was about to give birth.

He stood there turning his hat and I asked him, "Uncle Ned, why didn't you already eat those hogs?"

Uncle Ned looked up at me and said he owed Squire Tally a big payback. When he was a young man he was owned by somebody else and was goin' to get sold off. Squire Tally found out he was sweet on Leah, here at Tally's Nook and Squire Tally went over to the other plantation where Ned was living and he bought Ned and brought him to Tally's Nook so he could marry Leah. He took them both down to the Methodist preacher and got them married before he would let them live together. He said that saving that pair of hogs was the best way he knew to pay him back. Then he said that when Mister Anthony and my Pa come back from the war we can use the hogs to start up with. He said we can build the smoke houses again. I told him that it would take money and we don't have any. Then he said the funniest thing. He said we have money. Real money like that that Mister Grenville hid. He said Squire Tally and Uncle Ned hid it together. Ned said we all could use it to start over.

He said his boy, Young Ned, was leaving. He heard tell of a place out west called Texas and he's goin' to go there and herd cows. There is no more Tally's Nook and Ned wants to stay here with Toby and Nellie if I would let him. I told him it was all right with me, but why didn't he just take the money and go away up north or something. He said this here's his home. South Carolina is the only home he ever knew. Said up north he would get cold. He always liked Mister Anthony Parish and wants to be here when he get back with my Pa. Said we could start both farms up again. So I told him he could stay. He and Toby can take care of the hogs. Maybe we can build up the river boats again. It sure is *something to think about now that this old war is over. I wonder if Mister Anthony and Pa will come back. Wonder if he and Pa are alive. Will Pa come back? Maybe if he knew Ma was dead he'd come. Wish I could let him know.*

The final entry in the diary was only one line. As Elizabeth read it, tears filled her eyes.

Yesterday, on Saturday, July 29,1865, I had a little boy. I named him John Charles Grenville, Jr.

Elizabeth sat quietly and very still for a long while with the diary in her lap. She stared out toward the river; gazing, looking for something to bring relief from the pain that reading the diary had brought her. Then she carefully folded the letter and returned it to the back of the book. She felt the anguish, the sadness, the agony of Margaret, the agony of Elizabeth, the agony of John and the others who had lived and suffered through those miserable years before, during and after the war. Even poor, simple Thad was to be pitied. She closed her eyes and rested her head on the back of the chair. Sensing someone behind her, she turned to see Jake standing there.

"I didn't hear you come up. How long have you been here?" she asked.

"Not long," he answered. "Long enough. I wanted to be here when you finished."

"Yes."

"Now you know," said Jake, coming closer behind her chair and placing his hand on her good shoulder.

"Yes. Now I know," she repeated his words. "I don't even know who should have most of my sympathy. Judging is..." Elizabeth hesitated, looking for the right words, "... judging is impossible. I think I won't even try. They were all caught up in such chaos; not only the war, but their private lives and their private demons."

"That they were." Jake came from behind her chair and pulled up another chair to sit close beside her.

"Sit more in front of me." Elizabeth motioned to Jake. "It hurts to turn my neck to look at you."

"Right you are." He slid his chair more to the front, close to her bundled knees.

Elizabeth looked directly into Jake's eyes for a long moment, then she asked, "She killed them both for a name? For a family? For status?"

"Ultimately, yes but I've always believed that at the time she saw it more as survival."

Elizabeth took the diary from her lap and turned it over in her hands. "Before reading this, I don't think I could have understood how anyone could do what she did, the way that she did it. Now, I think I can. Anyway, a little bit." Elizabeth reached over slowly and placed her hand over Jake's as he spoke.

"Margaret killed them in a state of... what? Insanity? Rage? Fear? Then she kept her secret for her son's sake, for a family, for a better life, for a name for him. She wanted her son to have and carry on a family name that was respected. I don't believe she comprehended much more than that. She had never had respectability. She killed and lied for it then and her great-granddaughter was willing to do it again."

"Harriet?" Elizabeth asked then answered her own question. "Yes, Harriet was after the same thing wasn't she?"

"Harriet knew the truth and it consumed her. The fear that somehow she was tainted; that she wasn't really quality, caused her to work for it more and more. She became obsessed with the idea of proving to others that she was who they thought she was so that she could make herself believe it too. If no one knew that her—our—great-grandfather was just a young simpleton who came from a low-class family, then she could pretend it wasn't so. Harriet could pretend that our ancestor carried the name and blood of American aristocracy. Way back then, during the War, Margaret wanted society to accept her son and wanted him to be brought up in the upper class. Both she and her son would be able to escape all the contempt and misery she had experienced. For her, the alternative was unthinkable—to return to her home with Sylvie, disgraced forever, herself and her son to always be classed as poor white trash. She was capable of murdering both the father of her child and her husband to keep anyone from knowing her secret."

Elizabeth interrupted him. "Most of all, I think she killed the father of the child because of what the man had done to her, don't you think? Then she killed John Grenville almost as a reflex. She just did it before thinking. While I was reading, I could feel her feeling his disgust. Right about then, she must have had contempt for the whole male species."

"I suppose you're right," Jake agreed. He paused, took her hand up to his lips and kissed the tips of her fingers.

"For Harriet, if anyone knew the truth, she believed that would bring disgrace too." Elizabeth looked puzzled then asked, "But how would anyone ever find out? Certainly she wouldn't have told anyone. And you never did. Would you have?"

"Remember, she never knew for sure who had the book, but she often said things that led me to believe that she thought I was the one who discovered it and took it away. I think she really believed that I was the only one besides her who would have kept the secret so long. And I did."

"Then why didn't she believe you would continue to keep it?"

Jake did not hesitate. He said it simply and directly. "Because she knew how much I love you. How much I always have loved you. And she knew that when your husband died, well then…"

Elizabeth knew she should be surprised by those words, but she was not. Somehow she had always known it. Remaining silent, she continued to look at him with that knowledge written on her face.

Jake continued, "She knew that if I had the book and had not told, it was because of my not wanting to hurt either of our families. She also knew that I had promised Julia to keep away from you."

"You what?" Finally Elizabeth was shocked. "When?"

"When we were very young. You must have been only about fifteen but I was coming close to twenty. I didn't think we were close enough cousins for it to matter; you coming down from Elizabeth Grenville Perry and me from John Grenville, but Julia must have. She knew how I felt about you and I think she was afraid we were getting too close."

"I wondered ... we were so close ... then nothing. I used to come to visit and you would be away. I never knew. Thought you just outgrew me."

"Never. But that is when I had to make my decision not to tell anyone. That's when I had to decide whether I would ruin my Momma and Daddy's lives and Harriet's to have a chance to win you, or to give up that idea to keep peace in the family. I was young. And every time since then that I wanted you, missed you, loved you, I chose that path repeatedly. Now, though, there is nothing standing in my way. Harriet knew that. She was afraid that with all our parents gone and no one left but her to protect, I would not deny myself again. She was right. I had planned to tell you everything."

Elizabeth started to speak, but Jake placed his fingers over her lips and shook his head. "Let me finish." He took his hand away and placed it over hers again. "I used to think when we were young that even though we were cousins, we were distant cousins; family but not too close. I thought they would let us be together. But I reckoned without your mother. When Julia realized what was happening, she was upset. There was a scene—a big family pow-wow with you not included, of course, but little Harriet knew about it. All the grown-ups—your Momma, your Daddy, my Momma and Daddy—made sure that I knew in no uncertain terms that I was to keep away from you. I remember your

Momma saying to me, there have been too many cousins married to each other in South Carolina'."

Elizabeth hung her head. "She said the same thing to me once when I asked her if I could marry you when I grew up."

"She did? You did?" Jake was astonished. "You actually asked her that?"

"I did. I must have been about twelve or so. That was her answer to me, also."

"I never really knew if you had thought of me that way. I wanted you to but didn't know."

"When I came, there was no family but Harriet left to protect?"

"Right again. I don't think she trusted me to keep it together this time. She knew I would tell you."

"What made her think you would tell this time? Except for the fact that when Momma died, you were the last one of the family except for Harriet?"

"She might have known that I didn't put so much store in background as she did. I don't care about whether a person is a blueblood, or quality, or a redneck or a mountain William or not. I care about what a person is inside. I expect people to accept me for the same reasons."

"Harriet thought that everyone else was like her. That no one could just accept her because they liked her and might be a good person?"

"Yeah, that's what she believed. That's what the atmosphere down here can do to a person. In particular, those high falutin' snobs downtown," Jake responded with the first bitterness she had ever heard from him. Then he smiled, "That's the worst of this place. And I still love it."

Elizabeth had a sudden thought and asked, "I wonder why Harriet kept the diary after she found it? Why put it back in the hiding place? Why not destroy it?"

"Destroying the book would have been sacrilegious to Harriet. That book came from her great-grandmother and as much as she hated the life Margaret had come from, she could not destroy the book. To destroy the book would have been the same as killing an ancestor. Even if someone read it and destroyed her good name, it did exist and it was part of her past. This diary was her great-grandmother. Considering to what lengths her great-grandmother had gone to give her son the family home, she could not do anything to destroy this. And she would let no one else destroy it. Better to kill again."

"How long did Margaret stay here at The Hill. Does anyone know? I mean, after little Andrew was taken away. He was my great-grandfather, wasn't he? Did the Perry women make her leave?"

"Don't really know what happened, but my guess is that she stayed here. The place went to the Elizabeth's son, Andrew Perry and the diary says he was taken away to grow up in Charleston. He made a career of the army. At least, I know he went to the Citadel. I think that's when it started, this tradition of the Grenville's living at The Hill, while the Perrys continued to make their careers in the army."

"At the very least," Elizabeth observed, "Margaret must be given credit for helping to keep the infant, Andrew Perry, alive. Under the circumstances, that wasn't a small thing. She must have cared for him ... I mean really cared for him."

"Yeah. Seems that she thought of people as the evil doers and the victims; the mean and the meek. Then she must have learned that those two parts might live side by side in everybody. She must've loved babies. How else could she have loved her own that much?"

"Maternal instinct," answered Elizabeth. "Throughout history, if all women had to depend on loving their husbands and having their babies conceived in a loving act in order to love the babies ... well," she stopped, unwilling to finish the thought, but her point made.

"Guess you're right," Jake agreed. "You know, she lived to be quite elderly."

"How do you know?" asked Elizabeth.

"Harriet told me." For the first time in a while Jake smiled. "I think she was born sometime in midcentury. 1849 or 1850, probably. Let me see," Jake began to calculate the number of years. "She lived until about 1930 or so. My God, that's ten years before I was born."

"Wonder what her life was like. I mean the rest of it."

"Wonder if she ever understood what she did and forgave herself for it?"

"Maybe as she grew old, she did," said Elizabeth. Then she changed the subject back to Harriet. "When did Harried find the diary? How long do you think she had been reading it before you found it?"

"I don't know," he answered, "but she used to play around in that room all the time when Momma and Daddy were in town. I used to leave her alone because I thought that she wasn't into any mischief if she was in that room. She'd be so quiet and I didn't think anything was up. She was probably reading that diary for years and then putting it back in that desk. If I hadn't seen her put it in there, I wouldn't have known where to find it."

"And then it was gone."

"And then it was gone. And then she began to be frightened because she didn't know who had it ... or when someone would use it against her."

"She became paranoid."

"Yes. And I blame myself. When I got a little bit older, I should've known. I should've seen it and made the connection. I ought to have told Mom and Dad ..."

Elizabeth cut him off, "No Jake. How could you have known what she would become? How could you tell anyone and take the chance of hurting your Mom and Dad? I think you did right, or at least the best you could have. Something like this is sometimes too big for one young boy."

"Harriet would've thought that I told just so that I could be clear to court you. She would've thought I did it out of sheer selfishness." He continued, "And you, does it hurt you? Knowing that I am the bastard great-grandson of a dimwitted woodcutter?"

"Jake!" She exclaimed. "Don't put yourself down like that!" Then she saw him smile and knew that he was playing with her ... trying to relieve some of the tension. Maybe there was time for that now. Maybe the past was over and the tragedies finished for them. Maybe the time for playing at The Hill had come again. Elizabeth looked out at the river and pointed to the rowboat tied up at the little dock, oars crossed over the seats. The sun was going low in the sky. Shadows had crept in. Birds began to look for their nighttime roosts. Whippoorwills called.

"This is the time that this place is beautiful. This is when I love it most," Jake continued to hold her hand as he spoke. "You have to stay for a while, 'til you're well, but will you consider staying longer? I want my chance. I've waited for it."

Elizabeth should have felt exhausted, but instead she felt light. She should have felt sad but did not. She had come close to death but felt more alive than ever. He would get his chance — and she, hers.

"When will you take me out fishing again?"

"As soon as you are well."

"Will you put the worm on the hook?"

"Anything you wish, my darling." He smiled at her, leaned over and brushed her cheek with his lips.

The End

To contact Dorothy or to see all books in this
series go to:
http://www.dorothykmorrisbooks.com or
Facebook Page: Mockingbird Hill Series,
Novels of Early South Carolina.